SCARLETT WRIGLEY AND THE LIGHT BENEATH THE VEIL

CHARMAINE MULLINS-JAIME

Sea Salt Press

Library of Congress Control Number: 2016918327

ISBN: 0999505007
ISBN-13: 978-0999505007

To sweet Scarlett for inspiration, John and Aggie-dear for magic and a sense of humor and Mimi for the final push.

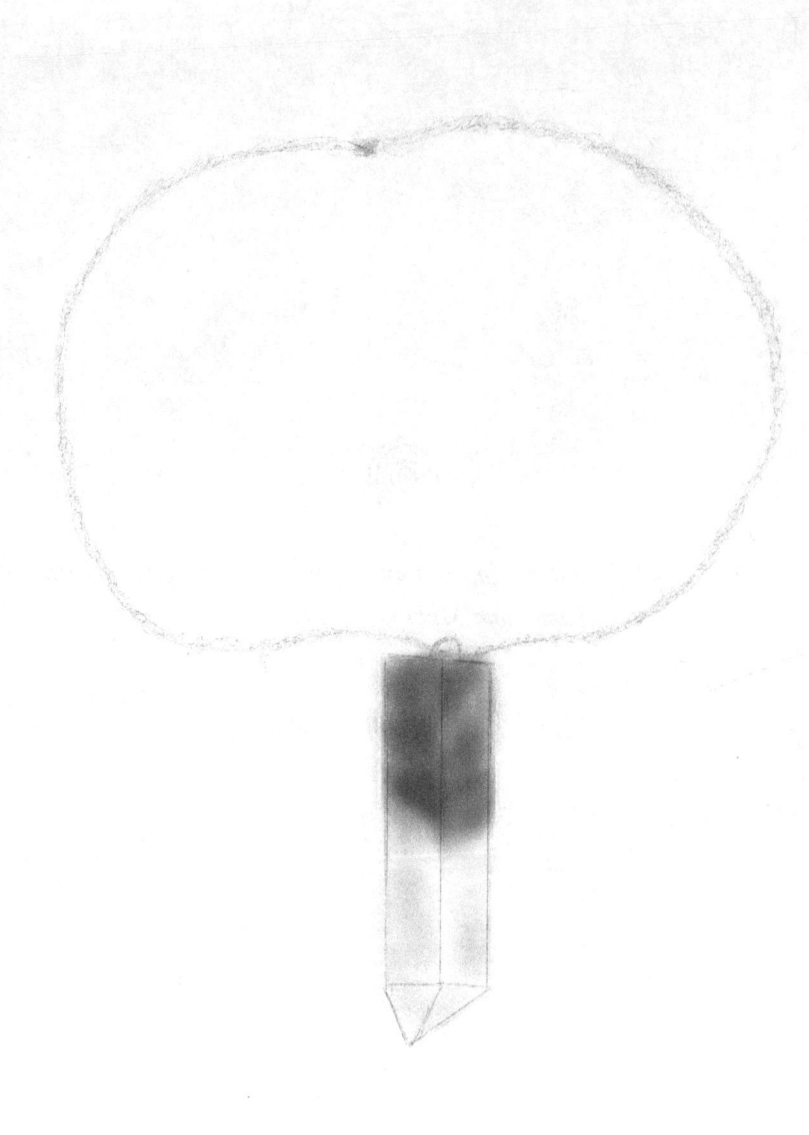

CONTENTS

ONE
STRANGE BEGINNINGS

All was quiet in the small Indiana town on that blustery winter's eve. Steam rose from the rooftops, encasing the neighborhood in heavy mist. Through the haze, a dark shadow advanced. It had set out at sunset, shrouding its surroundings, casting shadows and darkness in its wake. It snaked through valleys and towns, snuffing out any illumination as it passed. It traveled with restless intent as if searching for something ever out of reach.

The shadow enveloped Deerbrook Drive with a hiss, extinguishing street lamps one by one until the entire street lay in darkness. On that very street, in an ordinary house, if one cared to look closely enough, they could observe something really quite extraordinary.

Thwack-thump. Tiny wings smacked against crib rails. The creature fell on the mattress with a soft thud, generating a tiny cloud of green iridescent dust. All three creatures held their breath and watched the baby's face with dread. The baby, levitating in her crib, just sneezed and turned her head, still resting sound asleep.

"Goodness, Precious, don't wake her!"

"Sorry, I can't help it. My eyes aren't what they were."

"Your eyes were never what they should be. Hurry up, Snuke! More dusting. Hurry, before someone hears us. Before we're found."

Three tiny winged humanlike creatures—similar in size, but very different in features—fluttered around the baby's crib, emitting flashes of green light as they moved. From a distance, the lights could be easily

1

mistaken for fireflies, but anyone who knew anything about the world beneath the veil would've known what they really were: fairies.

Precious was long and thin with a narrow face and sharp features. A shock of red wiry hair protruded from her head with a streak of white fuzz through the middle. A pair of thick round spectacles rested on the end of her long hooked nose, magnifying her beady brown eyes and making them appear disproportionately large for the rest of her features. The mole on the left side of her nose seemed to help keep her spectacles from falling off her face.

Precious was blind as a bat—in fact, she was one-sixteenth bat. Her great, great, great, great, great grandfather, Rory Mcflaterhearn, who didn't have the best eyesight himself, overindulged in too much honeywine one evening and ended up falling in love with and marrying a bat. It was a happy marriage in the early years, but in the end, the bat got tired of his roving and carrying on and had him for dinner. Of course, not before giving birth to Precious's great, great, great, great grandmother.

Snuke was young, as far as fairies went. She was only seventy-seven. In fact, her adult wings had only sprouted last year. Snuke's long electric blue hair framed her delicate features and contrasted with her amber eyes. A pretty little thing, indeed. Honeybee saw something in Snuke, despite her young age and inexperience, and hand chose her for this mission.

Honeybee was portly and rosy-faced. Her blonde hair, piled high in a bun on top of her head, had many streaks of silver. As the eldest, she had assumed a matronly role in her later years. While she had a naturally good disposition, given the dark circumstances of events, she had taken on a rather authoritative demeanor as the 'expert in all things important'.

"We were lucky to get here first," Honeybee whispered.

"Aww, she is beautiful! Look at those rosy cheeks. And those ears!" Snuke clapped her hands excitedly as she sprinkled green iridescent dust over the baby's head.

Precious perched on the crib's rail admiring the baby. "My

goodness. In all my years, Honeybee, I've never seen one more darling. I can feel the Juma from here."

"How wonderful! I feel so alive!" Snuke darted up to the ceiling, did a somersault mid-air and then fluttered back down to the crib's rail. She brushed back her long blue hair from her face as she perched alongside Precious and helped her sprinkle more dust over the baby.

"More dusting, you two," Honeybee guided them. "Just a bit more. There we go."

"Ooh ooh, I hope this works!" Snuke cried in a sing-song voice.

"Yes, yes, deary. I think it will." Precious slapped her knobby knees. "It has to."

"SILENCE, YOU TWO, WE MUSN'T BE FOUND!" Honeybee, red in the face with her hands on her hips, struggled to regain her composure. "Just a bit more dusting and we're ready for the incantation," she managed to say in a softer tone.

"Yes, the incantation. Yes…yes…hmm…oh…now…where did I put that? I wrote it down so I wouldn't forget. Oh my goodness!" Snuke squeaked as she fumbled through her tiny satchel.

"You didn't bring the incantation?" Honeybee huffed. "How in the world did you forget to bring the incantation? This is the most important thing you've done, probably the most important thing you'll ever do. HOW COULD YOU HAVE FORGOTTEN TO BRING THE INCANTATION? I'LL HAVE YOUR WINGS CLIPPED FOR THIS." Her face turned bright fuchsia as the tips of her pointy ears wriggled and flapped in outrage.

"SHHH, loves. They'll hear us," Precious whispered.

"Easy, Honeybee. Umm…I didn't forget. I put it in a good place for safekeeping is all and now I….oh me." Snuke, fumbling and breathless, finally managed to retrieve a tiny piece of parchment from her satchel. "Oh there now. Here we go. Gather 'round now, loves…ready…say it slowly."

All three fairies encircled the tiny babe. "*Oowatha cabada caluooh.*"

The baby, levitating above her crib, floated back down and landed softly on the mattress.

Snuke squeaked, "Did it work? Did it?"

"Quiet. Someone's coming. LIGHTS OUT."

At that very moment, the shadow, just outside the window, halted its advance. It retreated like a hound that loses a scent or one called home by its master. The twinkling stars and street lamps illuminated the neighborhood once again. In the very same moment, the door to the nursery swung wide open, casting an amber light into the room.

Mrs. Wrigley rubbed and blinked her eyes a few times because the source of the tinkling chimes she had faintly heard appeared to be coming from three tiny green lights that fluttered and flashed around her infant daughter's crib. The three tiny winged figures froze and held their breath. At a second glance, the green lights were gone, leaving Mrs. Wrigley perplexed and looking for a rational explanation as to what she saw. "My eyes are tired. Must be the reflection from the light on the humidifier," she muttered to herself.

Mrs. Wrigley stood over the crib admiring her baby girl. Her heart swelled with love as she looked over her sleeping daughter. She leaned over and drew in a breath, taking in her sweet smell, like fresh cream and honey. She caressed the baby's cheek and kissed her forehead. Then, she turned and walked toward the hall. For a brief moment, Mrs. Wrigley looked back over her shoulder to see if she could see the green lights again, but they were gone. She shook her head. "I need to get more sleep," she muttered as she walked out of the nursery and closed the door.

"All clear, loves," Precious announced. "She's gone."

"Did it work? Did it?"

"I think it did, Snuke. I don't feel it as strong anymore. As she gets older, it'll get more and more difficult to hide," Precious warned.

Honeybee perched over the crib rail, crossed her arms, and dug in her heels. "Well, we'll be here when the time comes."

***

The tiny babe grew to become a sweet, vibrant little girl, always curious about the world around her. Her curiosity often got her into trouble with the Wrigleys, but only because they loved her so much and tried to keep her safe. The child's name was Scarlett—her mother was a fan of *Gone with the Wind*.

The curious thing about Scarlett was that odd things seemed to happen around her. It wasn't so much that she had several imaginary friends, and it wasn't the fact that she could often be found in strange predicaments, like the time Mrs. Wrigley found her napping in the chandelier when she was a toddler. It was that strange things seemed to happen to people whenever they were around her.

One time while making Scarlett's lunch, Mrs. Wrigley could have sworn she saw a leprechaun fixing himself a sandwich in her kitchen, but in the blink of an eye, he was gone. Another time, while watching Scarlett playing in the living room, Mr. Wrigley could have sworn he heard their pet beagles, Betty and Elvis, having a conversation with one another over who was going to keep watch that night until the haarrybee—or something or other—came back.

One day, when Scarlett had just turned three, she played outside in the front garden as the mailman approached to deliver the mail. He claimed that a black furry creature with red eyes chased him away from the mailbox. It took the Wrigleys three months of complaining to the post service to have their mail delivered to their door again. When the mailman did add thirty-three Deerbrook Drive back to his route, Scarlett again played nearby as he approached when he claimed eleven miniature men blocked his path and wouldn't allow him to pass.

It was a bizarre story for anyone to believe. The mailman had clearly lost his grip on reality, but after twenty-one years of service, the post office manager didn't have the heart to discipline him or let him go. Instead, he sent him for psychiatric therapy, and thirty-three Deerbrook Drive was taken off the delivery route permanently. Mr. and Mrs. Wrigley had to rent a post box, and that was how they'd gotten their mail ever since.

***

The moon gave off its last light as the sun broke over the horizon on the dawn of the winter solstice of Scarlett's third year. "Honeybee, this is all getting out of control. We can't protect her if we can't hide

5

her Juma—or at least hide it until she's old enough to know how to use it. She sees us now, and her parents are starting to see," Precious pleaded as she wrung her hands, looking up at the moon.

"No, she's still just a baby."

"Something must be done, Honeybee. We can take her to River—"

"Ah. Don't even say it, Precious. Haven't you considered that I might have thought of that already? It's too close, and there are too many there. It's the first place they'll look."

"Exactly, Honeybee. With all that extra Juma, how in the world will anyone ever know what she really is?"

Honeybee looked to the horizon. She squared her shoulders, her expression resolute. "We'll do another cloaking incantation and a muddling spell. That should buy us more time. We'll call in reinforcements, and we'll do it tonight. Not another word about Riverstone."

Precious sighed. "Ho hum. Very well, Honeybee."

And the incantation worked, indeed.

TWO
AWAKENING

She could see her breath as she walked barefoot down the long damp hallway. The only light came from torches spaced along one side of the stone wall. The cold made her bones ache and her breath catch in her throat. Her nose burned with the acrid smell of sulphur. At the end of the hall, a stone gargoyle with glowing red eyes, its menacing deep voice cut through her like a razor.

"You think you can defeat me? You can't. Let it go. It's easy." She couldn't move a step closer, frozen in fear. "You are going to have to choose sides," it hissed as its red eyes glowed.

Scarlett woke gasping for air, her pajamas soaked in cold sweat. She pushed away her sweat soaked hair and looked around the warm familiarity of her bedroom. With the morning sun streaming in through her window, she took several deep breaths until her heart stopped racing and her breathing returned to normal. "Just a dream," she said to herself. She stretched, rolled out of bed and headed into the bathroom to get ready for school.

A haze covered the room. It looked like she was seeing things as if looking through a veil. First, she thought it was smoke, but after glancing up at the smoke alarm's green light, she knew it couldn't be fire. It must be just sleep in her eyes.

It was the morning of her thirteenth birthday. Ten years had passed without incident. Scarlett had no knowledge or memory of strange creatures or any unusual circumstances for that matter. Up until now, her life had been ordinary. Just a girl, with an uncanny talent for playing music, who lived in the Midwest with her adoring parents.

While her life seemed perfectly ordinary, there was still something a bit peculiar about Scarlett. Even though she liked things that other kids her age enjoyed and had little difficulty getting along with others, she often found herself yearning to find a deeper meaning to the world around her. As the child of scientists, she questioned everything. Why do we live in towns and cities? Why do we get our food from the grocery store? Why do I have to go to school? Why do you have to go to work?

Her quest for a better understanding tended to make some people uncomfortable. While normally soft and expressive, her cerulean blue eyes could also be piercing—as if they could penetrate flesh and bone to gaze upon one's soul. As the subject of one of her many inquisitions, under her gaze, she was even known to make some adults squirm from time to time.

After getting showered and dressed for school, Scarlett went downstairs. Her father looked up from the news on his laptop. "Good morning birthday girl. Have a good day!"

She kissed the top of his mop of dark curls. "Is it smoky in here?"

He raised his eyebrows and shot her a strange look. "No."

"Hmm."

Stepping into the kitchen, she ran into her mother, who was frantically fixing coffee in her takeaway mug. Her red hair fell in her face, and she hurried to get ready to rush out the door to work. She was late, but her mother was always late.

She flashed her green eyes on Scarlett. "I have a surprise for you tonight, birthday girl. *Mwah.*" Her mother kissed her on the forehead. "Have a good day, honey. We'll go out for dinner tonight, *Castilianos.* Your favorite!"

Scarlett smiled and nodded. "Sounds good, Mom." She stuffed a banana and a muffin into her bag, waved goodbye and walked to the end of the lane to catch her bus.

The haze was no better by the time she stepped off the school bus, but, when she blinked or rubbed her eyes, it seemed to go away for a while. By lunchtime, it hadn't improved and, every now and then, she could see a flash or sparkle from the corner of her eye. She saw Mrs. Goodspeed, the school nurse, who told her it didn't look like an infection but to have her parents follow up with an eye doctor if it didn't get better by tomorrow.

Even though some of her classmates came up to her to wish her a happy birthday throughout the day, it didn't help distract her from thinking about the horrible dream. She couldn't remember much other than the red eyes and the menacing voice, but it was enough to disturb her. She shuddered, remembering the sound of the gargoyle's sharp metallic voice and how the red demonic eyes pierced her like a jolt of electricity. Even now, with the afternoon sun blazing through the classroom windows to warm her, the memory made her shiver and left a bitter metallic taste in her mouth.

She made it through last period, Algebra, rubbing her eyes whenever the room filled with haze. The strange thing was that the cloudiness didn't seem to affect the clarity of her vision. She could easily see the formulas on the blackboard just the same—with or without the haze. The bell rang. She gathered her books and rushed to get the bus home. She had thirty minutes to change and un-disaster her hair before her parents got home from running "errands" after work.

***

"Ugh!" She grunted as she looked at herself in the mirror, trying to pin up pieces of her hair in a sophisticated half up and swept to the side do she saw in one of her mother's magazines. Scarlett had a hard time doing anything with her wild golden hair. She could never get the hang of braiding it, despite her mother trying to teach her. She cut it short a few times thinking it might help control the mess, but that only made it worse. The ends kept sticking up in several places, and no amount of styling product could make them stay down. At least with long hair, the weight of it kept it from sticking up, and she only had to worry about keeping it from becoming a tangled mess; which, if she wore it down, it was a mess within the hour.

STOMP…STOMP…CRACK…BANG… Scarlett heard noises downstairs. *They must be back early.* She started changing out of her jeans and into the new outfit her mother bought for her to wear for her birthday dinner. *Castilianos* was her favorite restaurant. They had the best vegetarian lasagna and a lot of non-dairy options for dessert.

Tap…tap…tap… She heard someone at the front door. Scarlett continued getting ready, hoping her parents would get it.

Knock…knock…knock… The tapping became knocking, but no one was answering. Frazzled, sweat formed on her brow as she struggled to pin the side without making any bumps or turning the rest of her hair frizzy.

KNOCK…KNOCK…KNOCK…. The sound became louder, more forceful. *Mom and Dad must still be out getting my "surprise" birthday cake,* she thought. Every year the Wrigleys have a cake made and hide it in the garage until just before bedtime. Then they would bring it out with candles lit and sing Happy Birthday, and they would all have a late night snack. Now, the knocking became loud thumping, *THUMP….THUMP….THUMP,* like the police, right before they kick the door in. Not that Scarlett had ever seen the police kick in a door in her neighborhood, but she'd seen it on TV.

Giving up on her hair, Scarlett threw it up in a bun and went downstairs. "I'M COMING," she cried out. She stomped downstairs, opened the door and held it open halfway so as not to let the dogs out, although the dogs were nowhere in sight. A tall, thin man stood on the porch. He had a long goatee and a mustache that curled around his red puffy cheeks. He wore a top hat and a long, old-fashioned coat with a red carnation pinned to the lapel—a very strange outfit for Indiana, indeed. His hands and arms were long. The nails on his fingers came to a point.

He spoke with a purr and flashed his pointy teeth. "Helllllooo, Scaaarletttt. Happpy Biiirthday! Youu probably don't know meee, but I am a cousinnnn of your motherss's, Felixxx McCaan." Felix took off his hat and bowed, revealing long yellow ringlets that bounced around when he moved as if they had a life of their own.

She stood in the doorway and blinked a few times, eyeing him up and down. She didn't recognize the stranger and everything about him—his appearance, his voice, his drawn-out manner of speaking—made her feel ill at ease. A shiver ran down her spine as the hairs on the back of her neck stood up. She began assessing how quickly she could slam and lock the door in his face and make it to the phone to call her mother or the police.

"Oh dear, she didn't tell you about meeee?" he purred. "Oh my, no wonder you look soooo concernnned. Here I am, a stranger showing up on your doorrrr minutes before you're about to leave for your birthday dinnerrr. You're going to *Castilianosssss* isn't that riiight, your favorite…hmm?" Scarlett just stared at him blankly. *Who is this weirdo? He looks so strange…creepy voice.* Instinct told her not to trust him.

"Well, my dear, I'm surpriiiisssed your mother didn't tellll you about meeee. I was passing through on busssinessss. I'm a busssinessssman you seeee and I contacted her because it has been yearsss since we saw eachotherrrr, and I thought it would be nice to connect and finally meet youuuu in personnn." He gave her a pointy-toothed smile, blinking several times.

Unconvinced, Scarlett stood in the doorway, blocking the entrance with her arms folded. The stranger continued, "I know so much about you, Scarrrlettttt. Anyway, I'm sure your motherrrr will be back in a few minutes after she picks up your cakke." Scarlett's eyes widened. *How could he know about my cake?*

"Oh deearr. I'm sorrrry. She told me it was a surprissse and here I've ruinnnned it!" Pouting, he batted his eyelashes, giving her an over exaggerated look of remorse.

Scarlett shrugged. *I guess he is mom's cousin. How else could he know about my birthday dinner and my surprise cake?* Reluctantly, she opened the door and gestured for the stranger to come inside. "My parents should be home soon. Why don't you wait in the kitchen?" Trying to keep some physical distance between them, she walked ahead of him as she led him down the hall toward the kitchen. She called back, "Where did you say you were from?"

"Kansasss, deearr."

Scarlett tried to make polite conversation with the stranger, but her mind reeled with suspicion. "Can I offer you a cup of tea?" Her mother's family was from the old country, where other than stout and whiskey, tea was the preferred drink. Her mother was raised on it. *"There's not a problem that a good cup of tea can't solve,"* was what her grandmother always said. It was a staple in the Wrigley household.

"Yes, deearr. Tea would be luuuvleee."

Scarlett busied herself putting the kettle on the stove and setting the cream and sugar on the table. At the sight of the pitcher of cream, the stranger's eyes widened. He began licking his lips and salivating quite noticeably.

"Would you like cream and sugar?"

"Only a bit of sugar for me, deearr," he said, rubbing his throat. He pulled out a handkerchief from his pocket and mopped up the sweat beading on his forehead. His actions told a different story: he really didn't mean what he was saying and would like nothing more than a large helping of cream for his tea.

Scarlett poured some cream for her own tea. Felix's eyes became wild, his desire for it unmistakable. At the risk of sounding rude, Scarlett thought it too odd not to question. "Why not cream? You look like you really want some."

"Oooh deearr, is it that obviousss? I recently found out I'm alleeerrrgic. But I do soooo enjoy all sorts of milk products, espeeecially cream." His eyes rolled to the back of his head, and he smacked his lips. "Oooh, my!"

Scarlett didn't discuss her own dietary choices but said, "I know the feeling," more or less to continue on with polite conversation. This was about the strangest interaction she'd ever had with a person. She watched the cat clock in the kitchen, counting the seconds as the cat's eyes and tail moved side to side, keeping rhythm with the ticking of the second hand. "My parents shouldn't be much longer."

***

Mrs. and Mr. Wrigley stared at the clock hanging on the back wall over the bakery counter. The minute hand had moved thirty times since they entered the shop and the baker still hadn't re-emerged from the back.

"This is getting ridiculous," Mrs. Wrigley hissed under her breath. "We've never had to wait this long."

After thirty years in business and thousands of birthday cakes, the baker couldn't manage to write *Happy Birthday Scarlett*. Although he'd written this phrase every year for the last thirteen years on the same type of cake—non-dairy double chocolate fudge—he kept messing up the word "happy" and had to clean off the icing seven separate times and start over. His hands shook with every attempt. By now, the Wrigleys were thirty minutes late for picking up their daughter.

"Oh, I hope she isn't waiting around on us and getting too hungry," Mrs. Wrigley sighed, looking again at the clock.

"No, she's probably trying to tame her hair," Mr. Wrigley mused.

Finally, the baker emerged from the back looking confused, his eyes bloodshot. He handed Mrs. Wrigley the cake. "Sorry...I...I had trouble with the lettering."

Honeybee and Precious watched silently. They were not accustomed to leaving Scarlett for any length of time, but Precious had a dream the night before of trouble on the horizon. They assumed it might be something mundane like a traffic accident, so they followed the Wrigleys on their errands to ensure their safety. But, when the baker emerged from the back, they sensed dark magic around him and flew into high alert.

Since muddling spells had been known to go awry with disastrous consequences, Honeybee wrung her hands, anxiously looking all around to find something to get the Wrigleys moving without making their presence known. Otherwise, she would have to risk casting a muddling spell to change how the events would be remembered.

Outside, a clap of thunder cut through the air. The sky darkened as heavy rain beat against the windows. Mrs. Wrigley paid the baker and looked to the storm raging outside. "We need to be getting back. We can pick up the candles at the gas station after dinner," she said to her husband. They hurried to their car and headed for home with the two fairies following close behind.

***

"You knooow, I'm surprised your mother didn't tell you about meeee. I know so much about you, my deearr," Felix purred, clicking his tongue on the roof of his mouth. "Yes, yes, yes, very much indeeed. That reminds me. I brooought you somethingggg." Fluttering his eyelashes, he pulled a box of finely wrapped chocolates out of his long and strangely old-fashioned coat. "Here you are, my deearr, the finest chocolates in all of Sidhe—er umm...Kansas. Doooo try the strawberry filling ones first. They are diviiine."

Scarlett narrowed her eyes. The polite thing to do would be to thank the stranger for the present, but somehow, she couldn't get the words out or make any gesture to accept or acknowledge the gift.

Mmmrlmrlmrl, thump, thump, thump. Scarlett turned and looked toward the coat closet where the noise had come from. *Mmmrlmrlmrl, thump, thump, thump.* Sometimes the dogs wrestled with one another. Although they were pretty old now, they still messed around and created a ruckus from time to time. But Betty and Elvis were nowhere to be seen.

Felix began unwrapping a piece of chocolate. "Here, my deearr. Try this one; it's filled with strawberry creeeeam. Who doesn't like strawberry creeeeam...hmm?" He held it out to her, waving it beneath her nose.

"Mmmrlemrrrmlee." *Thump, thump, thump.* Scarlett thought she head a muffled voice say, *"Ooont ake ihh."* *Thump, thump, thump.* *"Oooont aaaake ihhh."* The sound from the closet became louder *THUMP, THUMP, THUMP.* The floor and surrounding door frame shook under the force. Then, a loud *bang* and *snap* as the door splintered into pieces and a small and strange looking man the size of a toddler crashed through.

It looked like his mouth had been sewn shut with twine. He frantically pulled at the stitches. One...two...three stitches came loose. "Ooont take it!" Panting and grunting, the little man rushed toward Scarlett and her strange visitor as fast as his stubby little legs could

14

carry him. Four…five…six stitches came loose. He reached the stranger and knocked the chocolates out of his hand. "DON'T TAKE IT!" he yelled as he tackled Felix to the floor.

Scarlett jumped out of the way just in time to not get taken down along with him. She backed away from the scuffle, leaning against the wall. Shaking and wide-eyed, she couldn't bring herself to speak as she stood staring at the strange little man and her mother's creepy cousin as the little man pummeled Felix's face with his tiny fists.

Betty and Elvis tore through the kitchen screen door and bit down on the downed stranger's wrists and ankles while the little man struggled to put him in a chokehold.

"Hold still, you!"

"*Ngéibheann!*"

A tiny winged blue-haired lady, about the size of a hummingbird, flew into the kitchen and shot green bolts of lightning from her fingertips. Thick vines appeared from nowhere and ensnared Felix. Within seconds, the vines had Felix hog-tied and gagged. With him subdued, Betty and Elvis limped over to Scarlett, whimpering from long sharp thorns sticking in their paws, necks, and mouths.

"I got here as fast as I could. A thorn bush caught these two, and it took me half a dozen spells to free them. I couldn't smell this one coming. Could you?" The tiny blue-haired lady asked the little man.

"Naah," he said as he spat the remaining pieces of twine onto the floor. "Blindsided me. All I saw was a flash o' red then BOOM; there I was in the closet with my pie hole sewn shut. She could see him, you know. She let him in. She was talking to him. I had to do something before she accepted his gift." The little man hung his head down. "I let her see me," he stammered. "She saw me bust through the closet."

"Well, we'll just have to muddle her when we get this mess sorted out. You did right, Nick dear. Goodness only knows what would've happened if you didn't stop him." The pretty little blue-haired lady bit her bottom lip and rubbed the tip of one of her sparkly wings. "Oh me. Where are Precious and Honeybee?"

Scarlett tried to pull the thorns from her poor dogs and soothe them, but couldn't take her eyes off the scene. She trembled, but couldn't bring herself to speak. *What are they?*

The ugly little man had a large bulbous nose. His skin was withered and his huge pointy ears stuck out like a bat's. Tufts of wiry black hair sprouted from his balding head. The only pleasant looking thing about him were his large green eyes that seemed to sparkle and shine when he smiled.

He was dressed in children's shoes and jeans except for his baggy t-shirt that hung down past his knees. It had a Led Zeppelin album cover printed on the front. *That shirt is familiar. It looks exactly like my shirt that went missing last year. It even has a chocolate stain on the bottom in exactly the same spot.*

"We need to clean this place up before they get back," the tiny winged blued-haired lady said as she looked around at the disaster in the kitchen. She and the ugly little man busied themselves picking up the knocked over chairs and wiping up the spilled cream and sugar.

"*Dheisiú.*" The blue-haired winged woman flicked her fingers and the closet door repaired itself completely. She then repeated this for the broken screen door. With Felix still tied and gagged on the floor, they went about the kitchen putting things away as if they had lived there for years and knew exactly where everything went.

A small frightening creature covered in black fur with red eyes flew in from the window and crashed onto the kitchen floor. "I'm here. Let me at him," it grumbled in a raspy voice. It sprang at the bound stranger and chomped on his leg with its razor-sharp teeth.

"YOWL!" Felix cried under his gag.

"We got it, Sweetie Pie. Enough till Honeybee gets home."

Home? They live here? Scarlett couldn't be more confused if a pack of three-eyed elephants riding winged monkeys flew around her kitchen. *Maybe I'm having an aneurysm.*

Betty and Elvis stood stoically at Scarlett's feet licking their wounds and couldn't help but give off little whimpers.

"Poor little loves…*leigheas.*" The blue-haired woman flicked some sparkly stuff on the dogs. Scarlett let out a gasp to see the deep wounds around their mouths, necks, and paws healed before her eyes.

Two more winged creatures came flying into the kitchen. "We got here as quickly as we could. What happened? Who's this?" the plump one asked.

The black furry creature grinned as he chomped on Felix's leg causing Felix to make muffled cries through his gag. *Maybe it's not an aneurysm. I'd probably be dead by now.* Scarlett looked down at her feet, then her arms and hands. She waved her hands in front of her face, and she saw a rainbow prism trail as the image of her hands passed before her eyes. Then she wiggled her fingers and toes. Again, prism trails followed her movements. *Nope, not dead. But I've definitely lost my mind. What are they?* Then all the childhood fables came back to her. "Fairies," she said under her breath with recognition. And as she said it, she knew it was true.

"How did you find her? Who sent you?" the plump winged fairy interrogated the stranger. She took off his gag as the ugly little man waved the pitcher of cream under his nose. The stranger's eye bulged as drool poured down his chin, creating a gross puddle on the kitchen tile.

"Come on now. You're caught. Take the cream and pay us your service," the little man barked. The stranger tried to resist, but his eyes bugged out more and more with each pass beneath his nose. Sweat poured from his brow, and his tongue rolled out of his mouth and wagged on the floor. "Come on…take it. I know you want it. Take it!"

The stranger, exhausted from struggling against his captors, gave a nod of acceptance. The vines holding him hostage loosened, allowing him to free his hands, grab the pitcher, and empty the contents in one gulp. Still panting and gasping for breath, he smacked his lips and rolled his eyes to the back of his head as if savoring the most delicious thing he had ever tasted.

"Who are you?" The plump fairy demanded.

"My naaame….*Gasp*…is Felix McCaan…*Gasp*…of the Borg County clan."

"Why did you come here?"

"I took a contraaact for 500 nuggets and a lifetiiiime supply of milk and honeyyy to find the girrl. Not hurt herrr, just find herrr and indenture herrr to follow me back to Borg County wherrre the gobliinnn who paid me said he needed to taalk to herr. He said he wanted to talk, that's alll! He said he would bringgg herr right backk when he was through, honnest! I wouldn't hurtt the girl," he pleaded as his eyes widened and he batted his lashes in an exaggerated attempt to appear innocent. By the twinkle in his eye, it was obvious Felix could care less what the goblin did with her so long as he got his payment.

The furry black creature bit down on Felix's foot.

"Yowl! My footsie! Make him stop. I tooold you what I knoooow."

The furry black creature let up for a moment, allowing the plump fairy to continue her interrogation. "What of this goblin? What is his name?"

"I don't knoooow. I just met him at the puuuubbb."

With a nod from Honeybee, the furry creature's red eyes flashed with delight as he sunk his teeth into Felix's leg.

"Yowl! Smorg...Smorg...he said his name was Smorg...yowl!"

The furry creature kept chomping, cackling with glee.

"Ok, Sweetie Pie."

Chomp, chomp.

"SWEETIE PIE, STOP!"

Groaning, the furry red-eyed creature opened his mouth, slowly withdrawing his sharp teeth from Felix's leg. With a huff, he stomped under the kitchen table to pout with his arms folded across his chest.

"Sweetie Pie, you must go to Borg County and find out what you can about this Smorg. Do it discreetly," the plump fairy ordered.

"And make sure you're not followed back!" the blue-haired one added. With a nod of his head, the black furry creature disappeared. They all looked at Felix, still bound on the floor.

"What do we do with this one?" the little man asked.

Creak. The door from the garage opened. Scarlett heard footsteps in the hall. "Scarlett, we're back! Are you ready?"

Scarlett turned toward the sound of her mother's voice, but she couldn't bring herself to respond. She stood still like a fly stuck in a web, a web of crazy, mesmerized by the spectacle before her.

"Honestly, hon, I can't believe that storm. It came out of nowhere." Her parents' footsteps drew nearer.

"Yes, it was strange, but it's all clear now. There you are! Are you ready?" her father asked.

Scarlett looked from her parents to the strange man bound and gagged on the kitchen floor and the motley crew surrounding him, then back to her parents. She expected some reaction, revulsion or shock or some gesture to acknowledge the events taking place in their kitchen. But they just stared at her, waiting.

"Scarlett? Hello? Earth to Scarlett. Are you ready?" her father asked again.

Scarlett began to panic. *Don't they see this? So, I am crazy then. I'm only thirteen. I'm too young to be crazy!* She looked back and forth between her parents and the bizarre group assembled in her kitchen. *Maybe it's taking them a minute to process.* But no, her mother stuffed her keys and a water bottle into her purse and gestured for Scarlett to get moving.

"Send him to the badlands," said the blue-haired fairy.

"No, too lenient for the likes of him. Take him to the judge," the little man gruffed.

"No, Nick. We can't draw attention to this situation, and you know how he likes to make an example," the blue-haired fairy argued.

"Well, how are we supposed to let him get away with this?" The ugly little man raised his voice, his cheeks turning red with rage.

The plump fairy intervened, "This situation is too delicate, indeed. We'll baffle him and set him onto the Seven Paths of Redemption. That'll buy us some time. We may still need him alive."

The little man, his face now beet red and stomping his feet, said, "Honeybee, he almost took her! We can't let him get away with this! We should've let Sweetie Pie finish him!"

The plump fairy they called Honeybee raised her voice as she pulled back strands of silvering blonde hair that had fallen from her neat bun. "NICK, YOU WILL OBEY. I AM THE AUTHORITY IN THIS

MATTER AND WHAT I SAY—"

"Honeybee," the thin red-haired fairy with thick spectacles, who had remained silent during this whole ordeal, interrupted. "Honeybee," she said again and pointed at Scarlett.

The hairs on the back of Scarlett's neck stood up as she looked at the red-haired fairy and saw that she stared right back at her.

"She sees us."

"Quickly," Honeybee barked. "Say it together."

All three chanted, "*Cuir tro-chéile.*"

Nothing happened. Scarlett continued to stare at the five creatures in her kitchen.

"Okay, try again." The three fairies flew around Scarlett's head, sprinkling green dust all over her. "One, two, three..."

"*CUIR TRO-CHÉILE*"

The dust tickled Scarlett's nose. She sneezed, and her eyes welled up. Sniffling and sneezing, she swatted at the winged creatures, trying to make them stop. The fairies maneuvered around, avoiding her blows. The Wrigleys tried to get Scarlett's attention while they watched their daughter jump around the kitchen swatting at something they couldn't see. Mrs. Wrigley pulled on Scarlett's arm.

"Snuke, a distraction," Honeybee ordered.

The phone rang in the living room, followed by a knock on the door. "I'll get it," her father said as he ran to the door while her mother went to answer the phone.

"This isn't working anymore," Precious sighed. "Honeybee, it's time." Precious turned to Scarlett and smiled at her with her brown magnified eyes. "Scarlett, honey, it's time you knew. You haven't lost your mind. Don't bother with the eye doctor, love. We are real. We've lived with you since you were a baby but no one—or usually no one—can see us, including your parents. Now, for the sake of your parents, love, pretend you don't see us. They'll not understand and only worry. We'll be with you at dinner. When they go to bed, we'll talk, and I'll tell you everything. Can you do that for me, love?"

It was as if all the blood rushed out of her head. Scarlett nodded, not knowing what to say.

"That's a good girl."

THREE
CHANGES ASTIR

Distracted by the three winged fairies flitting about, picking away at the various dishes and desserts as the waiter brought them to the table, Scarlett could barely concentrate at dinner. Precious managed to nick a few sips of Mrs. Wrigley's wine before Honeybee gave her a smack.

"These are dangerous times. You need your wits about you, fool!" Honeybee hissed.

Mr. Wrigley talked excitedly about their latest project. "This could mean big changes for us, hon."

"Uh huh, that's great Dad." Scarlett, already dizzy from watching the fairies flutter around the table, didn't even look up, opting to give her vegetarian lasagna her undivided attention out of fear she might get sick—or worse, look crazy as her eyes darted around the room looking at nothing.

After dinner, they stopped for gas. The fairies followed along outside the car. Scarlett watched in wonder at how quickly their little wings could move to keep up.

***

Nine p.m., time for Scarlett's "surprise". The Wrigleys ran out to the garage and returned with a large wrapped package and a birthday cake in the shape of a music note with thirteen lit candles.

"Chocolate cake, my favorite!" Scarlett clapped her hands, feigning surprise and amused they would still think it would be a surprise to her since they "surprised" her with cake every year. But her parents seemed to get so much joy out of it; Scarlett didn't have the heart to spoil it for them. They sang Happy Birthday to her and told her to make a wish before she blew out her candles. She took a deep breath and closed her eyes. *I wish I wasn't crazy. I wish the haze and the vision of winged creatures, ugly little men, and the pointy-eared stranger still tied up on the kitchen floor right in front of me will be gone when I open my eyes.* Then, she blew out the candles, snuffing out every last one. Unfortunately, when she opened her eyes, the motley crew remained staring right back at her. She pursed her lips and sighed. *Well, at least I tried.*

Scarlett gasped when her parents handed her a large wrapped present. She didn't even have to unwrap it to know. Its shape was unmistakable: a brand new guitar. Butterflies fluttered in her stomach before she let out a squeal. "I can't believe you bought it for me. I love it!" Scarlett played guitar, violin, and piano, but guitar was her favorite instrument by far. She had been saving up all summer to buy the very same one, but she still didn't have enough. It would have taken her until at least Christmas.

She tore open the wrapping and ran her fingers along its smooth body. She could see her reflection in its smoky finish as she began to tune the strings until her strumming produced rich, warm tones that resonated through the house. For a minute, she forgot about the fantastical creatures in her kitchen. "Thank you, thank you!" She hugged her parents and played them a tune.

***

After her parents went to bed, Scarlett crept downstairs into the kitchen. Felix still lay bound and gagged on the floor, and the ugly little man they called Nick sat on top of him.

"What are you?" she asked.

"I'm a leprechaun."

Scarlett raised her eyebrows. "But you don't even sound Irish."

Nick clicked his tongue on the roof of his mouth. "What, you expect me to have an accent and dance around in a green suit with a hat? Or maybe wear pointy little shoes and play a flute? Jeez, talk about stereotypes. This is America, sweethaahrt. Hmmff." He crossed his arms in a pout.

"I'm sorry. I didn't mean to offend you. I just always heard about leprechauns being from Ireland, and you don't dress like one, and you talk like you're from the Bronx."

"Yeah, well everybody's from somewhere, ain't they?" Nick climbed down from Felix's back and paced the room. "My mother was from the old country, but I've never been. She followed your grandmother to America when your grandmother was a little girl. I'm the twelfth generation leprechaun of the O'Bannister clan. My ancestors have been living with your ancestors for years. We've become attached to the women in your family, and for generations, we've taken up house wherever they live. My mother was pregnant with me when she came over with your grandmother and, I've been attached to your mother ever since she was born. She doesn't know it, of course, but I try to help her out wherever I can. I repair the heels on her shoes—my god that woman can wear out a pair of heels. Sometimes, I fold the laundry or clean the bathroom. Basically, I just try to keep her safe."

Scarlett couldn't help but laugh thinking of what her mother might do if she knew a leprechaun followed her around.

"Since we live for hundreds of years, I suppose I'll follow you around and live with you too until you have kids or probably even your kids' kids."

Exhausted from the day's events, she tried to digest the fact that this little man had been living with her all her life. Then, an icky thought crossed her mind. "You don't follow us into the bathroom, do you?"

Nick stopped pacing; his ugly face turned red as a tomato. It looked like steam could shoot out from his bat-like ears. "OF COURSE NOT. Silly, what do you think I am, some kind of sicko? Yuck!"

Scarlett breathed a sigh of relief. "What about the black furry thing?"

"Aww, Sweetie Pie? That's your father's bogey."

"Bogey? Like, bogey man?" Nick nodded. "But I thought bogeys were wicked creatures that tried to scare children."

"They are. Nasty things." Nick stuck out his tongue. "When your father was little, Sweetie Pie and his two sisters were out scaring kids one night when they came into his room trying to terrify him. While it worked, the poor kid slept with his parents for a month afterwards, but Sweetie Pie took one look at your father's cute face and fell in love. He came back night after night to check in on the tyke. He fought off his sisters one night when they came back to scare him again. He sent 'em packin'. Despite his nasty nature, he has a real soft spot for your dad—and for you too, you know. He's been shunned from the bogey community, of course, and the entire darkling community, for that matter. That don't bug Sweetie Pie; he's lived with your father ever since. I guess he's not so bad. But sometimes, he can't help but play tricks, like turning on all the lights in the middle of the night or opening the garage door or tearing apart the garbage in the kitchen, so the dogs get in trouble. His name's not really Sweetie Pie, it's Belzamoyle, but everyone calls him Sweetie Pie, although he hates it." Nick snorted.

"And what about him?" Scarlett pointed at the hogtied Felix.

"Him? He's an elf gone bad."

"Perimeter is secure," Honeybee announced as the three fairies appeared in the kitchen. "First things first: we need to find out more about the goblin who sent for her and if there are others. What with the trap set for the dogs and the bewildered baker that delayed our return home, we know he didn't act alone."

Honeybee tidied up her hair bun, wiped her hands on her tiny apron, and resumed her interrogation from this afternoon. "How many others know about her?" Nick propped Felix up and removed his gag so he could talk, but climbed on top of his shoulders and put him in a headlock for good measure. Nick was surprisingly strong for being the size of a toddler.

Felix opened his mouth to speak. "There are—" Just then, an arrow flew in through the window and pierced Felix's heart. He slumped over on the floor before he could utter another word. Scarlett could hear her heart thudding in her ears as her eyes darted around the room frantically looking for the attacker.

"Someone else is here. Quick!" Honeybee sprang into action, directing Nick and the other two fairies to follow.

In a *poof* of green sparkles, they disappeared outside to chase after the source of the arrow, leaving Scarlett dumbfounded and alone in the kitchen. She'd never even seen a dead body before, let alone watch someone die. She stared at the elf and the blood pooling on the tile beneath him. *Who was this creature? Did he have a family? Would anyone miss him? Was he really bad or just misguided?* She knew he didn't come here to do her any favors. From what she could gather from the conversations between Nick and the fairies, he planned on taking her somewhere where a goblin intended on hurting her. Maybe he did deserve to die, but staring into those dead glassy eyes, Scarlett couldn't help but feel sorry for the pitiful creature.

***

Shrill cackling echoed among the oak trees. The source, a pair of glowing green eyes. "*DÍBIR*," Snuke cried out. A flash of green filled the night sky and then the creature was gone.

"Where did you send it, love?" Precious asked.

"Along the Seven Paths of Redemption. It won't know where it is or how to get back at least until next spring."

Nick, Precious, Snuke, and Honeybee returned to the kitchen and stood over the body of Felix McCaan. "Well then, I guess that's that. I'll bury him in the yard before he starts to stink." Grunting, Nick began to drag the foul elf's body outside.

Precious sighed. "We can't hide her Juma anymore. There will be others more nasty and powerful than these two. Eventually, it will come for her, and when it does, she'll need an army behind her. Honeybee, it's time you consider Riverstone."

Flustered by the day's ordeal, Honeybee's round cheeks flushed. She perched on the edge of the sugar dish, wringing her hands. "It will take months to arrange. We'll have to create circumstances to cause the family to move; there are letters to be written…arrangements to be made…surely, you'd not have me separate her from her family?"

Blinking her magnified brown eyes, Precious tweaked the sole hair sprouting from the mole on the side of her nose, rolling it between her tiny fingers until she mustered the courage to confess. "Honeybee, I know I went behind your back, but I've been expecting this for a long time. The arrangements have been made. The family will be ready to move within the month."

Precious waited in silence for a thorough tongue lashing, but Honeybee only gave a weak smile and nodded in acceptance. "Good thing, Precious. I'll call in reinforcements till then."

While Snuke remained as sentinel outside her bedroom window, Precious and Honeybee tucked Scarlett into bed and told her about the world that lived beneath the haze; which was a preposterous story, indeed.

Portly, rosy-faced Honeybee patted Scarlett's shoulder and fluffed her pillow. "We live in a time, my dear, where there's too much darkness in the world. Most people live under a curse, and they don't even know it. The world is full of magic and magical creatures, you see, but most people don't see because the human world has been shrouded from its energy sources. The world has fallen out of balance, tipped to the side of darkness. The earth and the other elements have lost much of their power."

Precious peered somberly over her Coke-bottle glasses. "Years ago, love, the darkness sought to control the earth and all things in it. There were many wars, and many lightworkers fell in battle. Now, under a spell, the darkness sleeps while its servants remain to carry out its work. In the battle between light and darkness, the darkness became the victor, but not before we lightworkers could diminish its abilities. In exchange for keeping the darkness at bay, the energy sources were shrouded and a veil cast over the world to keep them separate. The veil weakens the abilities of all living things. For many humans, it keeps them from knowing their true selves and makes them too weak to cast off the darkness that overshadows their daily lives and keeps them enslaved. The haze in your eyes, love, is you looking through the veil to see the magic all around you."

"You see, people are magical too," Honeybee said. "They've just been separated from their energy sources for so long that they've forgotten themselves."

With raised eyebrows, Scarlett remained silent until they were finished. She had so many questions. "But, I don't understand. How—"

"Shh, child. It's time for sleep. Tomorrow is another day." Honeybee sprinkled dust over her head. Scarlett's eyelids grew heavy and drew closed before her head could even hit the pillow.

***

The next morning, Scarlett woke to the smell of fresh brewed coffee and pancakes and bacon frying in the kitchen below. It was Saturday. Her father liked to make the family a big breakfast on Saturday mornings. Scarlett rolled over and stretched. She couldn't believe the dream she had about fairies and a leprechaun living in her house, and an elf that tried to kidnap her.

The dream was all very heavy and too nonsensical for Scarlett to understand. Something about the energy levels in a person—or Juma, they called it—determined how in tune someone is with the magic in the world. According to the fairies in her dream, Scarlett's Juma was powerful, which made her special, but it also made her a target for creatures who served the darkness. She rolled over again. "What a crazy dream." Rubbing her eyes, she rolled herself out of bed and looked for her slippers.

Knock...knock... "You decent in there, sweethaahrt?" Her bedroom door swung open, and the ugly little man from her dream strolled in.

Scarlett gasped. "You're real."

"Yeah, doll. Of course, I'm real. C'mon, get dressed and have breakfast with your parents. They got news." Nick stopped at the door before leaving to go back downstairs. "And now that you can see us don't act like it around other people, okay? Or they'll think you're nuts and lock you up."

Scarlett took a deep breath. "Got it," she said under her breath as she threw on her housecoat and went downstairs.

"Good morning!" her father greeted and kissed the top of her head.

"Honey, she's up."

"Good morning!" Her mother beamed her a smile from across the kitchen.

They're both in a cheerful mood, Scarlett thought as she sat down at the table while her dad piled pancakes and bacon on her plate. She slid the bacon onto a separate plate. She had gone off eating meat ever since she watched a documentary on slaughterhouses. That was two years ago—not that her father had a head for these details. Her mother joined her with a mug of coffee in hand. As much as Scarlett loved the smell of coffee, she wasn't allowed to have it until she was sixteen. "It will stunt your growth," her mother always said.

When her father joined them at the table, her mother began, "Honey, we have some wonderful news. The work your father and I have been doing has gained quite a bit of recognition. The magnet train will be starting its trial runs this month, and we've been asked to head the program through the Environmental Protection Agency in Washington DC."

Scarlett just stared at them blankly, trying to ignore the pretty blue-haired fairy slurping maple syrup from her mother's pancakes while giving Scarlett a good morning wave.

Her father interjected, "Now, I know it's a big city, and we are all used to living in a small town, but there's this wonderful community not far outside of the city called Riverstone. It's really a nice town. It's nestled in a valley with mountains and a beautiful river runs through it."

Mrs. Wrigley interrupted, "But it gets better: there's a prestigious art school there!"

Her father continued, "The tuition is something your mother and I couldn't even dream of affording, but we made tuition coverage and a nice home close by a part of our contract. So you can go."

"They have a whole music program, hon—just as good as Juilliard," Mrs. Wrigley added.

As realization set in, it felt like Scarlett had the wind knocked out of her. Her breath came in gasps, her head reeling, her stomach twisting in knots. *I think I'm going to be sick.* In the past twenty-four hours, her life had been turned completely upside down. *Magical creatures exist, but no one but me can see them. I can't talk to anyone about it otherwise they'll think I'm crazy and now I have to leave everything I've ever known.*

She thought about her life in Indiana. While she would miss school parties and get-togethers with Jenny Spencer and Margo Brown, she couldn't honestly say she connected with either of them on anything more than a superficial level. Margo obsessed about her clothes to the point where she was mean to other kids who didn't meet her fashion standards. And Jenny was too preoccupied with boys and what other people thought of her to care about anything else. Sure, they went to parties and sleepovers together, but Scarlett didn't think she could call either one of them a best friend.

Over the summer, Scarlett found herself spending most of her time at the lake located behind her neighborhood with her beagles or at the library. Lately, she had become fascinated with stories of ghosts, mermaids, elves, and other fantastical creatures as well as Roman Catholic Saints and she spent a great deal of time reading about them. And of course, there was music. She could imagine her world without Jenny Spencer and Margo Brown and rest of the kids at Columbus Junior High but a world without music? Unfathomable. She dreamed of going to a place like Juilliard, but she knew that even if she was talented enough the only way was to luck into a scholarship.

The Wrigleys waited expectantly for her reaction. Indiana was all she had ever known so it was only natural her parents would expect Scarlett to be upset. But Scarlett was now preoccupied with the fact that fairies, leprechauns, and elves were real. And if Precious and Honeybee were right about her, then at some point there might be hundreds of foul creatures that would try to kill her and maybe even succeed. Scarlett gulped down the lump that had formed in her throat and shrugged. *At least I can still play music,* she reassured herself. Then she drew a deep breath and exhaled slowly. *I can handle this.*

"Well?" her mother asked.

She squared her shoulders and met their eyes. "That's great news.

When do we leave?" She forced a weak smile—it was all she could muster—stuffed a piece of pancake into her mouth, and continued to ignore Snuke and Precious as they fought over sips from the coffee creamer and Nick as he smacked his lips and licked bacon fat from the pan on the stove.

FOUR
NEW BEGINNINGS

Scarlett felt a distinct change in the energy around her as she passed through the town limits. Nestled in the Blue Ridge Mountains, Riverstone was a beautiful town. Plenty of trees with vibrant fall colors covered the beautifully rugged landscape. A hazy white and purple light radiated over the misty mountain range. It was fall. She was going to start her new school halfway through the semester. While this would normally be a source of great anxiety for anyone, Scarlett had become somewhat indifferent to it. She had bigger problems now.

Two days after her birthday she could fully read auras—not just pick up on the energy of people and things, but see it. She could also see any and all magical creatures that lived beneath the veil. She didn't even notice the haze anymore. Everything just appeared more vivid now.

Over the past month, her senses had heightened. She was sensitive to the slightest touch. With an acute sense of smell, her taste buds could detect the most intricate of flavors, making food so much more enjoyable. Or at least good food. It also made some food that much more unsavory. Unfortunately for Scarlett, her mother's cooking often fell into the latter category.

Her energy vibrated throughout her body, buzzing like an electric force field around her. It looked like bands of light around her body. Sometimes it was hazy white. Sometimes it took on a specific color, often dependent on her mood and sometimes it looked like all the colors of the rainbow. She noticed it seemed to vibrate at a higher frequency whenever she was close to nature. She could see her energy take form outside herself and feel the tingle of electricity when it came into contact with other living things.

She was amused and a little scared to find there was a symbiotic relationship between people and those behind the veil. A person's energy seemed to determine what kind of other-worldly creature was attracted to them and the human and creature seemed to feed off one another's energy.

Mr. Davis, the realtor they used to sell their Indiana house, was a petty and hateful man who went through life with a ghoul hanging around his neck. The ghoul had thin, sallow skin with pieces of its flesh rotting. Although no one else could smell it, the ghoul gave off a nauseating stench. Scarlett almost threw up the first time she met Mr. Davis and she held her nose whenever he came around to keep herself from gagging. The ghoul hissed at Scarlett whenever it saw her, but quickly retreated and hid behind Mr. Davis when she came near.

Past the scenic town limits was the lively town center. A farmers market, several coffee shops, and a few pubs lined the streets. She heard live music coming from one of the pubs as they drove by. Town square shopping area consisted of a used bookstore, an antique store, several clothing stores, a few boutique gift shops, a crystal shop that was hard to see inside because the windows were full of crystals and plants, and a tall abandoned Masonic looking building. Town hall was a quaint classic building with a steeple and a clock tower. Several wooded parks and walking paths extended beyond the main streets and square. All paths seemed to lead, at some point, towards the river that meandered through the town.

During their drive, Honeybee, Precious, and Snuke followed along outside the car while Nick rode in the back of the Wrigleys' Subaru next to Scarlett. She tried not to talk or look at him while her parents were paying attention, which was easy enough to do because he slept for most of the trip with his head on her lap, snoring and grunting the whole way. She had to wear headphones to drown out his snorts and groans. Sweetie Pie had still not returned as he was now deep undercover trying to find everything he could about the goblin Smorg and anyone else involved in the plot to capture her.

They finally rolled onto Riverside Drive, the street that would be their new home. The neighborhood was older and more established than her former neighborhood. Many mature trees and colonial style homes lined the streets. They pulled into the circular driveway of a brick mid-century colonial home with two bay windows with copper eaves. A stone birdbath sat in front of one of them.

"Home sweet home," Scarlett muttered as she hopped out of the car to check out her new digs.

***

Scarlett's stomach churned as she walked up the front steps of her new school, a massive stone building with a large balcony on the third floor. A knot formed in her throat when she saw two stone gargoyles perched on each end of the balcony, reminding her of the horrible dream she had the morning of her thirteenth birthday. It had only been a month, but it seemed like an eternity ago. She took a deep breath and walked through the large wooden doors. Inside, kids milled in and out of the halls, fumbling with their lockers and talking amongst themselves.

By now, Scarlett was used to seeing people's energy, but she was surprised by how many kids here had creatures associated with them. She saw a tiny dragon, a flower fairy, two elves, a gnome, and some creatures she didn't even recognize. She looked down at her registration instructions: report to Mr. Lechey for class schedule and locker code.

Mr. Lechey, the school administrator, seemed like a friendly man with rosy cheeks. He dressed in mismatched bright colors, orange shoes, purple pants, red shirt, and yellow tie. "Welcome to Rosemont School for gifted young people, Miss Wrigley. It's always nice to see new students," he drawled with a lisp and gestured for her to take a seat in his office.

He made small talk, asking her questions about where she moved from and what brought her to Riverstone. She answered politely as she played with the ends of her hair to calm herself. Giving Mr. Lechey her undivided attention proved to be impossible, distracted with the anxiety of starting a new school and the fact that a large pegasus sat on the floor next to Mr. Lechey. It neighed quietly, shook its mane, and nuzzled up against his thigh. The pegasus took up most of the floor space in the office and had to keep its wings tucked close by its sides to fit. Scarlett blinked a few times, still somewhat disbelieving what she saw. As quickly as she could, she got her locker code, school map, and schedule and backed out of the office. *I don't think I'll ever get used to this.*

Looking down at the map, she slammed right into a girl standing in front of her, knocking the girl to the ground and sending her books flying.

The girl let out a grunt as her butt hit the floor.

"I'm so sorry!" Scarlett cried, turning three shades of red.

The girl looked up at her and smiled. "That's okay."

"Here, let me help." Scarlett reached to grab the girl's hand to pull her up, and as she did, she saw the energy radiating around her hand wrap around and intermingle with the energy that radiated around the girl's hand. It tingled as their auras melted into one another. The girl smiled, causing her hazel eyes to smile too.

"Are you okay?" Scarlett asked as she pulled her to her feet.

The girl nodded. "You must be new." She was short and had light blonde hair with pink streaks. The pink streaks stood out against the gray uniform everyone was supposed to wear at Rosemont. A bright pink aura radiated around the girl. Scarlett could tell she wasn't a mean person and could let her guard down.

"Yes, first day," Scarlett said as she scrambled to pick up the girl's books.

"Are you sure you're okay?"

"Yes, I'm fine," the girl replied with a laugh, sticking out her hand to shake Scarlett's. "I'm Michelle."

"I'm Scarlett. Thanks for being cool, Michelle. Again, I'm really sorry about knocking you down."

"No worries. I'm kinda short, so I'm used to people tripping over me." Scarlett stared down at her map. "What are you looking for?" Michelle asked.

"I'm trying to find my locker; then I need to find room 206, first-period History."

"Oh, you're in my group." Michelle looked over the map. "That's right by mine. Here, I'll show you on the way to class."

As she guided Scarlett around, Michelle gave her the lowdown on Rosemont. "This school is over two hundred years old. Supposedly, it's haunted. It's well known for being a good school for music and the arts. Did you know Joan Byans went here? And so did Julia Divas."

"No, I had no idea." As if she wasn't already intimidated by the school, Scarlett looked at the framed alumni pictures along the hall and recognized a lot of the faces as famous musicians and artists. *Jeez. Am I talented enough to be in a place like this?* Joan Byans was a famous folk singer from the 60s who later became a peace ambassador to the UN. And Julia Divas was a famous movie star in the 1990s and early 2000s who now did Broadway shows.

"Anyway, there's a lot of really talented students here, but not everyone is that good. It's also just a place where rich people send their kids because there's nothing a person who has everything likes to brag about more than the fact that their kids are 'gifted'." Michelle rolled her eyes. "Some kids do get in on scholarships because they're talented, but it's so close to Washington that a lot of rich people from the city just make big donations to send their kids here. I'm kind of a mix: my parents aren't rich, but my dad's a senator. But, I'm a wicked drummer, and I dabble with poetry from time to time. We're from Iowa. Dad spent so much time in the capital over the last four years that Mom got fed up traveling and packed up me and my sister and moved us to the city. I just started coming here at the end of the summer. There are dorms here but a lot of kids are from the city, so they don't use them anymore because of the new magnet train line."

"Uh, yeah. That's kinda why I'm here. My parents developed the idea of the train, and they talked about it and promoted it so much that the EPA took it on as a project. So now they're heading the program here," Scarlett explained.

"That's so cool! Your parents must be geniuses. You must be really smart. I love the train. It's so fast. It only takes me twenty minutes to get here in the morning. If I started last year, it would've taken me over an hour by car each way. I'd probably have to live in one of the dorms. But now I can see my parents and hang out with my little sister at night."

Scarlett flushed and shrugged. "Uhh, I don't think I'm all that smart. I mean, I never had to repeat anything in school, but I don't get straight A's either. But I'm glad you like the train." Scarlett smiled. She didn't think what her parents did was all that impressive, but apparently to Michelle, it was. As convenient as the train was, Scarlett was grateful her parents had the option to do most of their work from home and only had to commute into the city twice a week, so she didn't have to live there. She loved the woodsy feel of Riverstone, and her house was so close, she could ride her bike to school every day and didn't even have to worry about catching a bus anymore.

A group of well-put-together girls walked past them. One of them, a tall, thin blonde girl, knocked into Michelle with her book bag. "Whoops! Sorry Michelle," she said with a sneer. It was obvious she knocked into Michelle on purpose and that she wasn't sorry. "Who's your new friend?" Michelle didn't say anything. She only sighed and shook her head. Seeing that she didn't get a rise from Michelle, the blonde girl continued, "Maybe she can help you fix your hair! It looks like a flamingo threw up on it." The other girls in the pack snickered.

Scarlett stared at the girl with her penetrating gaze. A creature lurked about the girl, but it was so translucent Scarlett couldn't quite make out what it was. Under Scarlett's scrutiny, a look of fear crossed the blonde girl's face. She put her head down and hurried on to class. The rest of the girls followed suit. Scarlett stared after them. She couldn't believe the assortment of dark brown auras intermingled with other colors that emanated from them.

"What was that?" Michelle asked with her mouth gaping open.

"What?" Scarlett asked.

"You just mean-mugged Vivian Patterson, and she took off like a scolded dog. That was fantastic!"

"I did? Huh."

"Anyway, don't mind them. They're like the 'mean girl' clique you see in movies only worse. But don't worry, I think they're only mean because their parents don't really care about them. They send them here and only want them home for holidays and parties where they can parade them around to look like the perfect family. I feel sorry for them."

They reached the door that read 206. Scarlett saw that all the seats were taken except for the two in the back. "You can sit next to me," Michelle reassured her. Relieved, she followed Michelle to the back of the class, grateful to have made at least one friend.

***

At lunch, Michelle showed Scarlett the cafeteria and gave her a forewarning about which meals were safe to eat and which cooks didn't wash their hands. Her uniform wouldn't be ready for another three weeks. Scarlett looked around at all the neatly dressed kids and all the older girls with their perfect makeup and sophistical hairstyles. Then she looked down at her Stone Temple Pilots t-shirt (her parents were 90s teens, so she grew up listening to their music) and jeans and wanted to shrink away until she was invisible. *I'll have to ask Honeybee if humans can even do that.*

They sat down at a long table with a group of kids. Out of the corner of her eye, Scarlett spotted a flash of Snuke's long blue hair and gossamer wings as she hovered nearby. Snuke waved and gestured the "okay" symbol. Scarlett nodded. *Just checking to make sure I'm alright.* Snuke fluttered out of sight. Scarlett smiled, happy to know that there were at least two friendly faces today.

"Who's this?" A tall dark-haired boy put his tray on the table where Michelle and Scarlett sat and plunked himself down next to them.

"I'm Scarlett," she answered and gave a small wave to everyone assembled around the table.

The dark-haired boy smiled. "Hi, I'm Grayson." He flashed her a smile, revealing his perfect white teeth. He was handsome and looked to be about sixteen. The energy bands flowing around him were very thick and opaque. While there were multiple colors in his aura, purple seemed to be dominant. Scarlett wondered what that could mean since she hadn't quite figured out the significance of aura colors or if there even was any significance. He scanned her features thoroughly. Scarlett wanted to shrivel up under his intense gaze.

"I'm Luke," a blond-haired boy with shaggy curls introduced himself. He seemed shy and a little nervous around new people. His aura was similar to hers only less intense and had a yellowish hue.

"I'm Louzanne." A pretty black girl with red frizzy hair and stylish thick-rimmed glasses waved at her. Her aura wrapped around her in waves and had many colors with maroon and earthy undertones.

"So what brings you to Rosemont halfway through the fall term?" Grayson asked.

"My parents were offered a job with the government, so we had to move."

"Where are you from?" Grayson asked.

"Indiana."

Grayson waited in anticipation to hear more, but Scarlett didn't elaborate. "It's hard to get a word out of you, isn't it?" he mused.

"Sorry, I…I just…this is a lot of change for me." Scarlett stared down at her shoes.

"Aww, never mind Grayson. Scarlett, you talk whenever you feel like talking, girl," Louzanne said as she punched Grayson's arm. "Just relax, it's not so bad here. I mean there are some jerks, snobs, and egomaniacs but it wouldn't be Rosemont without that, would it?" She gave Scarlett a reassuring smile. Then she leaned over so no one else could hear her. "I knew you were coming. I've been expecting you."

Scarlett's eyes widened, but before she could get her to clarify what she meant, Michelle interrupted with questions about her class schedule. By then, she had the group's undivided attention and couldn't ask Louzanne what she meant without everyone else hearing.

Instead, she asked each of them questions about themselves, where they were from and what kind of classes they liked at Rosemont.

She found out Louzanne's mother was a famous R&B singer, and while rock and roll was mainly Scarlett's forte, she was a big fan of Louzanne's mother. She was always on the road touring or away in treatment for her various addictions, which left Louzanne alone most of the time. While these circumstances were unfortunate, this didn't seem to affect Louzanne's outlook on life. She had an aunt who she had spent most of her life with that loved her like a daughter. So at least that somewhat made up for having an absent mother. After learning a little about each of them, they all seemed nice, although she couldn't wait to get Louzanne alone to find out what she meant.

***

When she registered online, Scarlett made sure to select music for every elective class. She knew they had an extensive music program, but her jaw almost hit the floor when she saw the music wing. It had a mini opera house complete with orchestra box and sound booths for kids interested in learning about recording arts. There were rooms filled with beautiful instruments behind locked cases. She learned that she could check out the instruments by signing the slip at the front desk. While her guitar at home was awesome, Scarlett couldn't wait to check out the Gibson Les Paul she eyed behind the glass.

Luke and Michelle were both in her last period class: Percussion. Luke was a gifted piano player. His parents were both elementary school teachers, and he attended Rosemont on scholarship for his talent. Scarlett was more fluent with the guitar than on the piano, but she could hold her own in a duet with most players—or at least in her experience, with most players from her small Indiana town. While she had never had much in the way of formal training, Scarlett had taken to music at a very young age and taught herself how to play. By the time she was three, she could play the piano, the violin, and of course her favorite, guitar.

Scarlett and Luke were paired up by Ms. Beasle during the last half of class. She sat beside him on the bench, closed her eyes, and listened to him play the most beautiful and haunting melody—airy but dark at the same time. It spoke to something deep within her soul. Her hands reached for the keys. With eyes still closed, she struck out a tune alongside him; which she thought to be a corresponding, however inferior, melody. He struck several more beautiful chords, and her hands moved to match his.

When the bell rang and the last note resonated through the room, Scarlett opened her eyes to find the entire class in silence staring at them. All in the room burst into applause.

"Beautiful. Just beautiful," cried Ms. Beasle, clapping her hands furiously, which caused her fluffy blonde ringlets to bounce and fly all over the place. "Luke is a savant of course, but Scarlett, I didn't know you were a natural! You must be in our variety show at the end of the year." Scarlett nodded and smiled and looked at Luke, who blushed and stared at his shoes.

Michelle caught up with them after class. "What was that, you two? I thought the heavens were going to open up and angels would fly through the ceiling at any minute!" Scarlett wondered if that was possible and she made a mental note to ask Precious if angels were real. "That was amazing, you guys. Anyway, I gotta run, I'll miss my train." She smiled and waved. "Luke, you coming?"

Luke nodded and turned to Scarlett. "I've gotta get the train too. I'll see you tomorrow?"

"Yeah, see you tomorrow." She waved goodbye to both of them.

Scarlett smiled to herself. Not a bad day, at least two new friends, and she was pretty sure Louzanne was shaping up to be a friend too. Although the bit about "expecting her" was a little unnerving. *Does she know about me? About fairies? Louzanne lives on campus. I could ask her now, but I'd better get home. Mom will be expecting a full account of my first day. I'll have to get Louzanne alone tomorrow to find out more.*

At the edge of the school property line, she saw a man with long brown graying hair and a scraggly beard wearing an orange toque that didn't quite fit his head right causing the hat to come to a point. He wore green corduroys and a purple vest. He looked like a brightly colored hobo except his shoes looked expensive. *He might just be an eccentric parent picking up his kid from school.*

The almost-hobo waved. *Who is he waving at?* She turned around to look for the kid behind her, but there was no one there. *Well, I don't know him. He can't be waving at me.* She shrugged, unlocked her bike from the rack, and set off for her house. The bike path leading there was part urban and part wooded. She had to pass the library, the crystal shop, the café, bookstore, and the old cemetery with beautiful old headstones and ornate wrought iron fencing before she got to the wooded path that snaked along the river and led to the back of her house.

When she made it to the bike path, about twenty yards ahead, the hobo sat on a park bench waving at her. *Does he know me? Maybe he thinks I'm someone else. How could he get here before me on foot? Maybe he knows a shortcut.* She decided to smile politely at him as she rode past but he waved at her again, and this time, he spoke. "Hello, Scarlett."

She hit the brakes, and the bike skidded to a halt. She looked from side to side for evidence of Snuke, Precious, or Honeybee nearby but couldn't see any of them. She narrowed her eyes, taking stock of him. *Okay, so it's a little creepy this hobo looking man can get here so fast, and he knows my name, but he doesn't look dangerous.* His sparkly blue eyes shone from a face wizened from many years of thinking. His appearance and demeanor didn't send shivers down her spine or make the hairs on the back of her neck stand up. In fact, just the opposite; she felt at ease. What did bother her was that she couldn't read his energy or get a vibe from him at all.

"I feel you sussing me out. That's good. You're learning quickly," he said with a laugh.

"I don't feel anything," Scarlett said. "You give off nothing!"

"Exactly child and that is what I am going to show you and more. You are giving off light like Vegas on a Saturday night, and it's drawing a lot of attention, some, not the kind you want. My name is Myles. I'll be your teacher."

Scarlett eyed him skeptically. She looked all around and still couldn't see any of the fairies. *How do I know I can trust him? Where's Snuke? I saw her behind me when I got on the bike path.*

The hobo spoke again. "I have a cabin down by the river. That's where I'll teach you how to use your Juma and how to hide it when you need to. Come with me." He gestured for her to follow him down a narrow wooded path darkened by tree cover.

Scarlett looked all around again. "Snuke? Where are you?" she called out. *He can't be serious. Is he out of his mind? No way am I going to follow some weird hobo down to a secluded wooded area just because he says he knows me and is supposed to take me there. What kind of a moron does he take me for? Way too creepy for me. I'm outta here.* She clicked her tongue, shook her head, and took off on her bike at full speed, not letting up until she was inside her house with the door locked behind her.

Honeybee greeted her at the door, drying her hands on her tiny apron. "Goodness, you're back early, love-dove. I thought Myles was going to give you a long lesson today before it got dark."

"You know about that guy?" Scarlett cried, gasping for breath.

"Oh yes, love. Myles is going to be your teacher. He is very old and very wise."

"I couldn't see any of you to know. Where were you? Why didn't you tell me? Besides, what kind of a moron goes off into the woods with a hobo just because he knows your name and says he's supposed to meet you?" Honeybee raised her eyebrows and patted her neat bun, baffled at Scarlett's frustration. "C'mon, they've warned me about this kind of stuff since pre-school!" Scarlett threw her hands up in exasperation.

"Scarlett, why did you take off?" Snuke asked breathlessly as she appeared in the kitchen.

"I couldn't see you. How was I supposed to know it was safe to go with this guy?"

"Oh, yes, I forgot Myles has that effect. He tends to mask all the energy in the area when he's trying to hide his own. I was there the whole time," Snuke reassured her.

"He was dressed like a lunatic!"

Precious sat on the edge of the counter and threw her head back and laughed, slapping her knobby knees. "Oh deary, that would be my fault. I told him to dress like that. I thought that if he looked like that he would seem hip and appealing to you young people. I could have sworn I saw those clothes in magazines. I thought you would be more accepting of him if he dressed like that."

With her hands on her hips, Scarlett shook her head and sighed. *Fairies.* "Well next time, tell me if you expect me to go off with some creepy stranger, kay?"

Mrs. Wrigley rushed into the kitchen, hugged her daughter, and kissed her forehead. "Hi, honey. How was your day? Who are you talking to, hon? I heard voices."

"No one, Mom. My day was good. I made some friends."

"Well, let me make some tea, and you can tell me all about it."

Scarlett told her mother about the music wing, the amazing instruments, how she knocked Michelle down by accident and how great she was about showing her around and about Luke and how amazing he was on the piano.

"Sounds like someone might have a boyfriend," Mr. Wrigley teased as he came in the kitchen for a glass of water. Scarlett blushed and shook her head. *Sometimes they're just so corny!*

FIVE
THE KROAKES

Scarlett's eyes snapped open to the sound of dishes breaking in the kitchen below. "BOO…BOO…BOO." *Bang, crash, smash.*

"I told you, you old goat if you said boo one more time I'd smash every dish in this house! How would you like that, Wilbur?" a woman's voice with a faint English accent came from the kitchen. "You go around saying boo hoping the new residents will hear you. Well, they can't hear you, you old fool! And why would you want to go and draw attention to us anyway? Next thing you know they'll be bringing psychics and mediums to the house trying to drive us out and making things complicated."

"Easy, Be," said the soft voice of an elderly man. "I was lonely is all. Just checkin' to see if anyone sees us. If you don't want the psychics and mediums here, why are you breaking all their nice dishes, huh?"

Scarlett crept downstairs, turned on the light, and saw an elderly man and woman arguing and a pile of broken dishes on the floor. The man was frail, medium build with wisps of gray hair. Warm kindly looking eyes peered out from his withered face. The woman was birdlike with pursed thin lips and a narrow wrinkled face. She wore rollers in her hair.

"Who are you?" Scarlett asked.

They both looked at her with mouths agape. "What did she say?" asked the old man.

"I think she asked us who we are, dear," said the old woman.

"You can see us?" the old woman asked.

"Yeah, you're in my kitchen. Who are you?" Scarlett sized them up. *Probably got confused and wandered out of an old folks home, but you can never be too careful these days.* She scanned the room for something she could use as a weapon just in case they got aggressive. Her father kept his golf clubs in the mudroom just off the kitchen, but she would have to pass right by them to get to there.

The woman cleared her throat, reaching for the string of pearls wrapped around her long, bird-like neck. "We are the Kroakes. Beatrice and Wilbur Kroake. Sorry about the dishes, deary. Err...oh my, this is a pleasant surprise. It's been so long since we've had someone other than each other to talk to."

Mrs. Kroake proceeded to tell Scarlett all about their lives, or former lives. Beatrice—Be to friends—and Wilbur Kroake were the first generation of Kroakes to live on twenty-four Riverside Drive. Wilbur had the home built in 1946 for his wife after returning from the Second World War. Wilbur was a fighter pilot in the forty-first regiment. He was an engineer by trade, and after the war, he took a job as an engineer at the local automotive factory. They raised three children in this home: Thomas, Gretchen, and William.

At the ripe age of eighty-three, Beatrice passed away in her sleep in this very house, in the master bedroom where Scarlett's parents slept. And Wilbur, not knowing what else to do, laid down beside her and died too. Their son William and his wife took on the house for a time but sold it to a young couple after their divorce. The house had seen three other owners since, none who died in the home, thus making the Kroakes the only resident ghosts of twenty-four Riverside Drive.

Scarlett eyed them skeptically at first, but after speaking with them and Mrs. Kroake's demonstration of walking through walls and disappearing then reappearing, she decided they must be telling the truth. It turned out they were a sweet old couple. They reminded her of her grandparents on her father's side.

"Well dear, that was rather a lovely chat. I must say, Wilbur and I are ever so happy to have you and your family here, what with all the guests you've brought with you. Are those fairies? And the other day

Wilbur met your leprechaun—charming fellow. Well, now that we know you can see us, we'll try not to be too much of a bother." Mrs. Kroake sighed. "We understand how busy the business of living can be, but would it be too much trouble for you to take the time to chat with us from time to time?"

Scarlett smiled. "Yes of course. I'll make a point of it." Then she added, "When my parents are out of earshot, kay? I wouldn't want them to worry that I've lost my mind."

Mrs. Kroake patted Scarlett's hand. "Of course. I understand, dear." Suddenly, Scarlett felt an intense jolt of cold shoot through her entire body. She gasped and recoiled. A puff of white mist escaped from her mouth when she exhaled. She shivered and shook uncontrollably, chilled to the bone by the encounter.

Mrs. Kroake gasped. "Oh no! So sorry, deary. I forget I have that effect on people. I'll have to be more careful next time." She disappeared momentarily, returning with a bulky sweater Mrs. Wrigley liked to keep in the coat closet for chilly mornings.

After putting on the sweater and drinking a hot cup of tea, Scarlett recovered from the icy blast. Then she helped Mrs. Kroake clean up the broken dishes, worrying how she was going to explain to her mother how they got that way. She looked at Elvis lying under the kitchen table licking his paws. "Sorry, buddy." Elvis perked up his ears and widened his eyes as if he understood he was about to be in big trouble. "Your mom's dog, she won't get too mad," she said as she reached under and scratched his ears.

***

Scarlett looked for Louzanne all day but didn't find out until lunchtime that she had called in sick. Disappointed about the delay in satisfying her curiosity about the whole "I've been expecting you" business, Scarlett quickly put it out of her mind with two back to back music classes: Woodwind and Strings.

Last period, Strings. She got her hands on the Gibson Les Paul and spent the remaining hour cautiously playing the untitled Led Zeppelin album. Her stomach fluttered both in exhilaration that she was playing such an elegant instrument and in terror that she might break it and her family would have to sell their car to replace it.

After school, Myles stood outside waiting for her, still dressed like a hobo but a little more muted today. He kind of looked more like a scruffy hipster and less like a crazy carnival hobo. "Are you ready?" He beamed a smile, and his blue eyes sparkled. Scarlett only nodded and followed behind him with her bike. Neither said a word the whole way.

When they made it to the wooded path that forked down to the river, Scarlett asked, "Why did you make it so I couldn't see Snuke? You scared me, you know."

Myles let out a long, deep sigh. "I am very old, and while I have accumulated a rather large amount of energy over the years, I am tired. It requires effort to be this close to regular people now without projecting my energy onto them. Much like you, my dear."

Scarlett crossed her arms. "So, what's that supposed to mean?"

"My energy allows people to see through the veil—to see things as they really are. They could start to see all sorts of strange things: fairies, bogies, auras…no, no, we cannot have that." Myles shook his head. "This could generate rumors of the strange sightings and occurrences in Riverstone and would attract much-unwanted attention. I can't take that risk right now, so I just try to stay close to the river."

This didn't make any sense to Scarlett. She looked at him with eyebrows raised. "Okay, so now I'm even more confused."

"The river is in a valley. The water and rocks help contain my Juma by absorbing my vibrations and sending them back to me. It helps me make sure my Juma doesn't get out and affect people in the area."

Scarlett gave him a blank stare.

"Think of it like a satellite signal. When you go through mountains or valleys, the signal gets interrupted by the rocks. While I'm farther from the elements that absorb my signal naturally, it is far easier for me to snuff out the energy in the area completely, rather than picking and choosing which energy waves to allow in and which to block out; which is why you couldn't see Snuke when we first met. I was cloaking my energy the lazy way by dampening all vibrations around me. In doing so, I overpowered yours so you couldn't see her. I do apologize for frightening you."

Scarlett studied him for a moment. His wizened face seemed sincere. Scarlett nodded by way of acceptance of his apology, even though his explanation still didn't really make any sense to her.

They made it to the riverbank. The small wooden cabin sat back from the river about twenty yards on a bed of quartz and limestone. Rings of smoke rose from the stone chimney and could be seen above the tree line.

"I put a fire on for a pot of tea later, but first things first: levitation." Myles grinned and gave her a wink. Then he planted his feet on the rocks and closed his eyes. With his arms spread out wide, he began to float.

Scarlett's jaw dropped. She didn't quite think he was serious, but there he was, levitating above the ground.

"Now you," he called down as he hovered above her.

"Me?" She snorted. "I can't levitate!"

Myles floated back to the ground, sat down on a rock, and rubbed his chin. "Hmm. I'm not sure what Honeybee or Precious told you. Scarlett, you can fly if you want to."

Scarlett blinked a few times. Staring blankly at the hobo, she shook her head and plunked herself down on the rock next to him. She threw her head back and laughed. "This is all too much! Fairies, leprechauns, dark forces, and now I can fly!" She threw her hands up, not even trying to hide her sarcasm.

"Well this might be all too much for you, but we can't hide it or make you forget anymore. We're all very tired. Scarlett, haven't you ever wondered why you can pick up an instrument and create a beautiful tune without ever having played it before and without any formal training? Or how you can sing and make up songs on any instrument just by playing what's coming out of your head? Music is the purest form of magic and, Scarlett, *you* are pure magic."

Scarlett eyed him skeptically but thought about what he said. "Hmm…well, yeah I guess it's a little out of the norm to be able to do that. But there's a big difference between being musical and being able to fly. This is crazy." She crossed her arms over her chest with a huff. This was all getting to be too much. *I wonder how long before I crack up completely.*

Like a balloon with all the air let out, Myles breathed a deep sigh, his shoulders hunched over in resignation. Her sarcasm and resistance were wearing on him. But despite her resistance, he still managed to give her a warm smile of encouragement. Scarlett felt guilty. She didn't want to hurt his feelings. After all, the whole past month had been lunacy, bogies, leprechauns, and ghouls that lived on people. Maybe flying wasn't all that crazy.

"So...umm...how do I fly?" she asked after a few moments of silence, more to lighten the mood than anything else.

His eyes lit up. "Excellent. Watch me." Myles stood up, closed his eyes, and spread his arms out with his palms facing upward. She could see his energy moving rapidly working to swirl the air around him. Then he began to float off the ground. "Sometimes it helps to say the words. Repeat after me: *"eitilt."*

Since she figured she wouldn't hear the end of it from Honeybee if she didn't at least try to humor him, Scarlett mirrored his actions. She stood up, closed her eyes and spread her arms out wide. The word *"eitilt"* no sooner passed from her lips when her energy began vibrating, and the air swirled beneath her. She opened her eyes and gasped to find she hovered three feet above the ground. In nervous disbelief, she threw her head back and laughed. Her laughter seemed to act as an accelerant, and she floated even higher.

"This is amazing!" Scarlett could feel the electricity tingling throughout her body, and the whoosh of air as her energy swirled the air to create lift. She'd never felt anything like this before, like a million feathers tickling her insides. It was euphoric.

"Excellent," Myles encouraged, "now move forward."

"What? How?" Scarlett flailed and kicked her arms and legs as if she were swimming, but it didn't seem to work.

"Just think about moving forward," he called to her from below.

She concentrated her gaze on a rock in front of her. She closed her eyes and thought very hard about inching her way closer to the cabin. When she opened them, the rock was two feet behind her.

"Good, now concentrate on moving backward," Myles called to her.

She closed her eyes again and, with little effort, she floated backwards. When she opened them and looked down, she was over the river. "Whoa!" she shouted. "I'm flying!" She floated even higher, and the wind rushed past her face. Her energy pulsed even more now and air whooshed all around her.

Beep, beep, beep, beep. Her mother's ringtone buzzed from her cell phone stuffed inside her pocket. With her concentration broken, next thing Scarlett felt was the biting chill as she plunged feet first into the icy river.

The current was strong. It thrashed her against the rocks and carried her downstream. She tried to fight against it. Thrashing, she struggled upstream, but her pant leg got caught on the branches of a downed log. The strength of the current forced her head under, and she could feel the branches dig into her thigh like sharp claws. The harder she struggled, the more the claws dug into her. She kicked and thrashed, but it didn't release her. Panic set in, making her feel shaky and weak. Then fear. *I can't get free.*

Her lungs burning, Scarlett couldn't hold her breath any longer. She gave another kick and reached around to try to snap the branches with her hands, but they seemed to grab hold of her wrists and pulled her down even further. For a moment, she thought she saw a pair of yellow eyes glowering at her from the deep. Scarlett gasped. Her lungs filled with icy water as the current forced her further below the surface. Above, the last of the day's sunlight glistened on the water's surface. Scarlett began to realize that this might the end for her. *I love you, Mom and Dad. I'm sorry it happened like this.* Then the light went out.

***

She heard voices, tinkling bells, and glints of sparkling lights. *This is the light that people always talk about.*

"Honestly, Myles, how could this happen?" sobbed Honeybee.

More sparkling lights. Scarlett felt hands pressing on her chest. She suddenly couldn't control her urge to vomit, and she coughed and spit up until her lungs were free of water. Finally, she gasped...*air!*

Rolled on her side now and still coughing, Scarlett opened her eyes and saw Myles and Nick kneeling over her looking concerned. Precious, Snuke, and Honeybee hovered above her with quivering lips and tears in their eyes.

"Scarlett, honey, you're okay!" Precious squealed.

Nick knelt over her looking as concerned as a leprechaun could. "We almost lost you, sweethaahrt. Boy, once you started to let it out, it got here fast."

Still coughing and looking around to get her bearings, Scarlett saw that the current had carried her one hundred yards downstream. She could barely see the cabin over the horizon. *Cough...cough.* "What are you talking about?"—*cough*—"It?"

"What grabbed you, sweethaahrt," Nick said, squeezing her hand and trying to wipe away the tears in his eyes so she wouldn't see them.

"What are you talking about?"—*cough*—"I got snagged on some logs."

"No, doll. You were in the grips of a vodyanoi." Confused and still coughing, Scarlett shook her head. "A water demon. Nasty things, like to drown people."

"I didn't see it," she said weakly.

"We fought it off, but wow, kid. It just came outta nowhere as soon as you started flying around and lettin' your light shine."

Myles tugged on his beard, looking up and down the riverbank. "We don't see much of those here in North America. It must have come from miles away, attracted to something. I'm going to check the river bed and make sure the area is clear." He dove head first into the icy river and disappeared.

Scarlett sat along the bank rubbing her eyes and looking into the water, waiting for Myles to re-emerge, but he didn't. Peering into the water, she saw no trace of him, no air bubbles or any signs of movement.

"You okay, kid?" Nick asked.

Scarlett coughed up the last of the water. "He…he…" She struggled to get her words out. "Myles?" She pointed to the river. "Is he okay? Shouldn't we go after him?"

"He'll be just fine, love. Come, let's get you inside by the fire." Honeybee tugged on her collar, gesturing toward the cabin. Too tired to protest, Scarlett just nodded and let the fairies help her up.

***

Curled up in an armchair in front of the fire, under a soft, warm blanket, Scarlett began to feel better. Her clothes hung over the fire to dry, and Precious found some loud yellow pants and a Grateful Dead t-shirt in Myles' dresser for her to wear. Nick busied himself about the cabin fixing a pot of tea while Precious and Honeybee flitted here and there casting spells around the cabin and Scarlett to ward off evil spirits. Snuke remained on guard outside the cabin. Scarlett's clothes were almost dry when the cabin door opened and Myles walked in, soaking wet and looking rather frigid.

"The river is clear. I found its living quarters about ten miles downstream. It doesn't look like it had been staying there long. Maybe four or five days."

Four or five days. That's about how long I've been in Riverstone, Scarlett thought.

Myles continued, "That was an Eastern European Water Demon. They don't usually venture this far west. It must have been looking for something." They all turned to stare at Scarlett. Myles smiled at her with his sparkly blue eyes.

He sloshed into his room, leaving a trail of drippings behind him. He returned in dry clothing and poured a cup of tea for Scarlett and himself. He handed her a mug and took a seat in the armchair next to her. He stared into the fire in silence. After several minutes, he spoke. "You did wonderful today—much better than I expected. I wanted to show you something fun first. Did you have fun?"

"Yes, at least until I almost drowned," she said wryly.

"Yes, that was unfortunate. I wanted you to believe in yourself first before showing you how to snuff it out, but now I see that was an unwise decision on my part. So, you flew. Do you believe it?"

Scarlett nodded. *How could I not?*

"Good. Now to dim your light a bit." He rubbed the tips of her ears, and the images in the room became a little less vibrant. The electricity around her body that she had become accustomed to traveled deep inside her until all that remained on the outside was a soft white glow.

"There now. That will have to do until tomorrow after you've rested. Scarlett, I don't know how much you've been told—"

"Precious and Honeybee told me that I have special abilities. I can see the real world, the one beneath the veil where magic is real. I can sometimes make others experience it with me too and, for that reason, dark forces—whatever that means—want me dead." She hoped the skepticism and frustration she felt over the whole situation was obvious in her tone.

Myles sighed and patted her hand. "You are so much more than that, my dear." He turned to Precious and Honeybee. "I'll call in the caravans tomorrow."

The words left Scarlett wondering what in the world she could expect from that. *Caravans of what?* But she was too tired to ask.

***

The last ray of light left the sky as Scarlett traipsed into her back kitchen door.

"Where were you?" her mother asked frantically. "I've been calling."

Scarlett's clothes had dried, but her hair was a mess—although this wasn't all that unusual. She remembered her soaked phone in her pocket. It would probably take a week to dry out, and it might not even work again.

"Sorry, I got busy with some new friends after school and I—"

"But why didn't you answer your phone?"

"I umm…" She pulled her wet phone from her pocket. "I…uhh

54

dropped it in the toilet at school." It was all she could think of on the fly.

Mrs. Wrigley's green eyes crinkled and she laughed. "Oh, I've done that before. Once on my first day of a new job and with a work phone too! Your uncle Shane's dropped more phones in the toilet than I can keep track—sometimes while I'm on the phone *with* him." Mrs. Wrigley's ribs shook with laughter, and Scarlett giggled picturing how clumsy her mother and her uncle could be. "It will probably dry out and work again. Good thing we didn't buy you a new phone for your birthday, huh?"

"Yeah," Scarlett agreed. "It's a lot harder to drop a guitar in the toilet."

"So, where were you? Who were you with and what did you do?"

"What?" Scarlett shook her head, tired and distracted by her ordeal at the river. She wasn't sure what truth was more overwhelming: the fact that a river demon almost killed her or the fact that she could fly. She looked at her mother. "Oh, I um…I was with Michelle, Louzanne, and Luke. We were playing music. We started a band, and we want to play at the year-end variety show."

Mrs. Wrigley's face lit up, and she clapped her hands excitedly. "Oh, that's wonderful, honey. Your father and I will be there, front row." Then she showed Scarlett the supper she was keeping in the warmer for her—mung bean soup and sourdough bread. She could see Nick out of the corner of her eye; he was sitting on the counter sticking out his tongue and making hacking sounds. *I guess the mung bean soup isn't that great.*

The Wrigleys normally watched TV or did some activity together in the evenings whenever Scarlett didn't have too much homework, but tonight she was too tired. After supper, Scarlett excused herself, mumbling she was tired from band practice and went off to bed.

Up until her thirteenth birthday, she'd never lied to her parents about anything but now found herself having to lie about everything. She went to bed worrying about how she was going to get Michelle, Luke, and Louzanne to start a band with her so she wouldn't have to fess up. She wondered if Louzanne even played an instrument.

SIX
THE ROMANASKI'S CARAVAN OF WONDER

"That's a wicked idea!" Michelle gushed as she picked the pickle off her ham and cheese sandwich. "I'm dying to show off this new beat I've been working on."

Scarlett opted for the vegetable soup and rye bread. "Awesome! Why don't we practice tomorrow night? Hey, I've been thinking about asking Luke to play keyboard, what do you think?"

"Yeah, he's the best."

"Does Louzanne play anything?"

"Uhh…yeah. Her mother is a musical genius, remember?"

Scarlett shook her head with a sheepish grin. "Oh yeah, I completely forgot." She had been so overwhelmed with the move, her new abilities and the entire "dark forces" being after her thing, that she really didn't have the chance to be completely star struck by the fact that one of her new friends was the daughter of one of the biggest names in music.

"She's a pretty good bass player, and she sings too." Michelle rifled through her bag for her notebook.

"That's great, I was thinking about asking her."

"Yeah, that would be awesome, but I think she's still out sick. Hopefully, she's back tomorrow. Here comes Luke." Michelle waved Luke over as he emerged from the cafeteria line with a tray full of food. "Scarlett has something she wants to ask you."

Luke blushed. "Uhh…hi," he said, giving Scarlett a quick shy glance before darting his eyes back down to this shoes.

"Hi, Luke." Scarlett smiled at him. "Will you be in a band with us?"

Luke lifted his head up from his feet to meet her gaze. "Yes," he said rather quickly, looking relieved.

Michelle, watching this exchange, couldn't help but interject, "What? Did you think she was going to ask you to be her date for the Halloween dance?" Luke blushed and shook his head nervously.

"There's a Halloween dance?" Scarlett asked.

"Yeah, we're both going, but not as dates, we're just going. You should come."

Scarlett loved Halloween. She made up her mind right away. "Okay, I'm going too."

Grayson joined them at the table. "Going where?"

"Halloween dance. You coming?" Michelle asked.

"Uhh, yeah, I guess."

"Hey Grayson, you play any instruments?" Scarlett asked.

He smiled and looked her over carefully. "Nah, drawing and photography are more my thing."

"Oh, I guess that's why I don't see you in class, huh?" she said more to herself than anyone else. Her cheeks flushed, embarrassed that she was about to ask him to be in the band.

"Yeah, that and I'm two years ahead of you." He reached over and mussed up her hair like an older brother does to a kid sister; it made her flush even deeper.

Michelle clapped her hands. "Okay guys, we've got a good group. This is awesome. Woo! I'm excited. What are we going to go as? Should we coordinate our costumes?" Her eyes lit up, and she clapped her hands again, getting even more excited at the idea.

Grayson groaned. "Whoa...stop. I'm not doing matching costumes, okay?"

Luke chimed in, "I don't wanna do that either."

Luke's support gave Grayson even more confidence. His chest puffed out further. "Yeah, let's just go as whatever we want and don't drag us into a lame dress up party, okay?"

Scarlett giggled at how difficult it would probably be to drag Luke and Grayson around looking for the perfect costume. "Okay Grayson, no lame matching costumes," said Michelle. Scarlett just smiled and kept quiet, wanting to remain neutral and grateful for the welcome distraction of a dance to keep her mind off flying lessons, fairies, and the vile creatures that seemed to want to kill her.

After school, Scarlett met up with Myles at the park bench at the entrance of the wooded path. She followed him down to the river, curious to find out about this "caravan" he promised to have there and hoping she wouldn't have another brush with death today.

Whoot whoot whoo…whoot whoot whoo…whoot whoot whoo. She could faintly hear a flute and tambourines rattling and what sounded like owls. When they made it to the clearing along the riverbank, she saw a giant Winnebago and three old-fashioned horse-drawn caravans. Three horses meandered around the clearing grazing on grass. They appeared to be wild. They looked unkempt and birds nested in their manes. She looked up and saw she was right about the owls. Three large barn owls circled around them, diving down and darting to and fro to the rhythm of the tambourines.

She looked all around to find the makers of this lively music and saw a little boy, who looked to be about the age of seven, a beautiful dark haired woman with brown eyes wearing large gold hoop earrings and a shiny red amulet around her neck, and a man wearing an old-fashioned shirt and pants with black curly hair and a bushy mustache. All three were barefoot.

They stopped rattling the tambourines when they saw her, and the owls took off back to their trees. They bowed their heads respectfully to Scarlett and Myles when they drew near. The beautiful woman smiled at her and said, "Scarlett, it is so nice to finally meet you. We are the Romanaskis. We are friends," the dark-haired woman, Yadira, spoke with a faint accent. Scarlett couldn't quite tell where she was from.

Yadira explained that they were a small family of gypsies who had been friends of Myles for many, many years. Although they looked young, like Myles, they were centuries old—not nearly as old as Myles, of course, but pretty old. They were human, not immortal. However, their ability to tap into the energy in the world had strengthened their Juma and gave them rejuvenating abilities. "We could still be killed just the same as anyone. Traffic accidents, plane crashes, you know, that happens. My heart still aches when I think about cousin Santi whose plane went down in '77." Yadira's eyes filled with tears.

To brighten her up, Scarlett changed the subject. "And what about your boy?"

"Gustaf? He's just a boy. We decided to start a family later in life, but God willing, he will be like his father and me. Come." Yadira took Scarlett by the hand, led her to the caravans and introduced to her seven cousins, their spouses, and their children. There was Kizzy and her husband Yoiko and their two daughters Rosabelle and Rosalee, Aishe and her husband Bioko and their two sons and daughter Franco, Milo and Tigris, Mirela and her husband Milosh and their daughter Lily, Lala and her husband Nicu and their son and daughter Nicola and Milee, Stefan and his wife Zelda, Yoska and his wife Gretchen and their three sons Tobar, Ferka and Samuel, Hanzi and his wife Rhianni and their two daughters Poppy and Posey.

If Scarlett's head wasn't already spinning, Yadira then introduced her to her husband Rolph's three brothers Bo, Fonso and Pesha, her grandmother, Yeeta, Rolph's great-aunt Yaw-Yaw and their pet pig Alfred. While being introduced some waved hello while others hugged Scarlett and kissed her on both cheeks. The Romanaski brothers bowed gallantly, while Yeeta and Yaw-Yaw flashed her toothless grins from beneath their afghans as they sat in their lawn chairs. Scarlett just smiled politely and nodded to each of them. She was sure she would never be able to keep all their names straight. There were thirty-five people in total that made up the Romanaski camp.

Scarlett looked again at the Winnebago and the three-old fashioned caravans and wondered how so many people could possibly live comfortably inside such small spaces until Yadira took her inside.

Scarlett's eyes widened at the sight. The outside of the first caravan looked small and old-fashioned with ornate hand carved trim. It looked like no more than four people could fit comfortably, but inside, it was bigger than her house! The caravan had all the amenities of a modern home: a large kitchen with dishwasher and double sink, a restaurant-sized refrigerator, and a huge wooden kitchen table with many mismatched chairs. Artwork from the various children plastered the refrigerator, held in place with souvenir magnets from all the places they must have visited. The living room had large, comfy looking sectionals and bean bag chairs strewn about the floor and a large flat screen TV on the wall. The curtains in the living room looked oddly familiar.

"My mom has those same curtains in our living room."

Yadira laughed. "Ikea. They go with everything."

A spiral staircase led upstairs to where the bedrooms were located, but Scarlett didn't get the upstairs tour. The other caravan was very much the same: old-fashioned and small on the outside but very spacious and equipped for modern day living on the inside. The living room in the second caravan was elegant and formal. It was decorated with many rich fabrics, velvet loveseats, and chaise lounges to give the feel of a lavish parlor. It also had a large flat screen TV. The Winnebago was very much the same as the first two. It was large and unexpectedly modern on the inside, except it was much larger than the other two caravans combined. It had a pool table, an arcade, and a bowling alley in the middle of it to entertain the kids.

The third caravan belonged to Yeeta and Yaw-Yaw. The inside looked much like the outside. Small ornately carved woodwork of angels, mermaids, fairies, dragons, and other mythical creatures that Scarlett didn't recognize accented all the rooms. The rooms were cramped and dark, lit only by the soft glow of the many old-fashioned lamps of various shapes colors and sizes scattered about.

The kitchenette was small, like one you would find in a small camper. There was a small bathroom adjoining the kitchen. The only furniture in this room were two padded benches that looked perfect to stretch out and read or to just sit and drink coffee and look out the window on a rainy day and a small round table that held a large crystal ball. A tiny hall off the kitchen led to two small bedrooms where Yeeta and Yaw-Yaw slept and to a third room on the left.

Two small oil paintings, side by side, adorned the hall. Intrigued, Scarlett stepped further into the hallway to take a closer look. Each was a portrait of an attractive young woman. The backdrops were similar to one another, showing an evening landscape with rolling hills beneath a dusky sky, although one background appeared more mountainous than the other. The woman in one painting had dark hair and the woman in the other had red hair. They dressed in clothing typical of the Renaissance era.

Scarlett stared intently at the two paintings. The luminescence of their features drew her in, and she couldn't quite put her finger on why. They reminded her of the Ginevra de' Benci or the Mona Lisa. The women were relatively attractive but not exceptionally beautiful. Maybe it was their smiles or how the light seemed to reflect on their skin and catch in their eyes. *That's it! It's their eyes.* She'd seen them before recently, but couldn't place where. She looked back at the kitchen to where Yeeta and Yaw-Yaw stood over the counter cutting out dough for perogies. They smiled and talked to one another in a foreign tongue, then Scarlett saw the light catch their eyes. *The same eyes as in the paintings. These are portraits of Yeeta and Yaw-Yaw when they were young!*

Yeeta's hair used to be jet black, and Yaw-Yaw's was once red. Scarlett stared back again at the now very aged portrait models. Yeeta's long braided hair had turned completely gray while Yaw-Yaw's hair was now white, kept back neatly in a bun. She wondered who painted these portraits to look like they were from the Middle Ages. When she saw the signature LDV at the bottom, she did a double take. Scarlett took every art and music class possible at her old school in Indiana. Anyone who knew anything about Renaissance art knew that the signature LDV belonged to the artist and scientist Leonardo DaVinci. *They must be fakes. Even if Yeeta and Yaw-Yaw were that old, what are the odds that their portraits were done by Leonardo DaVinci? Probably done by an artist at a fair. Nowadays, anyone can go into a portrait studio and put on a costume to look like they're from any era they choose.*

Yadira was talking to her about something, but Scarlett wasn't listening. She made out a few details about how Yeeta and Yaw-Yaw came to live together, but her mind was turning. She couldn't take her eyes off the paintings. *They have to be fakes,* she thought. But yet, she found them so interesting to look at. The door to the third room creaked open, breaking Scarlett's concentration. She drew near its threshold and peeked inside.

The third room was very dark. The walls were lined with ornate mirrors of various shapes and sizes. A large mirror hung over the ceiling. Candlelight was the only illumination except for the pulsing glow emanating from the large colorful crystals and gemstones scattered on shelves throughout. Scarlett found herself attracted to this room. Standing in the threshold, she could hear soft voices calling her. Some voices came from the mirror, while others seemed to call her from the stones.

Yadira was still prattling on, this time about her cousin's baby shower and Yaw-Yaw's cabbage roll recipe when Scarlett, attracted to the large red glowing gemstone, stepped through the door. It called to her in a soft voice. Scarlett could hardly feel her body moving towards the stone until her hands were upon it.

At that moment the soft voice became a hiss. "Got you!"

Electricity traveled through her body like sharp bony fingers that gripped and pierced her until the pain was excruciating. The pain only lasted a second when Yadira pulled her from the grips of the stone and out of the room, closing and locking the door behind her. "That place is not for you," she gasped, trying to catch her breath.

Scarlett was breathless and shaken. "What…was that?"

Yadira hugged her and rubbed Scarlett's arms. "There'll be plenty of time for that," she said with a smile. "Come, Lala is making fudge and Myles is waiting for you."

***

Myles stood before her on the river bank. "Learning to mask and block. It's a little like putting on a hat and coat and bundling yourself up for a cold winter day. I want you to imagine covering yourself with a blanket, even your head, so none of your body heat can escape and no cold air can get in."

Scarlett, still drained from her brush with the red stone and all the introductions, closed her eyes and imagined how nice it would feel to get in under the covers of her nice warm bed and throw the blankets over her head all snug and warm. She began to look forward to going home to her real bed and hoped this lesson wouldn't take too long. As she imagined wrapping herself in an invisible blanket, she sensed some of the electricity around her body—which she had become accustomed to over the past month—dissipate from the outer ring and travel inward, so she felt warm and glowing on the inside.

Myles grinned. "Good. You're doing it! Very good." When the warmth inside her body became hotter, she began to panic. *What if I burn up?* Frightened by the heat, she shook out her hands as if throwing off her "blankets." "I'm too hot!" she shouted. Once again, her energy took form outside her body.

"Yes, sometimes I need to get in the water or out into a cavern or valley so I can let it go when I get too hot, but don't worry, I've never been so hot that I burned up. You'll be fine too." He gave her a reassuring smile.

"Okay...good to know." She took a deep breath and imagined covering herself again and felt the tingling warmth of her Juma travel to the core of her body. She took a few deep breaths.

"How does that feel?"

Scarlett thought about it. *A little warm but not too bad.* "Pretty good."

"Good. Some days you'll find when other people are wearing coats, you'll only want a sweater or maybe even a t-shirt, but you'll get used it."

She spent the rest of the afternoon working with Myles, Yadira, and Rolph practicing cloaking her energy and drawing it into her core so it wasn't as noticeable. At first, they worked with her by trying to detect her Juma while she tried to hide it from them, and when she mastered that, they tried to penetrate her cloak with their own energy. By evening, she had it down pat. "Excellent, excellent leetle one!" Rolph cried. "She's really a natural."

***

Yeeta and Yaw-Yaw began setting up campfires and making supper. It looked like it was going to be a tasty cookout. While waiting for supper, the Romanaski men practiced sword fighting with real swords, while showing the little ones the art. The children practiced alongside them with wooden swords. The assorted savory vegetables, onions and garlic roasting over the fire smelled delicious. Scarlett wished she could stay for supper but knew her parents would be worried if she stayed out too long after school.

She told the Romanaskis about the band she was going to form with her new friends and how it would be a good excuse as to why she didn't come home for hours after school.

"Friends for the sake of having friends is important too, Scarlett, not just for excuses." Yadira patted her hand. "Never forget that." Yadira was right. She was happy and grateful that she'd been able to make so many friends in only her first week here.

When the sun began to set, she said goodbye to her new gypsy friends and set off for home just in time for supper, hoping it wasn't leftover mung bean soup.

SEVEN
KINDRED SPIRITS

"Yeah, I play bass." Louzanne stood in her dorm room archway, propping the door open with her elbow.

"I heard you can sing too." Scarlett held a pot of chicken soup, and her arms shook under the strain of carrying it across campus and up three flights of stairs. She looked past a disheveled looking Louzanne to see the room dimly lit with candles. The bookshelves, desk, and floor showed an accumulation of dried candle wax where it had spilled down the edges and onto the floor. Used tissues littered every surface and the smell of incense burning tickled Scarlett's nose. In the center of the room, two middle-aged women sat on Louzanne's stuffed armchairs. Even though it was four p.m., Louzanne was still dressed in her pajamas, a fuzzy pink bathrobe, and bunny slippers.

After the third day of Louzanne not showing up to class, Scarlett could no longer contain her curiosity. She had asked her mom to help her make a pot of chicken noodle soup the night before so she could bring it to school with her. She kept it in the cafeteria fridge all day to bring to Louzanne after school. She hoped it would help her feel better and it would also give her an excuse to ask Louzanne to join her band and find out more about the comment she made to her when they first met.

"Are you going to ask me inside?" Scarlett stared down at her trembling arms. "I think I might drop this if I hold it any longer." Louzanne sighed, rolled her eyes, flung the door open, and gestured for the two women to get out and for Scarlett to come inside.

"Come back later ladies," she called out to the women as they left. Scarlett put the pot of soup on the desk and sat on the edge of the bed while Louzanne plunked herself down on a chair and swung her legs over one of the arms.

"So, umm…do you have a cold? Who were they?"

Louzanne sighed. "I gotta make my money somehow. This is how I do it," she said, gesturing to the tarot card deck scattered on the bed.

Scarlett scanned the cards. They had gold lettering and beautifully drawn pictures of men and women dressed in old-fashioned garb and strange looking symbols. "But I don't understand. You don't have to do this for money. You can just do it for fun; your mom's rich."

Louzanne jumped up from her chair and started pacing the room. "*Pfff*…she can keep her money. I haven't taken that woman's money in over a year. The tuition and my board, well I'm only fifteen, I don't make that kinda money. There's nothing I can do about that. She pays for that, but pocket money? *Pff*... I haven't taken a cent from her. Her attorney mails me a check every month. I rip it up. I don't need it. I got some good clients here. Business is boomin', especially ever since you showed up. All sorts of people are coming into town wanting readings. Girl, what is your deal?"

Scarlett's only response was a shrug and raised eyebrows.

"I don't mind the paying customers; it's the spirits that drive me nuts. They show up at all hours. It's got me run ragged. My grandma had the talent, see. I guess it skipped my mother and came straight to me. It's been a lot worse since you showed up, though. Now I even got ghosts bothering me, 'Ooh call my son Vince and tell him I'm all right' and 'Could you contact my wife for me?' Like I got time to be chasin' down some stiff's relatives."

Louzanne can talk to ghosts too! As troublesome as Louzanne's predicament seemed, Scarlett couldn't help but feel a little bit happy that she and Louzanne had that in common. *Can she see through the veil like me? Can she see fairies and leprechauns too? What would she think if I told her? Better not; Honeybee would blow a gasket.*

After a few minutes of pacing, Louzanne sat back down in her armchair and let out another big sigh. She told Scarlett about the many new people she had seen around Riverstone over the past week. She even thought she saw a band of gypsies at the town grocery store. She told her about how her abilities had gotten stronger over the last week to the point where carrying out a regular day had become almost too distracting. "Between that and the ghosts that never leave me alone, I'm run down. I can't shake this cold." Louzanne blew her nose into a used tissue crumpled up on the chair.

"Three sisters bought the Lincoln Building on the corner of town square. I ran into them yesterday on my way back from the drugstore. They said they were going to turn it into a yoga studio and coffee bar or something. They're beautiful but really weird. They dress funny and they have super long hair. And they talk funny too, like they're from another time. But what's weirder is they kept reaching for my hand and calling me sister. I booked it outta there after that. What's creepiest is the man in black. I've seen him at least seven times since last Friday. I never get to see his face, but he's tall and thin, and he casts a long shadow. Gives me the creeps." Louzanne shivered and rubbed her arms.

Scarlett bit her lip and opted to just nod sympathetically. She didn't know what to say. *Is it okay to tell her about the Romanaskis? Myles? The fairies?*

Louzanne continued, "It's not even the newcomers that are weird. It's like everything is changing. I have my regular clientele, but now I'm getting so many more people wanting their fortunes told. Some of them come to me with all kinds of strange stories looking for explanations, talking about seeing elves in their kitchen or gnomes in their garden or now they see ghosts and want me to explain it to them. And it's not just the town wackos. Even Mr. Smith, the Biology teacher, came to me the other day wanting an explanation as to why his dead Aunt Myrna keeps turning up in his kitchen for tea. A lot of them just come for readings because suddenly they realize their life isn't meaningful and they want to know what they should do with their lives. I don't know what to tell them, Scarlett. I'm so tired! And it's all since you showed up."

Scarlett shrugged, feigning ignorance and squeezed Louzanne's shoulder. She heated up a bowl of chicken noodle soup in Louzanne's microwave and stored the rest in her mini-fridge. "Here, this will make you feel better."

After Louzanne finished her soup, Scarlett asked, "So you're coming back to school tomorrow?"

Louzanne nodded. "I guess so. I can't get any peace around here. I might as well be in school."

"Awesome. So tell me about this 'I've been expecting you' business."

Louzanne laughed. "Nah, it's weird."

"Come on, weirder than ghosts? I'm good with weird, trust me," Scarlett reassured her.

"Well, I keep having this dream. I'm standing on the edge of a cliff, and it's cold and windy, and there's snow on the mountains. Like an idiot, I'm standing on the edge. Then, I fall. I'm falling backwards, and I can feel the wind rushing over me as I watch the edge of the cliff getting farther and farther away. Then I turn to face the rocks below. I feel more scared than I've ever felt and, just as I'm about to smash into the rocks, your face flashes in front of me. Then I hear chimes and someone whispers 'She's coming,' but I never do hit the rocks. I've been having the same dream for over a month."

Scarlett's stomach churned. *Why is she having this dream about me? What could it mean?* She tried to keep her face neutral. "Phew, that sounds like an intense dream," she said trying to sound casual.

"Let me see your hand." Louzanne grabbed Scarlett's hand and stretched out her palm. She spent several minutes studying it. "Jeez, girl! You have a strange life. I see some things, but I can't make any sense of it! Do you have a dwarf or a little person in your family? Who are you and why has everybody gone crazy since you came?"

Scarlett was trying her best to mask her Juma. *Had it affected her ability to read my palm? Should I let my guard down? What would Myles and Honeybee think? They both seemed so regimented on security details, especially since the vodyanoi. I hate to think how they might react if I let someone I'd only met once before read everything about me. How would Louzanne react to know how weird my life really is? How would she react to the idea that fairies live with me? Or about my training at the river, the gypsies, and the fact that dark things are after me? Better not say anything.*

Instead, Scarlett just shrugged and said, "Hmm, that's strange, but yeah, my mom's cousin is a little person. He stays with us from time to time."

"Emilio….Emilio." A woman appeared in the middle of the dorm room. "Emilio? Where are you?"

Louzanne rolled her eyes. "Go away; there's no Emilio here." The woman began to sob.

Scarlett turned to the woman. "Don't worry, Miss. I'll help you find Emilio."

After getting the details and last known address, Scarlett agreed to write a letter to the late woman's husband telling him about the money she hid on the family property. The woman had taken up bootlegging many years before her death as a past time and found that people loved her moonshine and still whiskey so much they came from miles around to buy it from her. She knew it wasn't legal, but it was a family tradition, and she enjoyed making it—especially after the kids moved out of the house. Afraid of implicating her family, she kept it secret from her husband and hid the money in a crate buried in the woods in the back of the family property thinking she would one day surprise her husband with a cruise around the world or give it to her grandkids for college tuition. Sadly, she fell to her death from a balcony seat at a basketball game and never got the chance to tell her husband about the money.

Louzanne sat back with her mouth hanging open while watching the exchange. When the woman disappeared, satisfied that she could rest in peace knowing her husband would get her money and her grandkids' education would be taken care of, Louzanne narrowed her eyes at Scarlett; then she laughed until tears rolled down her cheeks. She threw her arm around Scarlett's shoulder. "I guess we're kindred spirits after all! Yeah, I'll be in your band."

EIGHT

KANONSISTONTIES

Louzanne, Michelle, Luke, and Scarlett got together as a band four times over the next two weeks. Each time they practiced, they got better and better. They already had the frameworks for four different songs, one written by each of them. When they put it all together they each added something unique to the sound. Scarlett had been meeting up with Myles after school regularly to practice cloaking and blocking Juma. After the second week, she felt confident that she could keep her energy under control.

The night of the Halloween dance arrived, and Scarlett had decided to go as a unicorn. She wanted to go as a witch—she'd always liked witches—but she had all the stuff at home to make a unicorn costume, and she hated to ask her parents for money. The doorbell rang as she was sprinkling rainbow sparkles over her paper-mache horn.

Michelle and Luke were taking the magnet train into town, so they all agreed to meet up at Scarlett's house and go to the dance together. Afterwards, Luke would spend the night at Grayson's dorm before catching the train home the next day, while Michelle and Louzanne planned to spend the night at Scarlett's house.

Because Louzanne lived on campus, the first plan was to have a sleepover at Louzanne's dorm. Scarlett felt this was a very grown-up thing to do and was excited at the prospect of a sleepover far removed from adult supervision. Of course, there were dorm supervisors at Rosemont, but they rarely left their rooms except for nine p.m. patrol.

This plan quickly came to an end after Honeybee threw a fit over security. "It'll take a month to reinforce that place with protection spells—absolutely not! I won't hear of it!" It wasn't worth the battle to go up against a red-faced and flustered Honeybee. Scarlett backed out, saying her parents would never let her and suggested they have the sleepover at her house.

Scarlett wasn't sure who was more excited, she and her friends or her mother. She had never asked her parents to host a sleepover before. Mrs. Wrigley, excited by the prospect of "girl time", organized for the girls to have decaf lattes and breakfast the next morning while they got manicures and pedicures at Lulu's Day Spa.

She heard the door opening and her father greeting Michelle and Luke below. "Ooooh look, honey," he called to Mrs. Wrigley. "A zombie and a ninja! Ahhh, I'm so scared!" He called up to her, "Scarlett, your friends are here."

She attached her sparkly paper-mache horn to her hair band, gave herself one last look in the mirror, and went downstairs to greet her friends.

"You look marvelous, darling," Mrs. Kroake crooned as Scarlett left the room.

"Thanks! I'll see you later." She called back to Mrs. Kroake as she went downstairs.

"Look at you guys!" Scarlett took in their costumes. Luke wore a tweed suit caked in mud with torn sleeves. His hair was messy and dirty, and his makeup was phenomenal. It really did look like his flesh was rotting.

"Wow, look at you!" Michelle patted Scarlett's soft white fur. Honeybee and Snuke helped her make the furry arm covers and leg warmers out of old stuffed teddy bears. "I love the leg warmers! You should make me a pair."

"Sure! Or you can have these ones after the dance tonight."

"I know you told me no big deal, but I couldn't help myself. I thought we could have a pre-dance party!" Mrs. Wrigley dragged Scarlett by the arm into the living room to show her the floor to ceiling Halloween decorations. Polyester cobwebs hung from the chandeliers where large rubber spiders had taken up residence. There were orange and black streamers draped from the ceiling and cardboard cut-outs of witches, vampires, werewolves, goblins, and ghouls filled the walls.

Mrs. Wrigley had set out caramel apples, candy corn, and an assortment of other treats on a side table. She even set up a fog machine and eerie flashing strobe lights. A spooky Halloween soundtrack played in the background to set the mood, and various activity stations were set around the living room. By the expression on Mrs. Wrigley's face, Scarlett could tell she and her friends weren't getting out of there until they participated in the activities she had planned for them. One table had a blindfold and various bowls of gross mushy food decorated to look like pickled body parts. There was even a bucket for apple bobbing. Precious and Snuke waved hello to Scarlett as they perched on the edge with baffled expressions as if observing some foreign primitive custom for the first time.

Michelle's and Luke's eyes widened when they saw the living room, and they dove into the mushy body parts right away. "Cool!" Michelle put the blindfold on and stuck her hand in one of the bowls. "Hmm…brains?"

"Nope, try again," Luke said.

While the idea was cute and her mother obviously went all out trying to make this party fun, Scarlett's face reddened. *This is babyish. All I wanted was to have somewhere for everyone to hang out for a while before the dance.* She looked over at Michelle and Luke, both laughing as Luke smeared ketchup—meant to look like blood—on blindfolded Michelle's cheek. *But at least they seem to be having fun.* Louzanne and Grayson were older; she cringed at what they might think.

The doorbell rang, and Scarlett ran to get it. She held the door open for Grayson, who was dressed in a black old-fashioned coat and suit with a withered carnation on the lapel. His rubber mask sported a black mustache that curled around his cheeks, with pointed teeth and long scraggly black hair and goatee. It reminded her of the bad elf Felix McCaan. Only Grayson's mask had black hair, not bouncy yellow curls like Felix. The mask's features were also grayer and sallow as if meant to look like the skin were dead and rotting. Even the rubber gloves, which looked like long monster hands with black pointy nails, reminded her of Felix.

"Great costume, Grayson."

Grayson didn't respond. He reached into his coat and held out a box of chocolates. Too fascinated with his costume, she ignored his gesture and reached to touch his mask. She pulled on it, but it wouldn't budge. She reached with both hands, pulling on his cold rubbery mask. Then, Scarlett looked into his eyes. A pair of cold black eyes met hers. *These are not Grayson's eyes.* She opened her mouth to scream.

"*Díbir!*"

Before Scarlett could make a sound, Snuke, Precious, and Honeybee attacked the elf. Green lightning bolts flashed everywhere. The elf disappeared, leaving nothing but a pile of chocolates and dust on the doorstep. When she regained her ability to use her vocal chords, Scarlett asked, "Who was that?"

"That was the ghost of Felix McCaan, love," Precious informed her as she picked off specs of glitter from Scarlett's costume that had gotten stuck to her wings.

Scarlett shook her head. "He's dead. I don't understand."

Precious tweaked the hair sprouting from the mole on her nose and sat down on Scarlett's shoulder and continued picking off the remaining sparkles. "Halloween is when the veil between the dead and the living is thinnest, love. By going after you, he committed a grievous act in life. He now has to pay for his wickedness for all eternity. He'll never be redeemed and pass on to the next realm in peace. He is doomed to walk this earth in misery, reliving his wicked deed. All Hallow's Eve is the time where it's easiest for spirits to connect with the living, you see. Elves are not normally wicked creatures, but they've been known to go astray, just like humans. Since you were his greatest sin, unfortunately for you, love, he'll likely reach out to you for every

Halloween after."

"He looked different. His face grayer and his hair was black."

"Yes. Unlike humans, elven hair is alive. When the body decomposes, so does the hair. Living things turn black when they rot. His body is dead. His remains are buried in the yard of your old house in Indiana."

"What about the chocolates? Why does he want to give me chocolates?" Scarlett pointed to the pile spilled on her front doorstep.

"Ahem." Honeybee cleared her throat with authority. Snuke sighed and straddled Scarlett's unicorn horn as if digging in for a long ear-bender. Scarlett got the sense she was in for one of Honeybee's long-winded lessons.

"Elves," she began, "like fairies, are bound by the ancient tradition of féichiúnas, an indebtedness for accepting a gift. The force of this magic is especially powerful when given their favorite things, such as sweets and cream. If one accepts a gift from an elf or fairy, the receiver will be compelled to carry out a favor in return."

Scarlett pursed her lips and eyed Honeybee with one raised eyebrow. "This doesn't exactly work that well on humans," Honeybee added. "Often because they're not aware that elves and fairies even exist, but humans also have a strong ability to exercise free will that other creatures do not possess."

Honeybee paused for effect to make sure everyone was still listening. "However, the subtle effects of this magic are evident in humans, especially if given a gift that they particularly like. If you couple this with a powerful potion to make the human more compliant, then *poof,* you have a willing participant to carry out whatever the gift-giver asks. In this case, you seem to like chocolate, love-dove. The chocolates were also filled with a potion intended to weaken your Juma and, in turn, your free will. So it would have been easy for Felix to get you to follow him willingly into the faery realm where he was going to hand you over to a goblin who planned to do God only knows what." Honeybee's lip quivered, and tears welled up in her eyes.

Scarlett shuddered at the thought of what a goblin might do with her. Not that she had ever seen a real goblin before or knew much about them, but given the intense reaction from Nick and the fairies the night of her birthday, she could imagine. "Speaking of nasty creatures, why hasn't Sweetie Pie returned?"

"He's deep undercover, love-dove. Darklings don't open up to strangers easily. He's had to take on a new life to convince them he's still a foul and wicked creature. Last I heard he was popping in and out of the fairy realm working part-time as a bogeyman, scaring children out of the Sacramento California area. Don't fret; he'll return when he has answers. My faith in him is unwavering." With her tiny hand, Honeybee squeezed Scarlett's finger in reassurance.

"Who are you talking to, Scarlett?" Louzanne squinted as she walked up the path to the front door. Grayson walked alongside her in a dark cape and plastic vampire fangs. Louzanne was dressed as a fairy godmother. She wore a sky blue ball gown with a set of gossamer wings sewn to the back. Her beautifully applied makeup was luminous against her brown skin, with sparkles around her eyes and cheeks. She held a sparkly wand in her hand.

"Err um…I was calling my dogs." Scarlett scanned the front yard to see if either of her beagles were around.

"I grant you the gift of wisdom my child," Louzanne said in an official tone as she waved her wand in front of Scarlett's face and tapped her on the shoulder with it. Scarlett laughed nervously, almost choking on the irony. *If Louzanne only knew three fairies were flitting around her right now, cracking up at her costume.*

"Good evening," Grayson lisped through his plastic vampire fangs, his brown eyes danced with mischief, then swept his cape over his face and bowed.

"You two look great!" Scarlett said, appraising their costumes.

"So do you, little miss unicorn. Sweet leg warmers."

"Thanks, I already promised these to Michelle, but I'll make you a pair."

Louzanne shook her head. "Nah, I don't think I could pull them off, but thanks anyway."

Louzanne and Grayson glanced down at the pile of chocolates on the front step. Grayson bent down to pick them up, but Scarlett grabbed his arm, just about tackling him to the ground. "No!" She dragged him away from the chocolates. Her friends both looked at her like she was a lunatic.

"Umm, err...it's a Wrigley tradition to leave sweets scattered on the front step on Halloween. If we pick them up before midnight, it will bring bad luck." As she said it, she became convinced this was a good excuse for her forceful reaction.

For a brief moment, Scarlett thought about all the little white lies that came so easily to her now and felt bad about it. She didn't like having to lie to her friends and wished there was a way to change it. *Well, there's nothing I can do about that right now.*

"Come on." She pulled them inside. "My mom set up some kiddy activities for us. She won't let any of you leave until you have some treats and do at least one of her games," Scarlett said, rolling her eyes and turning beet red. *I wish she didn't put on such a fuss. They'll probably think I'm a baby.* She was beginning to feel kind of cool having older friends; the last thing she wanted was them thinking she was a baby.

"Awesome!" Grayson lisped through his fangs. Their eyes lit up when they saw the decked out living room and all the sweets and fun activities. To Scarlett's surprise, Louzanne and Grayson joined right in with Michelle and Luke.

"Hey, guys!" Michelle now blindfolded and bobbing for apples called out to them when she heard them enter the room. To avoid ruining his zombie makeup, Luke stood back watching Michelle enjoy the game while he wolfed down Mrs. Wrigley's spider cookies.

Everyone ended up having a great time at the Wrigleys. All the activities her mother had planned for them turned out to be fun. Luke and Grayson polished off the caramel apples except for the three Scarlett saw Nick skirt off with earlier in the evening. Even Nick, who tended to be a bit of a grump, got into the festive occasion. He wore orange and black striped stockings and a tiny witch's dress and hat. From what she could remember from photographs, it looked like the Halloween costume Scarlett had worn when she was two years old.

After the unexpected visit from the ghost of Felix McCaan, Snuke, Precious, and Honeybee were on high alert and didn't have time to partake in the festivities; rather they kept to patrolling the perimeter of the house. Mrs. and Mr. Kroake seemed excited to join in on the festivities too. Mrs. Kroake had even taken her rollers out and styled her hair but, since on Halloween they could be easily seen, they kept to the shadows, peeking their heads into the living room from time to time to listen to the laughter and watch. It was pretty strange to see a ghost's head pop right through the wall while its body remained on the other side, but Scarlett was getting used to it.

When they did peek their heads in, Louzanne could see them plain as day. "I didn't know you had ghosts in your house," she whispered to Scarlett.

"Yeah, umm…they're really nice," she said, hoping Louzanne couldn't also see Nick and the fairies and she wondered what she was going to say if she could.

At seven forty-five p.m., Mr. Wrigley loaded everyone into his car and drove them to the school dancehall. "I'll be here after the dance to pick you up. If you need anything at all, call me right away."

Scarlett nodded. "Yup, got it. Thanks, Dad." She pecked him on the cheek as she hopped out of the car. They all waved goodbye to Mr. Wrigley and watched him pull away.

"Your parents are adorable, girl. I felt like I was on a modern day episode of *Leave It To Beaver*—in a fun and cool kinda way…uh, no offense," Louzanne said with a grin.

Scarlett knew her parents were sweet and a little corny. "None taken."

Unlike most schools that held their dances in the gymnasium, Rosemont had its own dancehall, an addition to the building commissioned after the civil war. Vivian Patterson and her nasty crew of friends were on the party planning committee. Despite their nasty personalities, they did a beautiful job.

The theme was Classic Hollywood Monster Mash. They had decorated various parts of the hall to look like the set of classic films such as *Dracula, The Wolfman, The Mummy*, and *Creature From The Black Lagoon*. There were even lifelike wax replicas of the films' characters, an impressive contribution by the fourth year Sculptures class.

Vivian Patterson, Jessica Benner, and Alison Mitchell dressed as scantily as Ms. Breesen, the young ladies' wing chaperone, would allow. They wore old-fashioned clothing and Scarlett couldn't tell who they were supposed to be but could only guess they were meant to look like the Hollywood damsels in distress, but Scarlett wasn't all that familiar with the films or their characters. The girls stood at the entrance greeting guests and handing out programs and raffle tickets.

"That's a boy's costume. Michelle, you look like a boy," Vivian sneered as she looked down her nose.

Michelle sighed and replied calmly, "Clearly, I do not look like a boy. You could recognize me and you know I'm not a boy. Honestly, you need to get a little more creative with your insults, Vivian."

Unable to come back with anything else, Vivian twisted her hair around her finger and pouted as she set her sights on Grayson. "You look great! Classic Dracula. I love Dracula. I love it so much I'm dressed as Mina."

"And I'm dressed as Lucy," Alison Mitchell chimed in, smiling coyly at Grayson while running her fingers along his cape.

"Oh…uh good costumes," Grayson said, trying to sound polite.

Vivian narrowed her cat-green eyes and shot Alison a murderous glare before plastering a sweet smile on her face and turning back to Grayson. "In the story, Dracula only loves Mina."

"Not before having some fun with Lucy first." Alison flashed Grayson a wicked grin.

Grayson didn't respond to either of their advances. "Have a good night, ladies," he said as he took the program and raffle ticket stub from Vivian and wandered into the dancehall.

Vivian was a year ahead of Scarlett, and her main stream of study was fashion and design, so she didn't see much of Vivian. Whenever she did, she could make out faint traces of a creature attached to her. The creature looked dark and scaly, but Scarlett couldn't tell what it was or make sense of the various colors in her aura. Scarlett couldn't help but stare at Vivian. *What's that thing attached to her?* Under Scarlett's intense gaze, Vivian began to tremble. To avoid further scrutiny, Vivian put her head down, handed out their programs and raffle tickets, and hurried them into the hall.

When they entered, Luke punched Grayson's arm, "Dude, you're the coolest! Vivian and Alison were falling all over you. How do you do it, man?"

"Err, I don't know." Grayson shrugged, seeming unfazed by the girls' flirtations. The movie set replicas and the monster sculptures drew his attention. He elbowed Luke and pointed. "Whoa, check out The Creature From The Black Lagoon!"

The DJ kept the crowd hopping. Scarlett couldn't remember the last time she danced so much or had so much fun, except for maybe a couple weeks ago when she flew. All the dancing made her thirsty, and she kept going back to their table for more punch. About two hours into the dance, the room became blurry. She felt giddy and laughed at the slightest thing. Then, the room started spinning. Her head thumped, and her stomach gurgled. *I'm going to be sick!*

A slow song came on, and the older kids got up with their dates to slow dance as Scarlett staggered to their table and sat down, nearly missing the chair entirely. She broke out in a cold sweat as waves of nausea overtook her. Leaning forward and taking some deep breaths seemed to help ease the nausea. *Oh my God, please don't let me puke all over the floor.*

A few minutes later, Grayson joined her at the table looking rather pale and shaky himself. Through her blurry vision and achy head, Scarlett clumsily reached for him. "What's wrong, Grayson?" she slurred.

Shivering, he couldn't get the words out. "I...I just spoke with my mother."

With the waves of nausea now passed, she giggled. For some reason, she thought this was hilarious. "Oh, is she in town visiting?"

"She died when I was five."

This snapped her out of her daze. Scarlett took his hand and tried to focus on Grayson, but her sudden movement sent the room spinning again. Grayson's face zoomed in and out of focus. She didn't know what to say, she couldn't speak. *I'm so dizzy. There's something really wrong with me.*

Snuke appeared in a poof of green sparkles. She bit her lip and tugged on Scarlett's ears to get her attention. "Scarlett...Scarlett!" But Scarlett was too dizzy to pay attention.

Luke joined them at the table and sat down beside her. With a furrowed brow, he took her arm. "Scarlett, are you okay?" He tried to focus his attention on her, but something distracted him. He blinked and rubbed his eyes a few times. Then he reached out to grab whatever it was that he saw.

It's Snuke! He can see her. Scarlett panicked through her nausea. Luckily, Snuke was too quick for him and flew beyond his reach. She fluttered back to Scarlett looking flustered, tugging on her unicorn hair band. "Scarlett, come with me. There's something wrong. You're not in control."

"I know. I think I'm sick. I'm so dizzy and thirsty," she slurred

"Here's another bowl of punch." Vivian smiled sweetly at the group as she set down the bowl, passing her hand over Scarlett's cup. Then she scurried back to her own table where she sat with her arms folded, glowering at Scarlett.

Scarlett rubbed her eyes, trying to bring the room into focus. *I'm so thirsty.* She clawed at her burning throat. Still holding onto Grayson's hand, Scarlett refilled her cup when Precious knocked the punch out of her hand. "Scarlett, you're not in control of your Juma! Your punch, it's been poisoned!"

Just then, shrill high pitch screams drowned out the music and the dancehall filled with hundreds of flying skulls. Thin, veiny brown flesh covered their hideous bony wings that made the most dreadful sound like bones breaking and crunching. Air whooshed beneath their flapping wings like a thousand hissing snakes. When they opened their mouths, screeches pierced the air.

They swarmed the dancehall, biting anyone they could sink their teeth into. The students began screaming and running from the hall. Some tried to hide in the locker rooms, while others made it upstairs to the classrooms. Two of the hideous heads ganged up on Jessica Benner and took a chunk out of her leg.

Through the commotion, Scarlett managed to snap out of her daze enough to realize her energy had projected throughout the entire building. Ribbons of it floated around the hall, up the stairs, and even out the front door. "Scarlett, you're lit up. You need to bring it in. You woke the heads. They're attracted to the light," Snuke shouted.

More alert now, through her foggy head, she began pulling in and cloaking her Juma. She didn't realize how far she had let her energy project while her defenses were down. *What happened to me?*

A man dressed as a harlequin grabbed her hand and began pulling her away from the dancehall. "Come with me," he drawled. Under his purple sparkly makeup, she barely recognized Mr. Lechey, the school administrator. He whisked her away from the chaos but not before Scarlett looked back to see Ms. Beasle, Myles, and the Romanaskis storm into the dancehall and attack the flying skulls.

A skull swooped in after a third-year boy, but just as it opened its hideous mouth to take a bite out of him, Myles threw a stone into its mouth. It chomped down on it and exploded into flames and disintegrated. The gypsies enlisted the help of Michelle, Luke, Louzanne, and Grayson, giving them stones and directing them to aim for the mouths.

Scarlett watched with her jaw hung open, still being dragged by Mr. Lechey, until he managed to get her down the stairs and into a darkened basement corridor. "Hurry! I have the perfect place to hide." Still disoriented, Scarlett struggled to keep up the pace without tripping over her furry leg warmers.

The lights flickered and went out. Fumbling in the darkness, Scarlett banged into a fire extinguisher that hung on a wall and a flash of searing pain traveled through her right arm. She put her hand over her arm, and it was wet with blood. She kept her left palm over the wound to put pressure on it to try to stop the bleeding while still scrambling to keep up with Mr. Lechey.

A few of the lights came back on, but flickered. What Scarlett saw ahead made her stop in her tracks. At the end of the corridor stood a figure dressed all in black. The tall figure cast a long shadow—so long it was halfway down the hall to where Scarlett and Mr. Lechey stood. The shadow crept over her shoes and began traveling up her legs. Her skin burned from the intense cold where it touched her. A mist emanated from the figure that seemed to act as an asphyxiant as it smothered the light and air from the room.

Scarlett shivered and gasped for air. *So cold.* Her energy left her body. Her bones ached, and she could see her breath when she exhaled. The shadow passed over Mr. Lechey completely. He fell to the ground and lay lifeless on the floor.

She looked at the figure ahead but couldn't make out any of its features. "Who are you?" she cried. "What do you want?"

The figure opened its fiery red eyes. The same eyes that haunted her from the dream she had on her thirteenth birthday, the last dream she had before learning the truth about the veil.

She knew the creature was killing Mr. Lechey and doing a good job at trying to kill her. At first, the fear paralyzed her, but that quickly turned to anger. *How dare you come here?*

"What do you want?" she shouted again.

Scarlett clenched her fists and locked eyes with it. Its red eyes burned into hers as its shadow crept further up her body. Scarlett grew angrier. "NOOOO!" With both hands, she threw the remnants of her Juma that she was holding tight inside her towards the figure. A large ball of hot white light shot out of her hands, filling the entire hallway. With a force like a bomb, it blasted the figure against the door.

Unsure what she was going to do when she got close to it, Scarlett charged headlong anyway. As she pounced on the figure, it disappeared, causing her to crash through the blasted out doorway. She pulled herself up again and looked around the corridor, but the figure was nowhere in sight. She ran back to poor Mr. Lechey, who lay lifeless, and dropped to her knees in front of him. Beneath his makeup, his lips had turned blue. She couldn't tell if he was breathing. He felt so cold.

Scarlett's heart thumped in her chest. *Oh, my God! I don't know what to do.* "Okay, stay calm," she whispered to herself. Then she remembered the First Aid and CPR class she took with her dad a few years ago and began giving Mr. Lechey CPR. When she breathed into him, Mr. Lechey's eyes fluttered open, and he began to breathe on his own. She hovered over him, rubbing his arms to warm him. His purple sparkly makeup ran down his face as he gave her a weak smile.

"There you are." Myles rushed toward them. He glanced at the blasted out doors. "Looks like you had no trouble looking after yourself."

"Irinius," Myles greeted Mr. Lechey, "I see you've encountered what our little firecracker can do." He flashed a crooked grin.

Mr. Lechey nodded, his eyes wide. "She...she brought me back, Myles. She has the healing."

Scarlett interrupted, "Uh...it's called CPR. I took a class." Scarlett held out her hand to help Mr. Lechey up from the floor.

Just then, the pegasus she saw on her first day hanging around Mr. Lechey came galloping down the stairs neighing. Scarlett cringed as it charged at them, but let out a sigh of relief when it halted at Mr. Lechey to nuzzle him with its snout.

"You're injured." Myles examined Scarlett's bleeding arm.

She rubbed her finger over the sticky gash. She had forgotten it was there. "Oh yeah."

"We'll get you to the school nurse," Myles reassured her. He took her hand and led her back upstairs.

Returning to the dance hall, Scarlett surveyed the damage. Myles, Ms. Beasle, Mr. Lechey, and the gypsies—along with some strange looking new people Scarlett had never seen before—rounded up all the faculty and students and began, one by one, casting muddle spells to alter the way they would remember this event. The injured were sent to the school nurse for treatment. The fairies worked their way through the building, repairing any damage and evidence of what happened.

The lineup for the nurse's office winded down the hall and around the corner. The lucky ones had cuts and bruises from bumping into one another or falling down trying to get out of the way of the ravenous flying heads. The unfortunate ones had chunks of flesh and digits missing from their bodies from where the heads managed to take a bite out of them. Scarlett heard about how great the new nurse was that just started at Rosemont but hadn't yet met her. *She sure has her work cut out for her.*

The line moved quickly. The badly injured ones were seen first, and they emerged from the nurse's office looking un-traumatized and good as new. Based on the look of Jessica Benner's leg before she returned from the nurse's office, Scarlett knew there was more than good medicine at play here. Finally, it was her turn. She entered the sterile office and first aid room. Mrs. Goodspeed, the nurse from her old school, looked up from her medicine bag and greeted her with a smile.

"What are you doing here?" asked Scarlett.

Mrs. Goodspeed didn't respond at first, rather she blew on her hands and rubbed them together in a circular motion. She then exposed Scarlett's arm and moved her palms back and forth above her wound several times. When Scarlett looked at her arm, it was completely healed.

Then Mrs. Goodspeed spoke. "I think you already know the answer to that, Scarlett."

"So, you're not from Columbus then?"

Mrs. Goodspeed shook her head and smiled. She peered down at her through her horn-rimmed glasses. "I think you already know that too, dear, but I'll tell you anyway. I was assigned to look in on you when you started school. After you left, my services were no longer required there, so Myles asked me to come here. Now, I suppose he could have asked the Appalachian witch who lives not too far from here to come, but I just can't imagine how she would react to having to deal with a bunch of teenagers day in and day out. Besides, not to brag, but I'm one of the best healers in North America. If anything were to happen to you before you get a chance to..." Mrs. Goodspeed paused. "If anything were to happen to you, I could heal you."

"A chance to what?" Scarlett pried, trying to get an answer but Mrs. Goodspeed only smiled and patted her hand.

"There's only thirty minutes left of the dance. Go enjoy yourself, dear." She shooed Scarlett from her office.

Scarlett returned to the hall and spotted her friends on the dance floor dancing and laughing as if nothing had ever happened. The dancehall and its Halloween décor had been restored back to normal, and the sound of the latest hit filled the room. In fact, everyone looked like they were having a good time. There was no trace of evidence that anything unusual had ever gone on.

Vivian Patterson was the only person who didn't look happy. Her eyes were puffy as if she had been crying. Scarlett watched Ms. Beasle, the Percussion teacher, escort her from the hall.

"Scarlett, where were you?" Michelle asked. "Are you okay? You missed it. Vivian got caught trying to spike our punch, but Ms. Beasle caught her. She's going to be in big trouble. I bet she'll get expelled!"

They obviously did a good job at muddling Michelle's memory since that's the only highlight of the night. And she didn't just try; she did spike it. Scarlett felt better after her visit with Mrs. Goodspeed, but whatever Vivian used in the punch, it sure did make her feel sick. *Why would Vivian want to spike our punch?*

"Oh," she said, opting not to correct Michelle since after tonight's events, having the punch spiked seemed like a minor detail.

Scarlett scanned the hall again for anything out of sorts and saw Myles leaning against one of the pillars with his arms folded. He smiled as he watched the students dancing and having a good time. Satisfied that everything was back to normal, he turned to leave.

"I had too much punch. You know I have to go again?" Scarlett excused herself from her friends and ran after Myles.

"Hey Myles, wait up!" She caught up to him in the hallway, but he continued walking. She followed outside. He sat down on one of the steps, and she sat down beside him. "What were those things?"

Myles let out a deep sigh. She could tell the evening's event had taken a toll on him. "Kanonsistonties, the flying heads."

"Kano-what?" Scarlett asked.

"Kanonsistonties. The souls of cannibals. Years ago, a tribe of cannibals used to live in these parts. Because they chose to eat human flesh in life, they're doomed to remain on earth in this hideous form, forever ravenous. They don't normally have the strength to break through the veil and actually attack humans, but they have been known to get through on occasion. We've discovered a few tricks as to how to kill them over the years. Hearthstones, for whatever reason, those little buggers gobble them up, and it makes their heads explode." Myles gave her a wink and grinned.

"Why did they come here? What did they want?"

Myles pulled on his beard, thinking carefully before responding. "Your particular energy represents the living. These monsters were attracted to it because the living means fresh meat. I suppose when you lost control, your Juma gave them enough strength to break through. Your schoolmates were also able to see the monsters because your Juma, when you let it, lights the way through the veil for others to see."

Scarlett was horrified. *How can I so easily attract these kinds of monsters? Am I dangerous?*

"Don't blame yourself. It wasn't your fault. You've been doing great, kid. Your drink was poisoned. You couldn't help it." Myles patted her shoulder.

"What about the man in black with red eyes? I dreamed about those eyes before, Myles. He's really scary."

"Him…well that's a conversation for later, my dear. Trust that you are safe tonight and leave that be for now." Myles' tone was stern. He seemed resolute in not telling her more, and Scarlett knew well enough not to push.

"Your father's here. You'll resume lessons Monday after school." He gave her a warm smile and, despite his fatigue, his blue eyes still sparkled. Resigned with shoulders slumped, Scarlett nodded and got up to meet her father.

Mr. Wrigley rolled down the window when she approached. "Who were you talking to, honey? It looked like you were by yourself." Scarlett looked over at Myles. *It's strange Dad can't see him.* "Uhh, no one. I was going over some lyrics I had in my head for a new song." *Again with the lies. Will I ever be able to stop?*

"Ahh, new song, eh? Cool."

The doors to the dancehall burst open, and the students began filing out. Michelle, Luke, Louzanne, and Grayson rushed over to Scarlett.

Michelle grabbed Scarlett by the shoulders. "Oh my God! That was the best! I hope they expel her until Christmas!" They all laughed.

"This was the best night ever!" Michelle raved. "Vivian Patterson is going to meet some karmic justice and—drum roll please—guess who won the door prize?" With a lopsided grin, Michelle held out the latest phone that tech stores couldn't seem to keep in stock.

"Well, we're going to walk across campus. See you guys Monday," Grayson said, tapping Luke on the arm to get him moving. They said their goodbyes and Grayson and Luke began their trek across campus to Grayson's dorm.

Scarlett, Michelle, and Louzanne piled into Mr. Wrigley's Subaru and headed for her house, where they would finish the night watching old horror films. Scarlett planned on pretending to doze off. She'd experienced enough horror for one evening.

NINE
WITH A MOTHER LIKE THAT

Mrs. Wrigley fussed over the girls all day on Sunday, treating them to pedicures, breakfast, and decaf lattes. Scarlett had so much fun she almost forgot about the horrible events that took place the night before. Almost, but not quite. On their way to get pedicures, she kept looking down alleyways expecting to see the man in black.

The girls agreed to get together over the weekend again soon. At the mention of another sleepover, to Scarlett's embarrassment, her mom could hardly contain herself. Mrs. Wrigley clapped her hands excitedly. "Ooh, that sounds like fun. We can plan a candle making night and a cookie baking night."

Scarlett tried not to roll her eyes or let out a sigh. She shot Louzanne and Michelle an apologetic look, but they didn't seem to mind. They seemed to like having a motherly figure around to spoil them.

***

A very scolded and withdrawn looking Vivian Patterson was present and accounted for at Rosemont first thing on Monday morning. Vivian sat outside Mr. Lechey's office with her head bowed and a somber expression on her face. Scarlett, Louzanne, and Michelle made their way to their lockers before first period when Michelle spotted Vivian, stopping dead in her tracks. "What's she doing here?" she hissed.

A refined nasally female voice came from Mr. Lechey's office. Curious over who might be inside, Scarlett motioned for Louzanne and Michelle to stop and listen. They lingered outside pretending they were waiting to see the administrator.

"Honestly, we pay you good money to provide support and guidance for our Vivian. My husband and I simply don't have the time right now to stay home with her. I'm expected in Beijing on Wednesday morning. Now, I suppose we could have the cleaning staff look in on her, but I'm sure you'll agree, Mr. Lechey, she really is much better off here at Rosemont where she belongs."

"Now, Mrs. Patterson," Mr. Lechey began.

"That must be Vivian's mother inside," Scarlett whispered to her friends.

"Please, call me Alexi," Mrs. Patterson interrupted.

"Alexi," Mr. Lechey continued, "your daughter stole isopropanol from the chemistry lab and poisoned another student's drink. The girl is very lucky to be alive."

"C'mon, Mr. Lechey. You can't honestly think my Vivian meant to kill the girl, do you? She probably thought it would just make her tipsy, like regular alcohol. You know, she's not very bright. I doubt she even pays attention in Chemistry class to know the difference. Her father was a moron too. She probably thought it would be funny to see someone drunk. But to kill someone? Honestly, Vivian doesn't have the guts to even try something like that." Even through Mr. Lechey's wooden double doors, the disdain Mrs. Patterson held for her daughter was palpable, like a thick blanket of toxic smog.

Scarlett, Louzanne, and Michelle remained silent outside Mr. Lechey's office wearing expressions of shock. *We can hear the entire conversation from the hallway, which means Vivian can hear it too.* Mrs. Patterson sounded like a horrible person. Scarlett couldn't help but cast Vivian a sympathetic look. Vivian's eyes remained fixed on the wall in front of her. Her mother's words had affected her because the strange creature attached to her seemed to have taken on a more solid form as if it had grown stronger.

Isopropanol can be dangerous, and I drank a lot of punch. That should've sent me to the hospital. I felt nauseous and dizzy, but then I was okay after. I should have collapsed that night, and I didn't. Why? And why did she do it?

91

"I thought maybe she spiked my punch with some peach schnapps or something, not a chemical from the lab," Scarlett whispered to her friends.

"Mrs. Patterson—Alexi—we have rules," Mr. Lechey said from inside the office. "We can't let this go unpunished."

"Oh, I'm all for discipline. You're the administrator. I'll leave that to you. Now not another word, Mr. Lechey. Here's the check for the design wing renovation. I trust our contribution is suitable, yes?"

Scarlett couldn't hear Mr. Lechey's response.

"Very good then. Have a nice day, Mr. Lechey."

A tall, beautiful blonde woman emerged from the office. She was fashionably and expensively dressed. When Scarlett got a look at her full profile, she recognized her immediately from old fashion magazines her mother kept around the house.

Louzanne covered her mouth and whispered, "Of course, Alexi Cierra—now Alexi Patterson. Vivian looks a lot like her. I knew there was something familiar about Vivian. She was a top model in the early 2000's. Her career ended when she got pregnant. She gained a lot of weight during pregnancy, and it took her several years to take it off." Louzanne giggled. "But by then, advertisers were on to the next fresh face, and she never had the chance to go back to modeling. Later, she married the real estate tycoon Ronald Patterson. Now she's the fashion editor for *Belle,* and she helps her husband with his business."

Scarlett couldn't stop staring at Mrs. Patterson and Vivian. With the mystery creature much more visible, she could clearly distinguish its scaly arms wrapped around Vivian's chest. It looked like it was making breathing more difficult for her.

Mrs. Patterson shot Vivian a look of disgust but pecked her on the cheek. "No more of this from you. I'm late. My whole day is ruined! I'll see you at Christmas. The Changs are coming for Christmas. This is a very important deal for your father and me. I expect you'll show their daughter, Fung, the city." Vivian nodded meekly, not meeting her mother's eyes. Mrs. Patterson patted the girl's cheek. "That's a good girl," she said as she turned and walked away.

The sound of Mrs. Patterson's designer heels reverberated off the granite tile as she walked down the hall. She gave Scarlett a quick head to toe disdainful look at the sight of her sneakers, ripped-up jeans, and t-shirt before continuing out the front door. She never once looked back at her daughter.

The bell rang, and Vivian hurried to class. Michelle's face flushed, and she exhaled heavily as if she could breathe fire from her nostrils. She waited until Vivian was out of earshot before blowing up. "How can Mr. Lechey let her get away with this? She belongs in prison! If you were some rich kid, she'd be expelled and yet, your parents weren't even called. This is class discrimination. I'm going to get my father involved. He was a civil rights attorney before becoming a senator." She clicked her tongue and put her hands on her hips. "It's just not right. You never did anything to her. Well, she's a little afraid of you, but you never did anything but give her that look you give."

"It's okay, Michelle. Really, I'm fine," Scarlett reassured her. "What look?"

"I don't know; you just stare at her really hard like you're looking through her. It's pretty intense."

"Oh, I didn't know I did that."

"I don't get it. You seemed totally fine at the dance. You looked giddy when we were dancing, but after that, you seemed normal on the way back to your house, and all day Sunday. That's a dangerous chemical. Did you barf? Is that why you disappeared?" Louzanne asked.

"Yeah, I barfed, but I felt better afterward. I thought maybe I had too much candy or something, so I didn't think much about it." Scarlett lied on the spot without even batting an eye and flashed them a persuasive smile.

It was enough to convince Michelle. "Maybe she only put a tiny drop in your cup, and it didn't affect you much because you drank so much punch. Maybe all the punch diluted what was in your system."

"Yeah, maybe," Scarlett replied. But Louzanne gave her a funny look as if she knew there was a little more to Scarlett than what she let on. Scarlett changed the subject. "You guys, did you hear her mother? I would die if my mom talked about me like that. I know she could've killed me, but I don't know...I kind of feel sorry for her. No wonder she acts out. It's gotta be tough with a mother like that. I don't care how rich you are."

Louzanne nodded. "Mm-hmm. Believe me, girl, I know."

"Mr. Lechey will decide the right thing to do," Scarlett said. Louzanne shrugged, but Michelle didn't look entirely convinced. "Hey, you guys go on. I need to talk to Mr. Lechey."

"Okay, see you at lunch," Michelle said as she and Louzanne headed on to class.

Scarlett knocked on Mr. Lechey's double wooden doors. "Come in," she heard from inside. She entered the office quietly. Mr. Lechey's face brightened. "Scarlett, I'm so glad you came. I was going to send for you today. I feel like, after Saturday, I can help explain some things to you. Please have a seat." Mr. Lechey gestured to one of his chairs lined up on the opposite side of his oversized mahogany desk. The pegasus slept on the floor beside it, taking up most of the floor space. "It's Melintha's nap time. We had quite a jaunty ride last night, so she's extra tired today. But don't worry, she's a sound sleeper."

Scarlett took a seat farthest to the right, so as not to step on the sleeping pegasus or disturb her while she pulled out her chair. Mr. Lechey took a seat behind his desk, tented his fingers beneath his chin, and gave her an attentive smile.

"Mr. Lechey," Scarlett began, "I don't understand what happened on Saturday night. The flying heads, the man in black, getting poisoned. What happened? And why did Vivian do it? After all the punch I drank, I should have been really sick or died, but I didn't. Why?"

"Ahh, well let me begin by telling you that I am sworn to secrecy about the man in black. Myles plans on telling you after you graduate from Rosemont and not a moment sooner."

"When I graduate? That's like five years from now. I can't wait five years to find out about something that tried to kill me—and almost killed you." Scarlett huffed and crossed her arms.

"I'm bound by a covenant of secrecy. My tongue will fall off if I utter even a teensy weensy peep." Mr. Lechey's pinched his thumb and forefinger together when he said this. It was clear Myles had some authority over Mr. Lechey. No doubt, his tongue might very well fall off if he told her about the man in black. She shook her head and clicked her tongue. *Myles must think I'm a baby and can't handle the truth. Mr. Lechey would tell me if it weren't for him.*

As if Mr. Lechey could read her mind, he said, "Now, don't go getting too upset with Myles. I entered the covenant willingly. I agree with Myles. This information is best kept from you until you're older. It's just that I have a tendency to get overexcited and blab about things that I really shouldn't. So, we felt the secrecy covenant was the best way to keep me from spilling the beans. Now," he clapped his hands three times, "on to your next question. I'm sure Myles explained the flying heads. Your Juma woke them, I'm afraid. What I did want to speak with you about is your tolerance and recovery from the poison is nothing short of remarkable. I think you're a healer. With Juma like yours, it makes sense, I suppose. I believe you healed yourself of the poison—unwittingly, mind you. And I also believe you healed me when you did this…what did you call it?"

"CPR."

"Ahh, yes. That. I believe you brought me back from the brink of death."

Scarlett rolled her eyes; she couldn't help it. *Ridiculous. He thinks basic CPR skills are magical. On second thought, I did fly. I did blast that creature with a force that came out of my hands. Compared to all that weirdness, maybe being a healer isn't all that weird. Right?* She wiped the scowl from her face and replaced it with a more respectful expression. "Mr. Lechey, why did Vivian poison us?"

"That's the strangest thing. Mr. Dogwood, our chemistry teacher, tested the punch and only your cup tested positive for isopropanol. The rest of the punch was fine."

"But why me? She seems to hate Michelle, but she doesn't even know me."

"I don't know. Ms. Beasle and I interrogated her while under hypnosis, and then Mrs. Goodspeed served her a helping of blabber tea. It seems Vivian has no memory of what she did. She doesn't understand it herself. After showing her the surveillance footage, she clearly understands that it was she that took the chemical from the Chemistry Lab, and it was she that poured it in your cup, but she doesn't remember doing it or why. I also have a knack for knowing what one is thinking, and I believe her. Regardless, her act cannot go unpunished, and I am currently devising a plan for atonement." Mr. Lechey tapped his hand on the desk by way of letting her know their conversation was finished.

Scarlett left Mr. Lechey's office with a new perspective. As crazy and dangerous as her new life was, she was surrounded by people who loved her. Seeing how Mrs. Patterson spoke about her daughter and the lack of affection she showed for the girl, Scarlett knew she wouldn't trade places with Vivian for anything in the world. As nasty as Vivian Patterson might be, and even though she tried to kill her—accidentally or intentionally—Scarlett decided one thing: she would try her best to be nice to Vivian. She knew any type of punishment that Mr. Lechey could dole out or any unkind word she could say to Vivian would pale in comparison to having a mother like that.

TEN
FEAR OR LOVE

"Ahhem." Mr. Lechey's voice crackled over the PA system. "I am pleased to announce that our school music department has been asked to perform at the symphony festival hosted in Washington DC this March." *Crackle crackle…* "We will be holding auditions. Those selected as orchestra members will perform at various venues throughout the city during the third week of March." *Crackle…* "There will also be a class field trip for first years in February, sponsored by the vocational department, to tour various industries in the community." *Crackle crackle…* "First years can use this as an opportunity to determine any future career interests. The vocational field trip will take place the last week of February." *Crackle crackle.*

"I'm trying out for the symphony. Are you?" Michelle asked over lunch. They both savored the macaroni and cheese from the cafeteria. Today was Rhonda's day to cook, so they took advantage, knowing the food was probably safe to eat. Thursday was usually Mary Kate's day to make lunch, and there were concerns over hygiene and food safety since many students often came down with a case of the runs shortly after.

Scarlett learned to play violin when she was three years old and had been practicing quite a bit since she started at Rosemont. She wasn't sure she was symphony material, but she imagined how fun it would be if she and her friends got to take a school trip.

"Yeah, I guess I'll audition."

Guitar was her favorite instrument, but she could hardly play the guitar in a symphony so she decided she would try her best to become a part of the orchestra by playing violin.

Michelle went on, "Drumming in an orchestra is a little different than in a rock band, but I do have formal training. Plus, Rosemont has some of the best music instructors in the country, so I've had a few months' exposure. I hope they pick me."

"I'm definitely auditioning as the pianist," Luke said.

"You'll definitely get picked," Scarlett reassured him. There was only room for one pianist in the orchestra, so this was the hardest one to get, but everyone knew Luke was the best at Rosemont. Luckily for Scarlett, there were eighteen spaces available for violin. There were a lot of talented students at Rosemont. She was only a first year; she hadn't even heard the fourth, fifth or sixth years play yet. *After six years under the direction of Ms. Beasle and the rest of the music department, they must be something else.* But Scarlett wasn't about to pass up on a fun trip, so she resolved to practice the violin every day and try to get selected at the audition.

***

There was a chill in the air as autumn leaves fell from the trees. Since she had learned to pull in her Juma, Scarlett rarely got too cold. A light sweater was all she wore to keep herself warm from the chilly breeze coming off the river. It was Wednesday afternoon, and she was about to receive a new lesson from Myles. Yadira stood by as his assistant.

Myles picked up a stick and traced a large circle around them in the rocks along the riverbank. "Okay, Scarlett. You can hold it in really well, and you can block—so long as you're not being poisoned, of course. Now, let's practice letting it out. Based on what you did at the dance, you seem to have a basic understanding of it. But I want you to learn how to control your Juma, so you don't have to be so destructive." Just thinking about that cold, shadowy man with red eyes made the hair on the back of her neck stand up.

With a motion from Myles, Yadira stood a plate up against a large river rock. "Try to knock this plate off the rock," he instructed. Yadira ran for cover just in case Scarlett wasn't able to control herself and blasted her to pieces by accident. Myles stood behind Scarlett. "Okay, now concentrate on moving the plate. Imagine your energy is like a long arm and you're reaching it out gently to move the plate."

She closed her eyes to center herself and reopened them. She imagined letting her energy out in the form of a long white glowing arm like Myles instructed. After a few moments' concentration, her energy ribboned outwards until it reached the plate. She made several passes at it, but couldn't manage to connect with the plate. After several more tries, she managed to make the plate quiver slightly.

"Good. Okay, that's a start. Keep it up."

After an hour of intense concentration, Scarlett could only make the plate vibrate. She couldn't manage to actually lift it from the rock.

"This isn't working," she huffed.

"Take a deep breath and try again."

"I'm trying!" she snapped. Just then, her Juma shot out from her like a laser. It struck the plate and smashed it into a thousand pieces.

"Good thing no one was near it." Myles gave her a lopsided grin. "What were you feeling that time?"

Scarlett stood still, shaken by what she had done. "I...I was feeling frustrated that I wasn't getting it."

"Why were you frustrated?" Myles prodded.

Scarlett thought about it for a moment. "I guess I was scared that I wasn't ever going to get it and that I might not be able to protect my friends or family if the man in black comes back."

Myles rubbed his chin thoughtfully. "Mmm hmm, okay. First of all, he will not come back. I promise. So you have nothing to fear. Yadira, could you set another plate please?" Yadira set up another plate on the rock and ran for cover even quicker than the last time. "I want you to try to move the plate again, but this time, imagine you want to move it out of love."

That sounded like the most ridiculous thing Scarlett had ever heard. "I don't understand what you mean. Move it out of love?"

"Imagine your mother or father was very hungry and unable to pick up this plate on their own. Imagine lifting up the plate and bringing it to them so they can eat."

Scarlett closed her eyes and remembered the time her mother broke her leg and couldn't leave her bed for a few weeks and how Scarlett would prepare snacks for her. She imagined setting plates out for her family at dinnertime. When she opened her eyes, the plate hovered mid-air above the riverbank, wrapped in a band of white light—her white light.

"Good...good, now set it down on the grass over there," Myles instructed. Scarlett imagined the grass was her dinner table at home. With her energy wrapped around the plate, she watched it move gracefully through the air as she moved it to the grassy area and set it down gently, as if setting the table. The plate remained intact. She let out a sigh of relief.

Myles flashed her a warm smile. "See the difference between fear and love?"

Scarlett spent the rest of the afternoon until sunset practicing moving objects with her Juma until she was able to get the hang of it. She even wrapped her Juma around Yadira and managed to lift her, but she chickened out when Yadira's feet hovered a foot off the ground, too scared she might lose her concentration and drop her.

***

The following Saturday after the Halloween disaster, Scarlett made her way down to the river after breakfast. In a few short weeks, they would be getting ready for Thanksgiving. Scarlett always looked forward to the holidays, although she was sure this year's would be far more interesting with a household full of fairies, a leprechaun, and ghosts. The temperature had plummeted, but it wasn't cold enough for snow yet, so she could still ride her bike down to the river. As her tires hit the path, she had a sneaking suspicion that she was being followed. By the time she made it to the riverbank clearing, the feeling was unshakable. She looked around everywhere, but there was no sign of anyone.

Puffs of smoke rose along the riverbank and ashes smoldered in the campfire pits from where the gypsies had left them burning the night before. Scarlett looked all around but found no trace of any person or beast that might be following her. *I'm getting paranoid.* She shrugged, walked up to Myles' cabin, and knocked on the door.

Myles greeted her with his warm smile. He was already up and dressed for the day in his usual hobo style. Today he wore a *Red Hot Chili Peppers* t-shirt, brown slacks, and a gray cardigan. Mrs. Goodspeed sat in one of his armchairs by the fire drinking a cup of tea.

"Good morning, Scarlett," she said with a grin.

Myles set about putting on the kettle for an extra cup of tea for Scarlett. "There's no need for outdoor practice. Mrs. Goodspeed will be giving your lesson, so you stay inside by the fire."

Mrs. Goodspeed remained seated where she was in the armchair. "Come sit down beside me, dear. Today we're going to learn healing and rejuvenation. Mr. Lechey is convinced you're a healer. So today, we shall see."

"All set then. I'll be back in a few minutes." Myles flashed them a smile as he left the cabin.

Scarlett took a seat alongside her in the other armchair and in the next moment, Mrs. Goodspeed pulled out a pocketknife from her purse, hiked up her skirt revealing her thigh and sliced it open just above the knee. Blood droplets oozed from the wound and Scarlett's eyes widened. *Is she nuts?* "What are you doing?" she shrieked. She wrapped her arms around herself and closed her eyes. "That has to hurt."

Mrs. Goodspeed smiled sweetly, as if her leg wasn't dripping blood. "I'm going to show you. Hand me that tea towel, dear, so I don't get blood all over Myles' nice chair." Scarlett handed her the tea towel from the tray set out beside them. Mrs. Goodspeed placed it over her leg to sop up some of the blood and keep it from dripping on the chair and onto the floor. She began rubbing her hands in a circular motion. "You see, I'm drawing out my Juma to the surface of my hands and I'm massaging it gently, creating a healing ball of energy. I have to pay attention to my thoughts and my feelings while I'm drawing it out. My Juma will only heal if my thoughts and intentions are for healing. I can't be thinking of anything else. Focusing your thoughts and intentions completely is what makes healing one of the hardest skills, and many magical people can't quite get it. Their minds are often on a hundred other things at once." Mrs. Goodspeed took a deep breath. "Now I'm emptying my mind of all things except the thought of warm healing light."

Balls of white light formed on Mrs. Goodspeed's palms. She held up her hands and exhaled onto the energy balls. This seemed to have a similar effect as if stoking a fire and the energy glowed with bright white embers. "Now, like this." She passed the palms of her hands above and over her thigh, back and forth, several times. The wound pulled itself together and healed more and more with each pass until there wasn't even a mark.

"That is the technique for wounds without complications. For infections or disease, you must draw out the sickness completely before you focus on closing the wound. Let's start with something simple, like a cold. Kizzy's little one, Rosabelle, has come down with a case of the sniffles. Myles is retrieving her now."

Myles opened the door and led in a sweet rosy-faced little girl about the age of four, with green almond-shaped eyes and a mop of dark brown ringlets. The little girl greeted her with a sneeze, "Hewwo Scawwett!" Streams of boogers ran down her nose and onto her lip where they jiggled as she attempted to sniff them back in.

"Come here, little one. Let's get you all better." Mrs. Goodspeed motioned for Rosabelle to come toward them. Mrs. Goodspeed paused for a moment in silence, rubbed her palms in a circular motion, and exhaled warm breath onto the balls of light she created. Instead of passing them over the child, she kept her palms still over the girl's nose and throat. When the balls of light appeared to thicken and turn opaque, she made grabbing motions with her hands until a thin film of green gooey substance came to the surface of her nose and mouth. Once Mrs. Goodspeed had a good grip on the film, she began pulling it out as if pulling in a fishing line. With three quick motions, the film was out. Then Mrs. Goodspeed spun it around her hand until it formed into a gooey ball and she tossed it into the fire. The fire gave a short burst of intense flame, then died down to its regular smolder.

Rosabelle took a few deep breaths through her nose. "I'm not stuffy anymore! Mommy said I can't play outside until I'm better and now I am." She hugged Mrs. Goodspeed and Scarlett and ran outside.

"See how that was different? It takes a lot of energy to find it and draw it out. And sometimes you don't get it all the first time. It takes a long time to get a knack for knowing when you got it all." Scarlett's jaw hung open.

"Now you try." The door opened, and Myles led in Yadira and Rolph's boy, Gustaf. He waved a friendly hello to Scarlett but gave Mrs. Goodspeed, who was a stranger to him, a weary look. "Scarlett is going to take care of you. Sit down on that chair there. Don't mind me, dear," Mrs. Goodspeed instructed the boy.

"Hi Gustaf," Scarlett greeted him with a smile. "Tell me, what's wrong with you?"

He pulled up his pant leg to reveal a scraped knee. "I got another one for my scar collection," he said with a grin. His tongue stuck through a gap in his front teeth where he had lost a baby tooth, and the adult one hadn't quite grown in yet.

"Well, Mrs. Goodspeed wants me to try and see if I can heal it, okay? Don't worry, I probably can't, and you can keep your scar. Will you let me try?"

Gustaf nodded.

"Now concentrate, dear," Mrs. Goodspeed instructed. "Clear your thoughts of everything."

This proved hard to do. Scarlett was thinking about the last band practice they had and the new song they were working on. She wondered how Honeybee, Precious, and Snuke came to live with her and what their lives were like before she was born. Did they live with other humans, or did they live in trees? Her thoughts always came back to the mysterious man in black. She hadn't gotten anywhere with Myles on getting him to open up about it.

"Concentrate, dear."

Scarlett took a deep breath and tried to clear her mind. Slowly, with great effort, the busy thoughts left her, and she replaced them with nothing but creating the intention to heal. Once she felt she had the intention, with eyes still closed, she rubbed her palms together until she could feel warm orbs begin to form on her palms. Then she exhaled onto her palms. She opened her eyes, amazed to see the energy balls glowing brightly as she breathed on them. Next, she passed her palms over Gustaf's bloody knee. The wound began to close right before her eyes.

The hair on the back of her neck stood up. She saw a movement from the corner of her eye. Were they being watched? She looked up at the cabin window where she sensed the presence, but nothing. When she looked back at her hands, the light orbs were gone.

"Ahh, I got distracted. Now I have to start all over again!"

"This is perfect, Scarlett!" Gustaf said, looking down at his knee. Rather than a fresh bloody scrape, it had healed together to make a pink scar. The wound wasn't deep enough to leave a permanent scar, but he could at least brag about it for a week or so until it healed completely and faded on its own. "Thanks, Scarlett!" Gustaf flashed her a crooked grin and took off outside to play.

She tried to heal the Romanaski kids' various injuries and illnesses, but she would get them healed halfway and then find herself distracted. Then she would lose the healing energy and have to start over again. To avoid leaving the kids half-healed, Mrs. Goodspeed had to take over several times to finish the job.

By lunchtime, Scarlett's disappointment in herself wore on her. With shoulders slumped, she was ready to give up. "I'm just not good at this. I guess I'm not a healer."

Mrs. Goodspeed took her by the hand. "Nonsense. You're as good as any. This is only your first day, and already you healed a sinus infection, an ingrown toenail, and you half healed a scraped knee. Many healers take years to learn their craft. I think you're a natural. The only thing stopping you is right here." She pointed to Scarlett's temple. "You have a very busy mind, my dear."

Myles entered the cabin. "Yadira is making goulash and perogies for everyone for lunch. I think you should both take a break and resume lessons tomorrow. Is tomorrow still good for you, Agnes?" Mrs. Goodspeed nodded. Scarlett's eyebrows rose when she heard Myles call her by her first name. She never knew Mrs. Goodspeed's first name was Agnes.

***

The Romanaskis sure knew how to have a picnic. Not only was there goulash and perogies, but there were several types of homemade baked breads, cakes, puddings, and pies. Scarlett made sure she saved enough room to taste them all. Some of the children were practicing sword fighting again. Like a beautiful dance, they pirouetted around the campfires, striking and dodging one another's blows.

Lala, Kizzy, and Rolph played beautiful music with drums, flute, and a sitar. Scarlett had never played a sitar before and asked if she could try. Once she got the hang of the different body and the strings, she was strumming along with the drum and flute in no time. Then she borrowed a violin to show them what she had been practicing.

After everyone finished all the deserts, Scarlett realized she only had an hour to get home, change, and meet up with Louzanne. They were going to check out the new café and yoga studio that had opened the day before. She said goodbye to her friends and agreed to meet with Mrs. Goodspeed again the following morning.

She was only on the bike path a minute or so when she sensed the presence again. It was coming from behind her, behind a group of trees. She hit the brakes on her bike and came to an abrupt halt. She paused for a moment to listen and couldn't hear anything. "Hello?" she called out and peered through the trees. She heard a faint rustling as one of the branches moved.

She didn't like the idea of someone sneaking around. *What if it's the man in black?* This made her angry—really angry. She balled her fists, leapt from her bike and ran toward the moving branches. She charged so fast that, without thinking or worrying about anyone seeing her, she began to fly. Behind the trees, the figure skulked about trying to remain hidden. She flew through the trees, rushed the stalker, and made contact.

The rest happened so quickly. She tackled him and the stalker fell backward into a deep ravine. As he fell, she recognized him. It was Grayson. His eyes widened, and he gasped. She tried to reach for him, but he fell so quickly. He landed below with a *crack* and a soft wet *thud*.

"Grayson!" she screamed as she flew down to the bottom of the ravine, landing softly on the rocky, muddy surface to find Grayson lying in a pool of blood with his arm bent in a horrible configuration. Blood oozed from the side of his head where it had struck a rock. "I'm so sorry," she sobbed. She looked around the ravine. She was too far away to scream for help. No one would hear her. *Can I fly and carry Grayson at the same time? Maybe I can catch up with Mrs. Goodspeed? Too risky. What if I drop him and make it worse?*

She could tell he was still alive from his ragged breathing and the fact that his eyes still moved around beneath his eyelids. She'd never seen anything more horrible, nor felt so guilty in all her life. If she didn't get help soon, Grayson was going to die, and it was all her fault. "Help!" she screamed, but it was useless. No one was coming. She grabbed him under his arms and tried to will herself upward. Air swirled beneath her feet as they lifted up. For a moment they both hovered slightly above the ground, but the weight of his body was too heavy for her arms. They dropped back down into the mud.

Scarlett felt hopeless. She sobbed as Grayson's breath became more ragged. He went into convulsions. She sobbed even harder as she watched him shake uncontrollably. For a brief moment, he opened his eyes and focused them on her. "Scarlett," he whispered.

That was enough to snap her out of it. She took a few deep breaths. "Okay, you can do this," she said to herself. Scarlett cleared her mind of nothing but the thought of healing. She wanted nothing more in this world than to heal Grayson. She rubbed her palms together in a circular motion. *Heal...heal.* She felt a warm tingling sensation as the energy orbs began to grow. After several seconds that felt like hours, she had accumulated large orbs on the palms of her hands. She passed her palms over his worst injury: the large wound on the side of his head where he hit the rock. She passed her hands above the wound over and over again. Intent on fixing her mistake, there was nothing in this world that could distract her now. *Heal...heal,* was the only thought that came to her mind.

The open wound began to stitch itself back together. She passed her hands over the wound several more times until the wound closed and no evidence of a scar remained. She then focused her attention on the rest of his body, first on his twisted arm. She laid it straight. After several passes, it too began to heal. Once the arm was healed, she made several more passes over his body. A fall like that had to have generated some internal injuries, and she wasn't going to let up until she was sure she had fixed all of the damage she caused. She passed her hands over his head one more time for good measure when Grayson opened his eyes and sat up.

He looked at her, then from side to side and all around the ravine to get his bearings, blinking several times. When she saw he was awake, she threw her arms around him. "Grayson! You're okay!" He rubbed the side of his head and then his eyes. He felt around in his pocket and pulled out his camera, looking relieved that it was still intact.

"Why were you following me?"

"I...I find you interesting," he said slowly as he looked around the ravine again. Then it all came back to him, how he came to be at the bottom of the ravine. "You...you flew!"

"You hit your head."

"You healed me. I know you can do that. I saw you and the new school nurse healing those gypsy kids. Were they real gypsies? I saw the old-fashioned caravans. I didn't think that was a thing anymore."

"How do you feel?" Scarlett asked, choosing to ignore his comments rather than argue with him. He smiled. Then he jumped up, picking her up and swinging her around. "I feel better than ever. Scarlett, that was amazing!"

"C'mon, let's get out of this ravine," Scarlett said, pointing to the rocky walls and the surface above.

Grayson eyed the rocks and branches along the upward slope, planning his assent. "Don't worry; I'm a pretty good rock climber." Scarlett had never been rock climbing in her life and didn't know how she was going to get herself out of the ravine without showing Grayson she could fly again. "Go ahead; you can just fly outta here. Go on; I'll meet you at the top." Scarlett hesitated. "Go on; I know you can. Just do it. If you try to climb, you'll get hurt. Just get yourself out safely, and you can convince me you didn't fly later." He winked at her.

She sighed and shrugged in resignation. She supposed she couldn't stay down there all day. She closed her eyes and willed herself up and out of the ravine. With a few bounds and leaps, Grayson was out almost as quickly as Scarlett. "Wow, you did that fast. Do you do a lot of rock climbing?"

"Yeah. It's weird, I've never been able to climb that fast before. Hmm…" Grayson scratched his head and looked around at the trees. "I wonder…" He leaped in the air and reached for a branch. With one arm, he swung himself up into a tree; then he jumped from branch to branch.

"What are you doing? Get down from there!" she shouted up at him. In one leap, he landed on his feet in front of her, giving her a goofy grin, his dark hair falling in his eyes. "Wow, Grayson. I didn't know you were a gymnast."

"Um…me neither. I feel different…I feel…more alive! Scarlett, what did you do to me?"

Knowing she wasn't going to be able to convince him that she didn't heal him, she decided to tell the truth. "I don't know, your head was bleeding, and your arm was broken, so I healed you the way Mrs. Goodspeed taught me this morning."

"Well, you definitely healed me. I feel great."

"Look, maybe I did something wrong." Scarlett questioned herself and began to worry. *What if I did something really wrong?* "I think we need to have an expert look at you."

"You mean Mrs. Goodspeed, the witch doctor?" he teased.

"Uhh, yeah."

"I feel fine. Never been better," he reassured her.

"C'mon." She led him back to the river.

With hands on her hips, Honeybee met them at the riverbank clearing. "Scarlett Wrigley, what is the meaning of this?" she shouted, looking red in the face and flustered. "Taking an outsider into our world!" They were footsteps from Myles' cabin. The Romanaski clan were going about the business of their other worldly lifestyle in plain view of Grayson.

"Honeybee, I have to take him to Myles. Find Mrs. Goodspeed. I injured him."

"He looks fine to me." Honeybee sniffed.

"I had to heal him, but I think I overdid it. He's different now. I need a professional opinion."

"Mrs. Goodspeed is gone."

Grayson squinted. "Who are you taking to, Scarlett? What's that ball of light floating around your head?"

Honeybee gasped. "He sees me?" She sniffed the air around Grayson. "He smells like you but a little like something else. He has quite a bit of Juma. Hmm, come, let's find Myles."

***

"So, she knocked you down, my boy? Myles asked Grayson, his eyes full of mirth. "That's a good girl." He didn't seem at all concerned that Grayson could now climb ravines in seconds or leap from trees or partially see through the veil. "You know you could have been a bogey or a goblin wandering around; the girl had to protect herself. It's a good thing for you, we arranged for her to have a healing lesson today. Well, it appears our Scarlett has not only healed you but improved you. Her energy has awakened your Juma."

Grayson raised his eyebrows. "Juma?"

"Your energy or your life force," Scarlett interpreted for him.

"Uhh okay," he said, pretending to understand.

"You see when people are not in tune with their Juma, like most people aren't, they're weak," Myles said. "They can't see the real world, the one where they have more power than they know and where magic exists. Scarlett has awakened that in you. You'll find your natural abilities magnified. You may have been naturally athletic; you will find yourself more so now. You will also begin to notice things that others don't. You may even see energies of other beings that live alongside humans, like our friend Honeybee here." Myles motioned toward Honeybee, who was huffing and flitting around the cabin grumbling to herself about an outsider.

Grayson squinted. "I can't quite see what you're talking about. All I see is a ball of white light moving around." He blinked. "What am I looking at?"

"That's our friend, Honeybee. She's a fairy who lives with me. I guess your Juma isn't strong enough to see her true form," Scarlett explained.

Grayson, still looking confused and overwhelmed by Scarlett's fantastical explanation, shook his head. "Fairies. That's nuts."

"Yeah well, so is flying, healing your busted head, and a wise man living in the woods with a caravan of gypsies. Welcome to the club," Scarlett said wryly.

Grayson shrugged and laughed. "Point taken."

Myles placed a hand on his shoulder. "You'll get used to it, my boy. I have no doubt, as you spend time with our Scarlett, the veil will become thinner and thinner for you."

"So, you're not going to wipe his memory or mask his Juma and make him forget?" Scarlett asked.

Myles rubbed his chin, pulling on his beard. "I suppose I could, but I think the universe works in mysterious ways, and these events have occurred for good reason. Besides, it would be good for you to have a schoolmate who understands your world."

Myles locked eyes with Grayson. "Do you like your new abilities?"

Grayson met Myles' penetrating gaze. "Yes…yes, I do, sir."

"Do you want to keep them?"

Grayson nodded.

"Do you swear to keep quiet about what you can see and what you can do in the presence of others outside of this group?"

"Yes."

"Finally, your friend here is very important for reasons that I cannot go into right now. It is imperative that she remains safe. Do you promise you will do your best to protect her?"

The final request made Grayson's chest puff out, and he stood a little taller. "Yes I will, sir," he replied.

"Excellent." Myles clasped his hands together and beamed at him. "Welcome to the world of the awakened, my boy. You will gain many new friends who will become like family to you."

Scarlett stood back and watched the smile sweep over Grayson's face. From what Scarlett had learned of Grayson's home life, the idea of having family other than his absent-minded father must have been a foreign concept to him. But it seemed to fill him with hope that maybe someday he might have more people in his life that he could be close to.

ELEVEN
AMONG THE COSMOS

They had just set foot on the path back to her house when Scarlett looked at her watch. "Ugh, I'm late!" She pulled her phone out of her pocket and dialed Louzanne's number. "I'm so sorry! I uhh…lost track of time."

"Scarlett, where are you, girl? I've been waiting for twenty minutes."

"I'm coming now. She looked at Grayson. "Grayson is coming too." She grabbed his arm. "C'mon let's go." She jumped on her bike and pedaled as fast as she could towards town. There would be no time to go home and change her clothes. Her pants were a little muddy from the ravine, but she could probably dust off most of the mud when it dried.

Grayson didn't have a bike, but he jogged effortlessly alongside Scarlett as she pedaled down the bike path at breakneck speed.

"Where are we going?" he asked as he trotted alongside her. His voice didn't even tremble. He didn't miss a breath.

"We're meeting Louzanne at the new café and yoga studio."

"Ahhh," he groaned. "I've never tried it, but I'm pretty sure I'm not a yoga guy. I just know."

"Fine, go home then," she replied breathlessly.

"No, way. Today was just way too awesome. I don't want it to be over yet."

Scarlett laughed. "Okay, fine."

They made it to the town square in under seven minutes. Louzanne sat sipping a hot latte at one of the café tables in front of the window.

She smiled and waved them over when she saw her friends. "I didn't order for you. I don't know what you like." Scarlett wasn't allowed to have coffee until she was sixteen, but they had a great selection of hot chocolates and smoothies. She ordered a hot chocolate and a banana nut muffin and joined them at the table.

The three sisters came out from behind the counter. Scarlett could tell they were the three unusual sisters that Louzanne described right away because of their beauty and formal way of speaking. She also recognized them from the Halloween dance. She remembered seeing them help Myles and the Romanaskis clean up the mess and muddle everyone's memory. Although, after the mind wiping and muddling spells, she was sure Louzanne and Grayson didn't remember them.

"Good afternoon, sister. We are so glad you could visit," they greeted Louzanne. "Welcome, I am Elan," the beautiful woman with long red hair introduced herself.

"I am Mya." Mya had long dark hair and violet eyes. The third sister, with long blonde hair and ice blue eyes, introduced herself. "I am Satine."

"Err… nice to meet you. I'm Louzanne, and these are my friends Scarlett and Grayson." The three sisters curtsied by way of greeting.

Scarlett waved. "Hiya."

"Uhh…hello," Grayson stammered, and his cheeks flushed, seeming unnerved by their beauty.

"After refreshments, won't you join us for a class?" Elan asked. "We are offering free classes during our week-long grand opening. One starts in fifteen minutes."

Luckily, Scarlett opted to wear yoga pants to the river today rather than her jeans, so she was ready. Unfortunately for Grayson, he wore a tracksuit so he couldn't use the excuse of not having the right clothing. The class was an hour long. Scarlett couldn't help but burst out laughing when she saw the confused and horrified expression on Grayson's face when the instructor told him to assume the position "happy baby." Afterwards, Grayson said, "That was surprisingly hard. I always expected it to be a bunch of women just stretching and chilling out, but the poses were difficult."

When everyone else left the studio, the sisters served them tea from tiny porcelain cups. After they drank their tea, Satine stood up and said, "Take your mats and come with me." She led them to a small room in the back with a low ceiling lit only by four candles. "Lay your mats here, and we will do a guided meditation," she instructed. They were joined by the other two sisters, Mya and Elan.

Scarlett lay on her mat and followed Satine's instructions. She breathed deeply with her eyes closed and concentrated on letting all tension out of her head and chest as Satine told them to. As Scarlett breathed deep and focused on letting go, she could no longer see the darkness from the insides of her eyelids, rather, she saw stars. Beyond her eyelids, constellations of light and beautiful colors flew by. She had the distinct sensation that her body was floating as if traveling among the stars.

Moving more quickly, the lights passed her in a blur. Now, she was on the coast. The glow of the sun rose over the water and, shining from the rocks, a glowing orb shone bright as the sun. Another blur of light and then she was in the mountains with the snow falling all around her. Then the light became brighter and there was a flash and an explosion, like a supernova. Suddenly, blackness. Then more images. Dimmer…muddier. A man—no, not a man—a god or deity and his three sisters sitting around a table breaking bread. The man's eyes turned red and began to burn with fire. Then his face blackened and faded away, replaced by that of a monster with skin covered in scales and two horns jutted out from its head. Then a flurry of loud crashes and light. The monster's face faded away, but the red eyes remained.

With a vividness greater than reality, behind her eyelids, Scarlett traveled through the cosmos. All the while, the red eyes followed her. They seemed to fill the universe. The eyes locked onto her. She could feel herself being drawn towards them, as if they were a planet that had some sort of gravitational pull. As they drew her closer and closer, a biting cold crept over her body, causing her to shiver and her bones to ache. The cold felt so intense, it was like being burned. She screamed as it scorched her skin. Now Scarlett felt another force, softer…warmer, pulling her back until the burning cold lost its hold on her. Free of its grip and traveling at the speed of light, the stars blurred past her.

"Scarlett…Scarlett," Louzanne and Grayson yelled, shaking her roughly. She opened her eyes and gasped for air. Louzanne, Grayson, and the three sisters knelt over her looking shaken, as if she had almost died. Snuke fluttered above her with a furrowed brow.

"That was close," Elan whispered breathlessly. "We mustn't tell Myles. He'll have our heads." She leaned in to Scarlett and squeezed her hand. "Scarlett, this isn't for you. You may come to yoga, but we will not repeat this exercise again." Then she turned to Louzanne. "You will return tomorrow. Seven p.m."

TWELVE
AUNT DANIELLE

Despite their extensive studies on climate change, the Wrigleys were most recognized for their efforts on the magnet train. It took ten years of research and engineering to develop the prototype. With government funding and support from various environmental protection interest groups, the magnet train began its trial runs this year. The Washington to Riverstone line was one of three currently up and running. The other two lines were within Washington DC city limits. Intended to dramatically reduce the amount of vehicle traffic inside the city, it was scheduled to run as a trial for one year to iron out any bugs. As far as the Wrigleys knew, the primary reason they relocated to Riverstone was to launch the magnet train and to better oversee studies on impacts the reduction in fossil fuel use may have on local ecosystems.

Scarlett didn't get the chance to spend much time with her parents during the whole month of November. Mrs. and Mr. Wrigley needed to work many additional hours preparing their case to secure funding and support to build additional lines. The Wrigleys' goal was to dramatically reduce pollution due to vehicle traffic nationally over the next ten years. Their dream could be realized by expanding the magnet train lines to every town and city in America and by ensuring it was the fastest, safest, and most convenient mode of travel.

With the December twenty-first deadline for their submission fast approaching, the Wrigleys wouldn't be around much until Christmas. Mrs. Wrigley asked Aunt Danielle to come and stay until the holidays to look in on Scarlett. While Scarlett was independent and fully capable of looking after herself, the Wrigleys would be more comfortable knowing they had a friend or family member around for Scarlett if she needed anything. Aunt Danielle wasn't really Scarlett's aunt, but she was the closest thing she had to one. She was her mother's oldest friend and had been a part of her family for years.

Aunt Danielle arrived on the Wrigleys' doorstep with her big tabby cat, Freckles, and a luggage set with lime green daisies plastered all over it. Scarlett answered the doorbell.

"Scarlett! Got a kiss for auntie?"

"Hi, Aunt Danielle," Scarlett greeted her and leaned in for a kiss.

Aunt Danielle, a round stubby woman, wrapped her chubby arms around Scarlett and squeezed her so tight she picked her up from the floor. Aunt Danielle was a jolly soul who always smelled like cinnamon and maple syrup. She was always giggling. She had an effortless way of putting people at ease, and anyone around her immediately felt right at home.

"Good to see ya, kid. Jeez, you're gettin' so big!" Aunt Danielle gave her another squeeze before putting her back down on the ground. Then she held Scarlett at arm's length to examine her. "Hmm…too thin. We'll fix that. Now, help Auntie with her bags, hon," she said as she started to lug her overstuffed bags up the steps.

Scarlett took the larger of the two bags from her and just about dislocated her shoulder trying to haul it up the stairs.

"That's a good girl."

She lugged the suitcase up the last step and showed Aunt Danielle to her room. Now that Scarlett could see people's auras, she could see that Aunt Danielle's dominant color was bright green. When they got to the top of the stairs, Aunt Danielle put her hands on her hips, panting for air. She looked appreciatively up and down the hallway and into the guest bedroom. "Huh, this house is a lot bigger than the last one."

"Yeah, Mom and Dad negotiated the house as part of their relocation contract. You know, so I could be close to school."

"Yeah...nice place. Okay, hon, set it down over there and let me get my things in order here."

Aunt Danielle plunked her small bag on the bed, almost crushing the top of Nick's head.

"Oh excuse me, dear," she said to Nick, who had been taking a nap on the guest bed.

Nick scowled and opened one eye. Then his face widened into a huge grin, and he wiggled his giant pointy ears. "Danny! How are ya?"

"Good to see ya, Nick." She picked Nick up off the bed in a bear hug.

Scarlett stood with her eyes wide, and her mouth hung open watching the interaction unfold. "You see him?" she asked, pointing to Nick.

"Sure I do. No point in hiding it from ya since I heard you woke up. Now, where's that bogey?" Aunt Danielle looked around and crinkled her nose as if smelling rotten eggs.

"He's on a special assignment for Honeybee," Nick explained.

"Hmmff." Relief washed over Aunt Danielle's face. By her expression, it seemed Aunt Danielle couldn't care less where Sweetie Pie was so long as he wasn't around her.

"Now let me see..." Plumes of sparkly dust dispersed into the air as she plopped the other suitcase down on the bed. She opened it up, spread it out, and began rummaging through. She pulled out various items: a hammer and nails, a tool belt, a box labeled "sparkles", and other such things; some half assembled toy trains and dolls, a set of red and green pajamas, and a stocking cap. Scarlett didn't know people still slept with stocking caps but could only guess that maybe they did up North since it got pretty cold.

A notorious tinkerer, Aunt Danielle was always working on one thing or another, whether it be making toys or crafts or cooking and baking. She always seemed to have a dozen projects going at once. Her suitcase was evidence of her latest projects.

"Hmm now, where is it? Oh, there...there it is. Ahh yes, yes, yes indeed, there we go." She pulled a red apron with a gingerbread man stitched on the front out of her suitcase, hung it over her neck, and tied the strings around her waist.

"Thanksgiving is in two days. We have cooking and baking to do," she said with a grin. "Now, show me the kitchen."

Honeybee, Precious, and Snuke waited in the kitchen, hauling out various baking items from the pantry in anticipation for Aunt Danielle. Precious perched on the edge of the sugar dish with her head back, smacking her lips as she sprinkled tiny granules of sugar into her mouth. Honeybee and Snuke each took an end of a bag of flour, moving it from the pantry to the kitchen table. If someone who couldn't see past the veil were to walk into the kitchen, they would think the bag of flour flew on its own. Scarlett was always amazed at how strong the fairies were for being so little.

They greeted Aunt Danielle with lots of hugs and kisses. It was very difficult to hug a tiny fairy without crushing it, so Aunt Danielle left the hugging part to the fairies. After a cup of tea and some cookies, they caught up on things since the last time Aunt Danielle visited. When they told Aunt Danielle about the foiled kidnap attempt on Scarlett's birthday and the shadow man that came for her in the school basement during the Halloween dance, she furrowed her brow. Her face turned ashen.

She looked as if she'd heard Scarlett had been diagnosed with some serious disease or as if she were in current danger. Scarlett had never seen Aunt Danielle so upset.

"I'm okay; nothing happened. I'm safe for now." *Aren't I?*

Aunt Danielle quickly changed her demeanor back to her jolly self. She clapped her hands and motioned for everyone to get moving. "Come on now, let's get busy."

Within the hour, Aunt Danielle and the fairies had turned the Wrigleys' kitchen into a high-capacity workshop of savory foods and delectable treats. Scarlett enjoyed herself while baking, cooking, and catching up with her aunt. Smelling the sweet goodness of cinnamon buns baking in the oven made Scarlett realize how much she'd missed her. It had been a long time since her last visit. As she watched her working in the kitchen, it occurred to Scarlett that she'd never noticed how pointy Aunt Danielle's ears and teeth were until now.

Whenever she thought about pointy ears and teeth, she thought about that awful elf, Felix McCaan. Her eyes flashed to Aunt Danielle's fingernails. They were pointy like his too, except Aunt Danielle's were painted with red, white, and green candy cane stripes. Scarlett gasped and shook as realization set in.

"You're an elf!" Scarlett cried and began looking from Precious to Honeybee to Snuke for a reaction and for their protection as she backed away from the kitchen, knocking over one of the chairs.

Aunt Danielle's eyes lit up. "Yes, dear! But only one fourth." She gave Scarlett a wink. "Don't look so scared. Not all elves are bad, ya know. Some of the world's finest people are part elf. You just ran into a bad one."

"Does my mother know?" *Does mom know about the veil? Has she kept all of this from me?*

"Heavens no, I think she would die of shock if she knew her oldest friend was part elf! No, hon." Aunt Danielle went on to explain her lineage. "I get it from my father's side. My grandfather took a Northern Diamond Elf for his bride while he was working in the Northwest Territories as a diamond miner. She was quite tall for a Diamond Elf— not that all elves are short, mind you, but Diamond Elves tend to be. So, it wasn't all that hard to pass her off as a human. My father was a short fella, like her, but he never had all the elven-like characteristics that I seemed to have inherited.

Scarlett raised her eyebrows; she didn't know all that much about elves other than what Honeybee had told her and what she'd read in children's books. "Like what?" she asked.

"Like being able to bake eleven-thousand cookies in a regular kitchen like this one in less than an hour, or be able to fix things no matter how badly they're broken. Yes, there's quite a bit of magic in me, that's for sure. I'm grateful, really. I can't imagine how dreadful it must be to have to do everything by hand. Roll out the dough and cut out the cookies. *Ugh*. All those sharp kitchen tools. Honestly, I don't know how more people don't lose fingers or an eye just from making supper or baking some treats."

Just then, Mrs. Wrigley rushed into the kitchen, tossing her purse and her keys haphazardly onto the kitchen table. She had just gotten back from a meeting in the city. The keys skidded to a halt but not before knocking Snuke off the table. Mrs. Wrigley hugged her friend.

"You made it early! Thanks so much for doing this. I know it's a lot right before Christmas. I know how busy you are."

Mrs. Wrigley was looking rather pale lately. It seemed all the work she'd been doing in preparation for this proposal was starting to wear on her. Mrs. Wrigley sniffed the air; the smell of cinnamon rolls had filled the house. "What's that?"

"Cinnamon rolls. They're almost ready!" Aunt Danielle said. Mrs. Wrigley took another sniff, and her face turned green. She excused herself from the kitchen. She came back a few minutes later looking shaken. "I must be coming down with a bug," she said weakly. Scarlett thought this might be a perfect opportunity to practice healing.

THIRTEEN
A DEMON FOR DINNER

Scarlett practiced violin until her fingers bled. She got together with her friends several times through the month of November to practice their music as well. Their sound was really coming together. While she enjoyed her lessons with Myles and her time spent with the gypsies, this was a creative and fun thing for her to do with kids her own age.

Grayson would sometimes join her down at the river and watch her practice her skills with Myles or just sit there and take photos of nature or draw and paint. Rolph had taken Grayson under his wing and was teaching him how to sword fight and how to use his Juma to do backflips and other tricks. Yadira worked with him on the more subtle art of tapping into one's own natural abilities, and for Grayson, it was all about visual arts. Since he'd been awakened to his Juma, his sketches and paintings had become more vibrant and textured. He was already a gifted photographer, but now his photos seemed that much more alive. Now, it seemed he could capture the emotion a squirrel felt as she cracked open a nut, or the love shared by two birds as they built their nest.

His photos had gotten quite a bit of attention from his teachers, who asked if they could display them in the main hallway at school. To Scarlett's shock and dismay, some of the photos were of Snuke, Honeybee, and Precious, hovering over the grass down by the riverbank as they gathered the last of the year's wildflowers. Scarlett could see the fairies plain as day, but to the Juma deficient masses, they would only see a picture with orbs of white light that floated over wildflowers set against a picturesque river valley. When Myles got wind of the display, he paid Grayson a personal visit at his dorm room and ordered him to take the pictures down immediately.

Michelle and Luke were going home for the Thanksgiving holiday to be with their families, and Louzanne would be at her aunt's house. Grayson didn't have any plans. His father worked a lot and, from the stories Scarlett had heard from Grayson, he probably didn't even bother to remind him that Thanksgiving was coming up, opting to let the holiday pass without occasion.

Knowing he would be around over the holiday, Scarlett invited Grayson for dinner, and he accepted graciously. Then she got an idea. *I'll invite Vivian. Her parents won't send for her, and she'll probably end up spending Thanksgiving in her dorm alone.* Scarlett cornered Vivian in the bathroom while she was away from the rest of her snobby friends.

"Why do you want me to come for dinner?" Vivian asked, hugging her books close to her chest.

"I don't know; I just thought you might like some company."

"But I poisoned you last month." Vivian snorted. "Why would you care?"

"Why did you poison me?"

Vivian looked away with tears in her eyes. She shrugged. "I don't know, you give me weird looks, and it makes me uncomfortable." Vivian shook her head. "I know that's not an excuse, but it's the only reason I have. I don't actually remember even doing it. I'm sorry...I really am."

Her explanation sounded sincere. "Look, you apologized, and Mr. Lechey made you do detention and community service, and you even donated most of your hair to charity— your new hair cut looks great by the way—so I'm over it if you are."

Vivian, sporting a short bob, patted her hair as if longing for the long blonde locks that were no longer there. As part of her punishment, Mr. Lechey made her cut her hair and donate it to charity to make wigs for cancer patients. She also had to do hair, nails, and makeup for the ladies at the local nursing home twice a week. Vivian had no choice but to accept the punishment. Otherwise, she would face even worse consequences if she had to go home to her mother and stepfather and tell them she was expelled from school and had nowhere to go. That would really inconvenience them and throw a wrench in their plans for a French Riviera cruise over the Thanksgiving holiday.

"Look, you don't have to come but here's my address if you want to." Scarlett handed her a piece of paper with her address written on it. "It'll be a good dinner; my Aunt is a great cook. I'll try not to give you weird looks, and Grayson Blackwell is going to be there too."

Vivian perked up at the sound of Grayson's name. The bell rang for third period. Vivian didn't say anything but snatched the piece of paper from Scarlett's hand and rushed out of the bathroom to get to her next class with her nose high in the air.

***

Thanksgiving dinner was delicious, thanks to Aunt Danielle. Along with a succulent turkey, an assortment of stuffing, variations of potatoes, marshmallow casserole, and mouthwatering vegetables of every shape and color lined the dining room table. While Scarlett didn't plan on eating any turkey, she sure was looking forward to all the sides. She wished her mother could cook like Aunt Danielle, but on second thought, if she could, Scarlett might weigh two hundred pounds by now. Scarlett and Mrs. Wrigley helped in the preparation, but most of the heavy lifting was due to the efforts of Aunt Danielle, Nick, Snuke, and Honeybee. Precious seemed to have no interest in kitchen duties unless her job was taste testing.

"Danielle, since you did all the work in preparing this amazing meal for us, could you please do us the honor of saying grace?" Mr. Wrigley asked when everyone assembled around the dining room table.

"Ah hem," Aunt Danielle cleared her throat. "We are ever so very grateful for the many friends, family, and new acquaintances," she said as she eyed Vivian, who, to Scarlett's surprise, had showed up at her door with a veggie tray in hand.

"We are grateful for the beautiful meal we are about to enjoy. I personally am also grateful for cinnamon and maple syrup. Cinnamon and maple syrup are by far the best food additives ever. They're nutritious and delicious. Cinnamon can ease swelling and irritation, and maple syrup just makes you feel good inside. Some doctors even call them super foods. Anyway, I'm grateful for cinnamon and maple syrup and for the beautiful gift of close friends to share the years with and for new additions to the friend and family circle."

"Hear, hear," Mr. Wrigley said, raising his glass and they all followed suit. Aunt Danielle tipped hers back and drank the entire glass of ice wine in one gulp. Then with a flush in her cheeks, she got the conversation going by telling some embarrassing but hilarious stories about when the Wrigleys were young, which led to everyone else sharing their funny stories, laughing, and having a good time. Even Vivian couldn't help but giggle at the last story about Mr. Wrigley locking himself outside in subzero temperatures in his birthday suit because he was sleepwalking.

"Good thing we got that sleepwalking thing under control," Mrs. Wrigley said as she squeezed her husband's hand. She looked pale and tired. She had been burning the candle at both ends with this proposal, and the dark circles under her eyes showed.

Scarlett was more than a little frustrated that when she tried to practice what Mrs. Goodspeed taught her on her mother, it didn't work. Over the past two days, she attempted to inconspicuously spread healing energy and draw out whatever infection or illness was keeping her mother down. Finally, she even flat out lied to Mrs. Wrigley, telling her that she and Louzanne had taken a reiki lesson at the yoga studio and wanted to practice on her just so she could spend time with her hands hovered over her mother without her wondering what in the world she was trying to do. And that still didn't work. Discouraged, Scarlett tried to talk to Mrs. Goodspeed about it but she had left town on urgent business and wouldn't be back until after Thanksgiving. In the meantime, her mother's health didn't seem to be declining. Rather, she maintained a steady malaise.

Grayson seemed to be enjoying himself too. He squinted as he struggled to make out the faintest outlines of Nick, Snuke, Precious, and Honeybee. His blinking and staring made it look like he was spacing out. When he began to point at them, Scarlett kicked him under the table. "Quit it," she whispered.

When it came time to share his story, Grayson told them about when he was younger, his father forgot it was Christmas Eve again for the fifth year in a row.

"When he realized what day it was, I guess he felt guilty about me not having any presents for the morning so he went out in a snowstorm to try to find a drug store or something open where he could get me some presents. It was just before midnight when he set out in the storm and was robbed at gunpoint."

Everyone around the table shifted in their seats and exchanged uncomfortable glances. This didn't seem like a funny story at all.

But then Grayson cracked up and slapped his hand on the table. "Not only did he have to return home with no presents, they also stole his shoes, his wallet, and his watch!" Grayson laughed even harder. "He didn't know Joany, Dad's assistant, already brought my 'Santa Claus' presents up to the penthouse earlier that night. They were spread out under the Christmas tree—which Joany also put up—waiting there for me to find on Christmas morning. Dad wouldn't know this—he doesn't go into the family room, at least not since Mom died. The best part is that he thinks the watch that was stolen was the watch my mother gave him." He laughed even harder. "But it wasn't. I nicked that years ago for safekeeping and had it replaced with an identical one."

Vivian hung on his every word and laughed loudly whenever he did. Everyone else just looked uncomfortable, not knowing whether to laugh or hug Grayson and give him condolences for having what seemed to be a cold childhood.

Aunt Danielle told another story about the first time she ever used a self-cleaning oven and how it was filled with turkey grease from a Thanksgiving turkey that was too big for its roasting pan, so the fat drippings spilled over everywhere. "I didn't think to wipe up most of the grease before setting it to self-clean mode. The oven got hotter than a billy goat with a blow torch, and the grease caught fire. The whole house filled with smoke and Joe and I had to evacuate the house until the fire department came."

By the time dinner was finished, everyone was laughing and at ease again. Vivian even opened up about the time her mother hosted a fashion party and fundraiser in honor of this woman who dedicated her life to helping blind children, but her mother couldn't get the woman's name right.

"She even misspelled it on the banners and invitation cards. The poor woman had to correct my mother after she mispronounced her name during her reception speech, like a dozen times. The ladies in her social circle gossiped about her for weeks!" Vivian gave a little snort as she laughed.

After seeing what little Scarlett did of Mrs. Patterson, she didn't blame Vivian one bit for taking some comfort in her mother's humiliation. Every time Vivian laughed or smiled, the creature that clung to her seemed to fade. As it dissipated, it would dig its claws into her as if to get a tighter hold, pinching her throat and squeezing her chest. While it didn't appear that Vivian noticed, it did affect her. As it dug in, Vivian's demeanor would return to her usual scowl. Freckles, Aunt Danielle's tabby cat wouldn't even go near Vivian, and he hissed at her when she first came into the house. Scarlett wondered if Freckles could see the creature too.

After dinner, Grayson, Scarlett, and Mr. Wrigley cleared away the dinner plates and began bringing out the desserts. The assortment was endless. She was quite the cook, but in the bakery department, Aunt Danielle reigned supreme. This time, she had outdone herself—even by her standards. There were cakes, pies, crumpets, toffee, cookies, cupcakes, and fudge.

Nick, Snuke, and Precious couldn't contain themselves and dove right in, picking away at little pieces of the goodies while Honeybee hovered over them piously, giving them disapproving looks until she too caved in and furtively made off with a crumpet. If one were aware of them, they would see winged fairies whizzing about the dinner table, nicking little bites from each of the plates and a leprechaun leaping up and down from the table as he snatched a treat.

Nick, being much larger than the fairies, tended to be a little more conspicuous. He was careful not to brush up against the dinner guests as he climbed onto the table to take a whole cookie or cupcake from the tray while no one was looking. With his hands full of goodies, he would scurry under the table and sit until he devoured his loot. Then he would come back for more. While reaching for a cookie, Nick accidentally brushed up against Vivian. She rubbed her arm and looked around to see if it could have been one of the dogs, but, Elvis and Betty stood eagerly by Mrs. Wrigley, who had been determined to be the weakest link and most likely to hand them some treats. Scarlett held her breath and waited for Vivian's reaction. Scarlett shot Nick a warning look, to which Nick shrugged and put his palms out apologetically.

"Sorry, 'scuse me for living. Jeez!" Nick grunted.

Vivian seemed to dismiss it and continued trying to make goo-goo eyes with Grayson while his eyes darted around the room to get a better look at the orbs of light.

Mrs. Wrigley asked, "What are you looking at, hon?"

It reminded Scarlett of how she must have looked her first night she could see fairies. She kicked him under the table to snap him out of it.

"Err...nothing. I was thinking about a homework assignment." Grayson rubbed the back of his neck and flashed Mrs. Wrigley a sheepish grin.

When it was time for refreshments, Mr. Wrigley poured himself and Aunt Danielle a glass of brandy. Precious dove head first into Aunt Danielle's glass, managing to slurp up a few swigs before Honeybee could give her a smack. Mrs. Wrigley opted for a cup of tea with milk and sugar, while Scarlett and Grayson couldn't resist the candy cane hot chocolate with a helping of whipped cream.

Vivian watched them with her nose turned up. *Tsk.* "The amount of sugar you just ate is disgusting. I'll have hot water and lemon please."

Scarlett got up to fix Vivian her drink, wondering if Vivian secretly wished she could indulge in dessert. *Probably scared if she gained weight she'd be disowned by her mother. She sure makes it hard to be nice to her.* As Scarlett waited for the water to boil, she eyed the matching pink piggy salt and pepper shakers on the shelf over the kettle, tempting her to pour salt in Vivian's cup. *It would serve her right for being so snickety.* With a giggle, she reached for the piggy salt shaker, its bulbous eyes egging her on. Just then, the kettle whistled. She sighed, flicked a slice of lemon into the cup, poured hot water over it, and took it out to the dining room.

At the end of the evening, Grayson walked Vivian home to her dorm. Scarlett and Mr. Wrigley cleaned up from dinner and did the dishes, while Aunt Danielle put her feet up by the fireplace in the living room—a well-earned rest from a long couple days of cooking and baking. Mrs. Wrigley excused herself and went off to bed looking pale and tired.

After cleaning up, Scarlett joined Aunt Danielle in the living room. "It's nice to see you've made so many friends so quickly, hon," Aunt Danielle called out from her armchair. Scarlett approached the fireplace and sat in the chair next to Aunt Danielle. Scarlett thought about how she'd never had so many friends that she actually felt close to in all her life back in Indiana. And yet, she had only been here a little over a month, and she could already count on more than both hands and feet the number of really great people who had come into her life.

"Although, I don't get the connection with the thin blondie. She doesn't seem the type you would pal around with."

"She wasn't very nice to me, but I think she has a rough home life and…I don't know; something tells me that I should be nice to her. I don't think she's all that bad. She has some sort of a monster attached to her. I don't know what it is, but I'm pretty sure that's what makes her act out. Do you know what it is?" she asked.

"Yes, poor dear. You see it then?" Scarlett nodded. "Well," Aunt Danielle sighed, "that's a demon. Thrives on misery. See how it faded a little when she started to have a good time? But then it fought to keep its hold. It wants her to be nasty so she'll feel alienated. It wants to bring her down. That's how it gets its claws in even deeper. Poor thing. Those are demons of the worst kind. Even if you're lucky enough to get rid of it completely, the moment you feel any weakness, it'll try and attach itself to you all over again. Sometimes they lie in wait for years after being cast out, waiting for their chance to get back in. Doctors call it depression but you and I see it for what it really is."

"How do you get rid of a demon?" Scarlett asked.

Aunt Danielle sighed and patted Scarlett's hand. "Love, dear. Lots of love."

Scarlett didn't think she really understood what Aunt Danielle meant in any practical sense but at least the explanation gave her confirmation that her decision to try to be nice to Vivian was the right one.

FOURTEEN
TROUBLE AFOOT

The night before the twenty-first of December Mr. Wrigley busied himself making final revisions to their proposal while Mrs. Wrigley rehearsed her speech. Mr. Wrigley was more of a technical guy and left the presentations and excitement to his wife, who was more outgoing and had a knack for generating enthusiasm in everyone around her. So while this proposal was the result of both of their efforts, people looked to Mrs. Wrigley as the spokesperson for the project.

By seven p.m., the Wrigleys resigned themselves to being as ready as they were going to be and settled into the dining room for their last meal together before Aunt Danielle's early morning flight. Her bags were already packed and waiting at the door.

"It was so wonderful of you to come and stay with us, Danielle. I can't thank you enough," Mrs. Wrigley said as she passed along the plate of roasted vegetables.

"Don't even mention it. I had a great time catching up with little miss Scarlett here. Jeez, I haven't seen her in years, so it was high time for a visit. It's important work you're doing. I'm glad I could help in any way I could."

Scarlett savored the flavor of her roasted veggie dinner before it was back to mung bean soup when Aunt Danielle left.

From the dining room, Scarlett heard the back door open and the sound of footsteps coming down the hall. Elvis and Betty, who sat at Mrs. Wrigley's feet waiting for a few scraps from the table, barked and stood on high alert. The footsteps became louder and louder. The intruder approached the dining room. A man dressed in dark clothing appeared in the entryway with a gun in his hand. He wore a dark balaclava over his face.

Scarlett gasped and jumped up from her chair. Freckles, Aunt Danielle's tabby hissed and arched his back. Betty and Elvis bared their teeth and snarled. The Wrigleys exchanged glances and stared at the stranger through widened eyes.

Before anyone could stop him, he pointed the gun at Mrs. Wrigley and pulled the trigger.

The next few moments happened in a blur. Mr. Wrigley pulled his wife out of her chair and onto the floor, and Scarlett stood frozen in shock and fear as if super glued to the floor.

The masked man aimed his gun and fired again.

Scarlett heard a scream.

"NOOOOOOOO!" Nick knocked the gunman to the ground, disarming him as he pummeled his face with his tiny fists. Betty and Elvis aided Nick by viscously biting the man's legs. The second shot barely missed the Wrigleys. Unable to will her body to move, Scarlett watched these events in horror as if unfolding in slow motion.

Aunt Danielle took charge and began giving directions. "Snuke, get Agnes immediately." Snuke was off with a nod, leaving a cloud of green sparkles behind.

"Precious, get Myles and the Romanaskis here now." Precious, already in motion, disappeared with a *poof.*

"Honeybee, secure the perimeter. There may be others waiting outside."

Mr. Wrigley sobbed, "Somebody call an ambulance."

The intruder lay on the floor grunting as Nick delivered heavy blows to his face. He squinted to get a look at his attacker, but each time he tried to get a look, Nick would punch him in the nose causing his eyes to well up with tears and blood to spurt out of his nose.

"WHAT IS GOING ON?" cried Mr. Wrigley as he took his eyes off his wife for a moment to watch the intruder, now laid out on the floor, frequently snap his head back and blood spew from his face as if he were under attack by an invisible force.

Mrs. Wrigley lay on the dining room floor in a pool of blood. Still frozen, Scarlett's eyes filled with tears until she felt Aunt Danielle's stubby fingers bite into her shoulders as she grabbed Scarlett and shook her roughly until her eyes rolled to the back of her head.

"You need to get to work until Agnes comes," barked Aunt Danielle.

Sobbing and gasping for breath, Scarlett ran to her mother's side. It felt like she herself had been shot. Her lungs burned as she struggled to breathe and the room spun around her. "Mama," she managed to say, the room growing dark around her.

She heard a crash from the living room window and the sounds of muffled curses. Rolph, Bo, Pesha, and Fonso Romanaski came bounding into the dining room and sprang on the intruder. In a blurred flash, they had him bound and began interrogating him.

"What the...who are they?" cried Mr. Wrigley.

"GET TO WORK," Aunt Danielle shouted at Scarlett.

Foggy headed and still sobbing, Scarlett held her mother's hand, watching the blood ooze out of her and onto the dining room floor. *She's losing so much blood. Oh my god. Please don't let her die!* It was all Scarlett could think of until it occurred to her that she had the ability to heal. This realization brought new hope, and the room came back into focus. She took several deep breaths to still herself. She closed her eyes then rubbed her hands together to prepare the healing energies of her Juma until warm glowing balls of light formed on her palms.

Pfff...pfff. She breathed deeply, her mind racing in a mad panic. "Easy, don't lose it. Keep it together," she whispered to herself. When she was satisfied that her light orbs would hold, she held her palms over her mother's chest for what seemed like hours until tiny shards from a metal bullet began to emerge from her mother's chest.

If she was focused on healing Grayson last month at the ravine, she was even more focused on healing her mother. Every fiber of her being vibrated with thoughts and intentions to help her mom.

Mr. Wrigley, white as a sheet, shook and sobbed while trying to comfort his wife. "It's okay; you're going to be okay. Everybody's going to be okay. Has somebody called an ambulance?" He looked at Scarlett with her hands hovering over her mother in a strange ritual. "What are you doing?"

"Let her be, Henri. She's the best hope right now," ordered Aunt Danielle.

Too shaken to protest, he remained where he was holding his wife's hand as she drifted in and out of consciousness. Scarlett knew she had to make sure she drew out all of the pieces of the bullet before sending any energy in to heal and before closing the wound. She held her hand over the entry wound for several minutes until three more tiny metal slivers emerged. When she was pretty sure she got it all, she focused her energy on sending the healing Juma inward to where the bullet and its shrapnel pieces had ripped through her mother.

The blood flowed less freely, and after several minutes, it stopped completely. Scarlett was reluctant to close the wound, scared she hadn't gotten it all. So she focused her energy back on trying to draw out any remaining pieces and on replenishing the blood Mrs. Wrigley had lost.

Mrs. Goodspeed finally arrived and knelt down beside Mrs. Wrigley.

"Who are you?' Mr. Wrigley cried, looking addled.

Aunt Danielle walked past Mr. Wrigley as he knelt beside his wife. Out of the corner of her eye, Scarlett could have sworn she saw Aunt Danielle sprinkle some sort of powder over her father's dark curly head. Mr. Wrigley fell silent again, directing his gaze back to his wife.

"Let me see, Scarlett," Mrs. Goodspeed said, ignoring Mr. Wrigley as she examined Scarlett's work. "Very good job," she said admiringly. "You didn't leave a trace. One more pass and close it up. Easy…steady…that's a good girl."

Mrs. Wrigley didn't recover consciousness, but Mrs. Goodspeed assured them she would awake in the morning. "Now help me get her up to bed."

In a daze, Mr. Wrigley picked up his wife and carried her upstairs to their bedroom. Aunt Danielle, Mrs. Goodspeed, and Scarlett followed to help get her settled. Mr. Wrigley laid her down on their bed with tears still in his eyes.

Mrs. Goodspeed gave Mrs. Wrigley one last inspection. "Scarlett got it all out and closed up things very nicely. There will not likely be any infection. She lost a lot of blood, but the baby is okay."

Relief washed over Mr. Wrigley's and Aunt Danielle's faces. Scarlett's expression, however, was one of confusion. *Baby?* Of course. It all made sense to her now. Her mother had been working so hard, but she was normally so high energy. No matter what Scarlett did, she couldn't heal her mother from feeling tired and sick. *I couldn't heal her because she wasn't sick!*

Aunt Danielle sent Mr. Wrigley downstairs and followed behind him. Scarlett remained with her mother holding her hand. She could hear voices below. After several minutes, Aunt Danielle returned to give Scarlett a report. "Myles is downstairs. The Romanaskis are camping outside the house tonight. Rolph's brothers are going to give up their caravan for a few months and move into the house next door until Sweetie Pie comes home.

Scarlett shook her head. "But the Jaimesons live next door."

"I'm sure they'll come into some money by New Year and decide to retire down in Florida where it's nice and warm." Aunt Danielle gave her a wink. "I'm still going to catch my flight in the morning. By morning, your mom will be good as new—probably better since you seem to have this little trick of igniting one's own Juma. When Myles is through, your parents won't remember what happened here tonight. It's probably for the best."

"What about the shooter?"

Aunt Danielle told Scarlett that the Romanaskis managed to pry Nick off the gunman and got him to talk. "Turns out he wasn't a darkling. This wasn't even darkling driven—mind you all acts of violence are ultimately driven by darkness, but this one wasn't aware of any dark forces. This was strictly for money. He was paid to make sure your mother didn't present the proposal tomorrow."

Scarlett sucked in a breath. "Well, the joke's on him." Aunt Danielle snorted. "We didn't phone the police. Rather than human jail, when the Romanaskis are through with him, he'll go before The Judge and live out whatever sentence is doled out to him. He may have him reincarnated as a lab rat or a slug. Who knows, The Judge is known to have an unusual sense of humor. Anyway kid, I'm off to bed." Aunt Danielle kissed her forehead and hugged her tightly.

She paused in the doorway. "Don't worry, your mother will be fine in the morning, you'll see. I won't see you before I leave but tell your mom and dad not to work too hard and come and see Joe and me soon, okay?" Scarlett nodded and gave Aunt Danielle one last hug goodbye.

Later on, Myles came up to the bedroom quietly and placed one hand over Mrs. Wrigley's temple, only for a brief second, then pulled it away. He smiled at Scarlett and squeezed her shoulder.

"You did really well today. Agnes might not have made it in time for your mother and the baby to make a full recovery. Thanks to you, all is well. You should be proud of yourself, my dear. You have come a very long way in such a short period of time. Your skills are developing fast. A little too fast...hmm." He paused for a moment, staring into nothing. He rubbed his chin and pulled at his beard with a furrowed brow. Then he sighed, and his expression relaxed. "Well, that is a subject for another day."

Myles turned and walked toward the door. "Your mother won't remember what took place here tonight and that is a good thing. Your parents are on the verge of doing something very good for the world, and we can't have them getting cold feet over concerns of safety. Good night, my dear." Myles walked back downstairs and into the living room. Scarlett could faintly hear Precious and Honeybee whispering below.

Scarlett remained by her mother's side watching her sleep. Her mother's long red hair framed her face, and she was no longer pale. The corners of her mouth were turned up in a smile, and she wore an expression as if she were having the most pleasant dream. When her father came upstairs, he raised his eyebrows to see Scarlett perched on the edge of their bed.

"What are you still doing up? Why are you watching your mom sleep?"

Myles obviously managed to wipe his memory.

"I…uhhh…couldn't sleep. I'm so nervous for you both for tomorrow. I hope everything goes okay." *There I go, back to lying again.* "Dad?" she asked.

"Yeah?"

Scarlett wanted to bring up the subject of the baby but decided not to at the last minute. There was so much she wanted to tell him—both of them—but she knew she couldn't. They would tell her about the baby when they felt the time was right. Instead, she said, "I love you." She stood up and kissed her father goodnight then stooped down to kiss her sleeping mother on the cheek and went off to bed with a heavy heart.

Lying in bed, Scarlett stared at the ceiling. She had a lot to contemplate. It was no longer just her "other-worldly" troubles afoot. Despite the perils she had found herself in lately, she somehow felt more comfortable with them than she had previously realized. Prior to this evening, she truly believed she was the only one in danger. Lying in the dark, she realized that as strange as the "other-worldly" stuff was, it was all okay with her. She accepted it like a new normal. The wicked elf, the vodyanoi, the man in black, they were dangerous, but—as crazy is it sounded—when it was just her at risk, she felt she had a great deal of control over the situation.

But tonight was different. Never in a million years would it have occurred to her that her parents might be in danger—and for something that didn't even have anything to do with her crazy life. Scarlett shuddered. *What if I wasn't home? What if I was still practicing at the river or with my band? Or what if it happened while my mother was at work or on the train?* This problem was bigger than her. It was mysterious. It was something she couldn't control. And that thought scared her more than anything.

FIFTEEN
THE WARLOCK FRANK

The next morning, Scarlett woke bright and early to the smell of bacon, eggs, and fresh brewed coffee. When she came downstairs, she saw that Aunt Danielle's bags were gone. Mr. Wrigley must have taken her to the airport before the crack of dawn.

"Good morning, baby girl." Mrs. Wrigley kissed Scarlett's forehead. She had color in her cheeks again for the first time in over a month, and she looked happy and energetic. Scarlett didn't say anything. She just wrapped her arms around her mom and hugged her tight.

"Well, that's an enthusiastic good morning!" Mrs. Wrigley smiled down at her daughter.

"Good luck today, Mom."

"Thanks, hon." Mrs. Wrigley checked her watch. "Gotta run." She took one last sip of her coffee, threw her coat on, and rushed out the door to meet up with Mr. Wrigley, who was already in the car waiting for her. They were going to park their car at the train depot and get the magnet train into the city for their big proposal.

Scarlett stood in the doorway and waved goodbye as they drove away. Nick rode along with them in the back seat, looking alert and determined to never leave Mrs. Wrigley's side. For that, Scarlett was grateful. She stood in the doorway for a minute taking in the beautiful morning outside. The air felt crisp, but the sun was warm. Scarlett didn't know what she was going to do with herself this morning. Classes were over for the semester, and she had the whole house to herself. After last night, she didn't feel like going down to the river for lessons. She needed to take a break and get her mind off things, maybe do something festive.

She walked back inside and looked around the barren hall and living room. Christmas was only a few days away. Normally, Mrs. Wrigley would have had the house all decked out by now. Aunt Danielle hung a few decorations, but she probably didn't know where Mrs. Wrigley kept the rest of the Christmas stuff. Aunt Danielle probably didn't want to bug her mom about where she kept them since she was so busy and tired. And if she did, her mother would probably feel bad having her friend do her decorating for her and would have ended up doing it herself when she really should have been resting.

Scarlett set about getting everything in order. By late morning, she had all the Christmas decorations hauled out onto the living room floor and organized into themes. Candy cane village will go over there. Santa land over here—which would also serve to cover a bullet hole in the wall until Scarlett could figure out how to plaster and paint over it— and of course, the nativity scene was reserved for the fireplace mantle.

She pulled out the homemade stockings with each family member's name sewn into them and began hanging them over the fireplace. She wondered if Grandma would knit another stocking—one for the new baby—and made a mental note to learn how to knit if Grandma wasn't up for it anymore. By noon, she had the place looking pretty festive if she didn't say so herself. The only thing missing was a tree. She left out the boxes of ornaments in the corner by the fireplace just in case she got a chance to put one up.

After she put the last empty box back down in the basement, Scarlett looked out the window and saw a moving van pull into the driveway next door. The Jaimesons, Judy and Frank, a nice couple in their mid-fifties, loaded boxes into the van. Scarlett pulled on her coat and boots and went outside to say hello.

"Hello, Scarlett," Mrs. Jaimeson greeted her.

"Hi, Mrs. Jaimeson. Are you moving?"

"Yes. We're moving to Florida. Just in time for Christmas! Frank's great aunt left us a rather unexpected large sum of money. We've been eyeing a condo in Florida for months, but we just weren't sure if we should retire yet. But with hearing the wonderful news this morning, we couldn't hesitate any longer. We made an offer on the place this morning, and it was a done deal before breakfast."

"No time like the present," Mr. Jaimeson said with a grin as he loaded the last cardboard box into the van. "Besides, Judy and I always wanted to have a beach Christmas, and we still have four days to get down there, so Carpe Diem! There's plenty of time to get down there and have few things set up in the condo before Christmas Day. Then we can stretch out and relax! Ahh, it's going to be nice watching the sunset over the beach."

"Sounds wonderful," Scarlett agreed and wished them luck.

"We're going to rent out the house for a few months until we have our affairs in order down in Florida and can find a buyer. Our realtor mentioned she might already have renters lined up. Please keep in touch and don't hesitate to let us know if the tenants become a nuisance. You and your family are such nice people; I would hate for anyone to bother you."

Scarlett took Mrs. Jaimeson's email address and assured her she would contact her if there were any issues.

"Merry Christmas!" Mrs. Jaimeson said as she hopped into the car and waved goodbye as she pulled out of the driveway. Mr. Jaimeson honked and waved as he pulled out in the moving van.

Wow, those fairies worked fast!

After lunch, Scarlett decided to take a walk downtown and do some Christmas shopping. She didn't expect her parents back until late that evening. After knowing the Romanaskis for over two months, she was convinced that there was something to crystals and gemstones. She was more than a little spooked from the previous night's experience, and she wanted to check out the crystal shop to see if there was anything she could get for her parents that might help keep them safe.

***

The door chimes jingled as she entered the crystal shop. "Good afternoon, Miss." A hunchbacked man limped out from behind the glass counter, dragging his left foot. He was short to begin with, but because he walked bent over, he could easily be mistaken for a little person. He had long wiry black hair that stuck up everywhere with streaks of gray speckled throughout. He was balding in the center of his head. One of his eyes was blue and the other brown. The blue eye was twice the size of the brown one. He reminded Scarlett of a Norwegian troll doll.

"Is there anything I can help you find?"

"Yes, do you have something that will protect a person?"

"Why don't you get a gun or a knife?" The hunchback slapped his leg and chuckled. "Just kidding. I have just the thing. Follow me." He led her to an aisle and pointed to an assortment of black and gold gemstones.

Scarlett glanced over the stones. "Hmm. I need one for a man and one for a woman, something they will keep with them throughout the day."

"How about a piece of jewelry? This is a lovely man's ring." He pulled a ring box from behind a glass case and opened it. It was silver with a black stone that gave off glints of green light at certain angles.

Scarlett examined it. The ring wasn't so busy or gaudy that her father would never wear it. He might even like it. "Hmm, yes okay."

"Over here is a beautiful lady's bangle." The man gestured to a glass case. The bangle rested on a purple satin pillow. The two sides met in front of the bracelet, then wove together in front to form a silver spiral with one large purple stone in the middle. The stone looked like an amethyst. She knew right away her mother would love it.

"These are perfect. I'll take them."

"Excellent." The hunchback flashed a smile, revealing a mouth full of crooked teeth. "Would you like them gift wrapped?"

"Yes please," she replied, grateful she wouldn't have to wrap them herself. She always made such a mess when she wrapped gifts. She could never get the paper lined up straight or the folded edges to look even. And being a lefty, it was hard for her to cut the paper straight with regular scissors.

"Now, I have one more thing to show you if you will just follow me, my pretty. Right this way." He led her down a narrow hallway, through a beaded curtain, and down a flight of steps into a dark, musty room which had many stones placed on shelves much like the room in Yeeta and Yaw-Yaw's caravan. Not all the stones were large; some were tiny, some were round and fat, and some were long and thin. But all gave off glowing embers that seemed to shine brighter and vibrate as her eyes scanned over them.

The hunchback peered over her shoulder. "See anything you like in here, my pretty? Anything at all, hmm?"

Scarlett did see something that caught her eye right away. A tiny pointed obelisk-like stone that looked much like the Washington Monument, only much smaller in stature. It was made of clear crystal that frosted at the tip and had purple, turquoise and green undertones at the base. It glowed magnificently, throwing rainbow prisms through the room when she drew near it. She loved it at first sight.

"Ah hah, of course. I should have guessed! Very good, my dear." The man took the stone from the shelf and brought it around behind a counter, where he mounted it to a small ring. Then he looped a silver chain through the ring. "There you go!" He held out his hand to reveal the stone was now a beautiful charm necklace.

"It's beautiful," she whispered.

"Here, put it on."

Scarlett hesitated, looking all around for Snuke, Precious, or Honeybee. She scanned his features to see if she could sense if he was anything more than a misfortunately unattractive man.

The hunchback narrowed his eyes. "Scarlett Wrigley, I'm no goblin. Don't you recognize a warlock when you see one?"

Scarlett didn't respond at first. She just sucked in a breath. She didn't know anything about warlocks but wasn't surprised to find out that they were real too, especially since she was pretty sure Louzanne was a witch. She was also pretty sure that Louzanne didn't fully know it yet. She could never get Louzanne talking about this sort of thing, afraid to reveal too much about herself if she did. And she knew the

Kaldife sisters at the yoga studio—Satine, Elan, and Mya—were definitely some sort of witches. But somehow she was still surprised he knew her name and talked about life beneath the veil so casually.

"You know me?"

"Of course I know you, my girl. I've been wondering when you would pay me a visit. Go on, try it on," he said, still holding the necklace out for her to take.

Scarlett looked around for Snuke. She couldn't see her, but she sensed her presence. "Snuke, I know you're here." Snuke appeared above one of the glass shelves. She gave her the thumbs up and disappeared again in a flurry of green sparkles. Relieved that at least Snuke didn't think any of this was odd, Scarlett shrugged and reluctantly held out her hand to take the necklace from the hunchback. She fastened it around her neck then stood in the mirror to admire it. She immediately felt happy and grounded. The stone sparkled beautifully, even in the low light. She wasn't much for fashion, but Scarlett thought this necklace would look fantastic with anything she wore.

"I love it. Uhh…how much is it?" The jewelry for her parents would drain most of her savings she had left over from when she'd been saving up to buy her guitar. She also wanted to pick up a few more gifts on her way home and wasn't sure she had enough money to pay for the necklace. But she did love it. "Do you have layaway?" She began to unclasp the necklace.

"Nonsense. I'll not hear a word of it. It is my pleasure and honor to be able to give you this gift."

"Oh no. This is too much…I couldn't—"

"Please don't embarrass an old man by not accepting it," the warlock interrupted her, folding his arms over his chest. Scarlett scanned his features. He looked sincere and resolute. He wasn't going to take no for an answer.

It seemed like too much to accept, but Scarlett didn't want to offend him. Instead, she said, "Thank you so much. I love it! But I'm paying for the ring and the bracelet, okay?"

"You have a deal." He grinned, revealing even more crooked and broken teeth.

Tinkle...tinkle...tinkle. "Excuse me, my dear, I think I hear another customer." The hunchbacked warlock disappeared upstairs to tend to his customer. "Good afternoon, young man," she heard him say. "How can I help you?"

She thought she recognized the other voice. Scarlett gave one last look around the room at the mysterious glowing gemstones and made her way back upstairs to pay for her parents' gifts.

"Yeah, I'm looking for a gift," said the customer.

"Uh huh, a gift. A gift for...?"

"For a girl."

"Ah hah, a love interest. How wonderful!"

"No, uhh...a friend. Just a friend but you know, like a real friend."

"True friendship is important. Indeed it is. Mm-hmm. Now let me see." With the customer's back to her, Scarlett watched the warlock rummage through shelves and bins looking for the perfect gift for his customer's friend. Red-faced and out of breath after pulling out several items from the top shelf, the warlock pulled out a cookbook. *Simple Meals from the Soul in 20 Minutes or Less.* "Here you go. This is an excellent gift. Your friend will love this."

"You think so?"

"Definitely."

Scarlett rounded the corner and saw Grayson hunched over the book. "Grayson! You're still here?"

Grayson quickly covered the book with his scarf. "Yeah, I'm not leaving until late tonight, so I thought I would check out this place since I've never been in here."

"Yeah, me too. I'm getting these for my parents. They're supposed to have protection properties to keep them safe." She held out the ring and bracelet for Grayson to see.

Grayson quirked up one eyebrow as he eyed the jewelry. "Oh yeah? They're nice."

By the confused look on Grayson's face, she remembered he didn't know anything about the attempt on her mother's life, but she decided not to tell him about it right now. The gravity of what almost happened was all still too much to process and talking about it would force her to relive the previous night's events when she just really wanted to keep her day light and festive. She also didn't say anything about the beautiful charm the warlock gave her. She was sure that Grayson wouldn't approve of her accepting a piece of jewelry as a gift from a stranger.

The warlock had taken the book from Grayson and wrapped it while Scarlett and Grayson were talking. Then he rang in her items and stuffed a book inside the bag: *Interpreting Light Orbs* by Wendy Dickenson. "Your friend would love to have this for Christmas," he said, eyeing Grayson. Of course, a Christmas present for Grayson! She completely forgot. She did manage to get a present for Michelle and Louzanne— certificates for pedicures at Lulu's—but for some reason, it never occurred to her to get something for Grayson or Luke. As if reading her mind, the warlock stuffed a medium sized yellow rock in her bag too. "This is for the other one," he said with a wink.

"Thank you so much for everything. I don't even know your name."

"It's Frank. Anytime. Come back and see me soon."

She paid Frank and thanked him again and promised she would visit. Then she got an idea: she could ask Grayson to help her haul a tree back to her house. "Hey since you're here for a few more hours, can I borrow your brawn?"

Grayson shrugged. "I don't have anything else planned. Sure."

First, they stopped into a sporting goods store and picked out a new hat for Myles. Scarlett hoped this one would fit his head properly, so it didn't look like he was going around wearing a pointy wizard's hat. She found a nice warm pair of toddler-sized long johns for Nick in the children's section. For Yadira, Rolph, and the rest of the gypsies, she thought she would make cookies and homemade Christmas ornaments for each family to hang on their tree. For the fairies, she planned on making tiny necklaces out of baby's breath and mini rosebuds. She stopped into the florist to pick up a few sprigs of the tiny flowers. Since the fairies were so small, she didn't need much material. She only needed one sprig of baby's breath and three rose buds.

The church parking lot two blocks down from her house was set up as a makeshift tree retailer for the holidays. The tree Scarlett picked out was enormous, but luckily they didn't have far to walk. Grayson helped her set it up in the living room and they even managed to get lights and quite a few decorations hung on it.

By then, it was almost supper time. Scarlett expected her parents to be home soon. She wasn't sure if they would be going out for a celebration dinner or ordering pizza at home. It all depended on whether her parents came home with good news or bad.

Grayson checked the time on his phone. "I need to get back and pack a few things."

"Thanks for everything." Scarlett gave him a hug and a kiss on the cheek. "Merry Christmas."

She slipped the book Frank selected for her to give to him into his coat pocket along with a note wishing him and his father a Merry Christmas. After he left, she stepped back from the tree to admire it and saw a small rectangular shaped package under it. She walked over and picked it up. The package had a tag with a smiling penguin wearing a Santa hat and read *To: Scarlett. Merry Christmas. From: Grayson.*

***

The Wrigleys came home laughing and talking excitedly. Nick looked exhausted. It was no wonder after an entire day cooped up in a building with so many people around that he had to try to keep away from Mrs. Wrigley. Scarlett could just imagine him flying into high alert mode anytime a stranger came near her mother. But she was grateful for his vigilance.

"We're home! Oh honey, look at the tree!" Mrs. Wrigley clasped her hands together. Tears glistened in her eyes. "Scarlett, you decorated the whole house!"

The Kroakes must have been in a festive mood because they finished hanging the rest of the ornaments while Scarlett was in the shower. They even put the light up star on top and plugged it in.

"Scarlett, honey, thank you so much for doing that. We've been so busy we haven't had time to make this place festive. It all looks beautiful. Let's go out for dinner. We have wonderful news."

***

They went out for Chinese with the fairies in tow. Nick pouted, not looking too pleased that he had to be out again. "I wanna put my feet up on the couch," he gruffed.

"Leprechauns tend to be homebodies, love," Precious explained, "but clearly after last night, I don't think he'll ever let your mother out of his sight."

Precious, Snuke, and Honeybee didn't pick at the Wrigleys' food much; they were too busy with security details. Myles and Ms. Beasle, Scarlett's percussion teacher, sat at another table to the left of the Wrigleys. They waved to Scarlett as if they were out enjoying a casual dinner. After last night, Scarlett was relieved to know they were taking this security thing seriously.

"So, now that we've got the funding we needed, we'll have the resources to hire a larger team and set up implementation centers across the country!" her father said excitedly. "Isn't that wonderful, honey?"

"Yes, I'm so excited for you both," Scarlett agreed, trying hard not to let her smile slip. It was also scary because there was someone out there that was willing to kill to stop their project. Since they didn't remember anything that happened last night, they wouldn't understand her concern, so she tried her best to keep a smile plastered on her face.

"After this year's trial, so long as nothing goes wrong, we'll be ready to expand the magnet train lines," Mrs. Wrigley said as she subconsciously rubbed her tummy.

"That's so great, Mom," Scarlett said, hoping they couldn't see her concern.

"And we have more exciting news!" Mrs. Wrigley added as she squeezed her husband's hand. "We were going to wait till Christmas to tell you, but we can't keep it from you any longer. There's just so much to be excited about. We're expecting a baby! You're going to have a little brother this June."

"What? Wow, that's so wonderful!" Scarlett hoped she was doing a good job at feigning surprise. The gender really was a surprise to her, and she hoped that was enough to pull it off. "This is going to be the best Christmas ever!" And she really meant it.

SIXTEEN
MYSTERY MAN

After they came home from mass on Christmas Eve, Scarlett left out a plate of cookies and a glass of milk. She was already too old to believe a large man in a red suit was going to fly around the world tonight and climb down her chimney just to eat milk and cookies and leave her a present. Then again, after the last few months, she was willing to entertain the idea of anything. Leaving out the milk and cookies was more of a nostalgic ritual for her now, since she did it every Christmas. It comforted her. For some reason, it always reminded her of Aunt Danielle. Now she understood the connection: Aunt Danielle was part elf, and elves were pretty Christmassy. Scarlett was still a little wary of elves since her first and only encounter with a full-blooded one, but since Aunt Danielle was part elf, she figured they couldn't be all that bad.

The milk and cookies were always gone by morning. Scarlett had figured her father ate them after she went to sleep, but she now knew that it was Nick that polished them off every Christmas.

"Right on time, sweethaahrt," he muttered as he padded into the living room wearing a tattered old onesie that Scarlett outgrew when she was a toddler. It was red and green with little Santa Clauses all over it. She could tell he wore it every Christmas. Nick thanked her for the treat, gulped down the milk, gobbled up the cookies, let out a huge belch, and went off to bed—which was now at the foot of her parents' bed ever since the shooting.

It was past midnight, and while the Wrigleys were already in bed,

Scarlett couldn't sleep. She wondered what kind of celebrations were taking place right now down at the river. The gypsies were never short on making a festival. She went into the kitchen to make a cup of chamomile tea and sat with Mrs. Kroake listening to her stories about Christmases past when she and Wilbur were alive.

***

The Wrigleys loved their Christmas presents. They put them on right away and swore to never take them off. Scarlett got a new case for her guitar, pajamas, yoga pants, and a watch. For some reason, watches seemed to stop working shortly after she wore them, so she rarely knew the time and was often late. Watchmakers were always puzzled as to why the mechanics would fail. Cheap ones, expensive ones, it didn't matter. They all broke eventually. She hoped her parents didn't pay too much money for this one and that it would last her at least a few months. Nick made her a strap for her guitar out of old shoe leather, and the fairies made her a beautiful comb for her hair made of rosewood and quartz.

After breakfast, Scarlett told her parents she was going out for a walk. While Scarlett wanted to get down to the river to wish her friends a Merry Christmas and give them the presents she had for them, she still felt wary of another attempt on her mother's life. She hesitated, reluctant to leave. Honeybee assured her that she and Nick and the rest of the fairies would remain behind to ensure her mother's safety.

"Dinner is at five today, hon. Be back before then," Mrs. Wrigley called out to her. She packed up the presents she had for Myles and the gypsies and made her way down to the river.

As expected, the riverbank was a flurry of activity. There was music and dancing and the Christmas lights strewn among the trees cast a cheery glow. Myles' new hat seemed to fit him a little better than his old one, but it still came up to a point on the top of his head. At least this one was a little less pointy. Yadira fixed Scarlett some lunch and Scarlett joined in with the Romanaskis singing Christmas carols. She borrowed Pesha's fiddle and played a jig for them. Then she played Monti's *Csárdás*—she had been practicing it ever since her school announced they would be holding auditions for the orchestra in the New Year. When it was time to leave, Yeeta and Yaw-Yaw sent her home with shortbread cookies to share with the fairies and Nick.

***

The Romanaski brothers, Bo, Pesha, and Fonso, moved into the Jaimeson's house over the holidays. While it didn't seem like they had much stuff, after going over for a visit, Scarlett could see the house was crammed with furniture, strange looking knick-knacks, instruments, various fighting swords, and other odds and ends.

Ms. Beasle started coming around to visit Bo. She visited so often that Scarlett wondered if they were a "thing". "I've been hearing so many wonderful things about the band you formed with your friends. I can't wait to hear you all play!" Ms. Beasle greeted her one morning as Scarlett was leaving her house on her way out to the river. While always pleasant and happy, lately, Ms. Beasle had taken on an exuberant glow.

"Yeah, we're having a lot of fun with it." Scarlett flushed and the tips of her ears burned. She never really knew what to say or do when someone complimented her. "Maybe you can watch us play one night? You probably have lots of good advice for all of us to improve."

Ms. Beasle beamed. "I look forward to it."

***

On New Year's Eve, the Wrigleys were to attend a fundraising gala in the city. Scarlett hated these superficial types of gatherings. "Why do I even have to go this stupid thing? Can't you just drop me off at Michelle's? I'm sure her mom would let me stay over."

"Well, honey, I hate these things too," Mrs. Wrigley said brushing Scarlett's hair back from her face. "Sometimes they make my skin crawl, but your father and I have accepted long ago that if we want our project to be successful then socializing and fundraising are all part of the job. Besides, it'll be fun. You'll see. And you're going to look so pretty in the dress I bought you."

Scarlett shuddered at the word "dress". "Mom, I hate dresses. I'm not a little girl anymore; you can't dress me up like a doll." Mrs. Wrigley

151

pretended she didn't hear her and laid out a beautiful indigo ball gown with a sweetheart neckline. The dress was a bit fussy for Scarlett's taste. She reluctantly put it on but immediately changed her mind about the dress when she saw how her charm necklace sparkled against the vibrant color. She admired herself in the mirror, amazed at how grown up she looked. *I even look pretty*—a thought that didn't often cross her mind.

To Scarlett's surprise, Vivian was at the ball too. They spotted one another from across the room. Vivian looked relieved to see a friendly face as she made her way over to Scarlett with an Asian girl in tow. "Scarlett, this is Fung. Her family is visiting mine over the holidays." Vivian leaned in to Scarlett and whispered, "They're closing an important deal together, and I'm responsible for keeping Fung entertained." Fung rolled her eyes, looking unamused to be there and barely even acknowledged Scarlett when Vivian introduced her.

"Where are the cute guys? Let's go look for some cute guys." Fung pulled on Vivian's arm until she gave in and let Fung drag her away.

"We'll catch up with you later, Scarlett," Vivian called out to her.

Mrs. Patterson gave a nasally speech about how pleased she and her husband were to be able to make a contribution to such an important environmental project. Since she had developed a genuine disliking for Vivian's mother, Scarlett had a hard time not rolling her eyes, but she managed somehow. Then, Mrs. Patterson introduced John Blackwell, another key benefactor, and owner of Blackwell Enterprises.

Scarlett's ears perked up when she heard the name. *Maybe Grayson is here!* She scanned the room to see Grayson in a tux, slumped over his table looking miserable. Mr. Blackwell gave a concise speech owing his selection of this cause to his late wife's interest in environmental protection and to his son Grayson, who personally selected the cause. Mr. Blackwell was very handsome with a velvety smooth voice. Scarlett could see where Grayson got his good looks, although Grayson's eyes were a warm soft brown unlike his father's, whose were steel blue.

Scarlett waved to get Grayson's attention. His face lit up when he saw her. He rushed over and swooped her up from the floor in a hug.

Vivian didn't miss his display of affection and scowled.

"I didn't think I was going to see any friends until after the holidays. I'm so glad you're here. Thanks for the book, by the way. I've been working through it. Do you know that your fairy friend, Honeybee, isn't the only one? There's more."

Scarlett laughed. "Yes, there's three that live with me."

Grayson's eyes widened. "I thought I saw a lot of activity at Thanksgiving. You never did tell me what they were and I forgot to ask you last time we were alone. I can't quite make them out all the time but sometimes I can. I've only seen two since you gave me the book. I saw one when I was having lunch with my father's assistant during the holidays, and I saw one here tonight. Right over there." Grayson pointed at Precious.

Precious patted her shock of red wiry hair and surreptitiously flitted around the bar, taking little sips from people's wine while glancing around the room—probably making sure Honeybee didn't see her. Then Precious, not having the best eyesight, smacked into a lady's wine glass and fell inside with a *splash*. Soaked in red wine, she had trouble getting her wings to work and had to clamber up the side of the glass. Scarlett and Grayson watched with dreaded anticipation. The lady raised the glass to her lips and tilted it back. Luckily, Precious swung herself out and over the side in time. She hung on the edge of the glass for a moment, shaking the wine off of her wings before darting off to safety.

Relieved she didn't have to tackle the poor woman to save Precious, Scarlett turned her attention back to Grayson. "That's Precious. She lives with me along with two other fairies and a leprechaun. They've lived with me all my life. There's usually at least one of them around me everywhere I go. That's what you saw at Thanksgiving: Honeybee, Precious, Snuke, and our leprechaun, Nick, hopping around eating our food.

Grayson shook his head. "I know you're not lying, but man, Scarlett Wrigley, you're so unusual! You've definitely made my life interesting."

Scarlett blushed. "See over there, that's Snuke and, of course,

Honeybee." She pointed to the dessert table, where Snuke and Honeybee perched on the edge of the chocolate fondue station stuffing their gobs with chocolate and fruit. They gave Scarlett a wave.

"And over there is Nick." He had his arms and legs wrapped around Mrs. Wrigley's leg like a scared animal ready to bite and kick any stranger who came too near.

Grayson squinted. "It's still hard to make them out, but I can see their outlines."

"Nick's been a little over protective of my mother lately. She's pregnant. That and the night before I saw you last, a man came into our house and shot her. She almost died, but I healed her. Myles wiped my parents' memory, so they don't remember any of it."

Grayson's eyes became softer, and he pulled her into a hug, "Scarlett, why didn't you tell me when I saw you? You must be so scared."

Scarlett shrugged. "I don't know. It just happened, and I didn't want to think about it too much, I guess. But I think we're a lot safer now. Bo, Pesha, and Fonso moved in next door and Myles and Ms. Beasle follow us sometimes to make sure we're okay. And poor Nick never leaves my mother's side. So I think we're okay, for now."

"Who did it? Why? I don't understand. Your mom is so sweet."

"Some goon did it for money. Somebody paid him to stop my mom from giving a proposal to secure more funding and support for the magnet train."

Grayson took her hand. "I'm so sorry."

"Well, it didn't work. She presented their proposal, and now they have the support they need."

"What happened to the guy? There wasn't anything on the news. Did you phone the police?"

"The Romanaskis took care of him. They sent him to somebody called The Judge. Apparently, he has a severe approach to justice. I didn't think much of it, really. I've been so focused on making sure my parents are safe to wonder what ever happened to him. But I do want to know who's behind it. "

They stopped talking to listen to Mrs. Wrigley give the final speech of the night. Afterward, the crowd applauded, and the band began to play. Scarlett and Grayson hung out together and danced all night. When their feet got tired, they sat at a table with Vivian and Fung. Vivian stared daggers through Scarlett whenever Grayson would laugh at Scarlett's jokes. Fung ignored everyone like they were insects, opting to focus her efforts on trying to catch the attention of the boy who sat at the table next to them. The boy was handsome and looked to be around eighteen years old, but Fung didn't seem to be having much luck.

It was a long time since the Wrigleys had gone out dancing. They kissed and hugged like a couple of teenagers. Ever since Scarlett had healed her, Mrs. Wrigley seemed like she was feeling much better. She still had the occasional bout of morning sickness—Scarlett could hear her barfing in the bathroom next door sometimes—but she wasn't exhausted like before. She also had more of a radiant glow.

Almost everyone, including Vivian, was on the dance floor at the stroke of midnight when the band counted down the seconds to the New Year. "Three, two, one…. HAPPY NEW YEAR!" everyone cried out. The band started in with a rendition of *Auld Lang Syne*. Mr. and Mrs. Wrigley made their way over to Scarlett to smother her with hugs and kisses.

"Happy New Year, baby girl." Her mother squished her and kissed her forehead.

Grayson gave Vivian a hug and a kiss on the cheek and wished her a Happy New Year. This took the scowl off her face and replaced it with a dazzling smile. *Vivian can be so pretty when she isn't in a snit.* Scarlett also noticed how the demon seemed to fade whenever Vivian truly smiled.

Then Grayson grabbed Scarlett and gave her a hug and a kiss on the cheek. He held her close and dragged her into a slow dance as the band continued to play. Scarlett could feel the daggers in her back from Vivian's glare, and when she turned around to look, the nasty demon had become vibrant again. It had one of its claws dug into Vivian's chest, and another one pinched her throat. Scarlett felt sorry for Vivian. She wondered what kind of a Christmas she had and if she was given any warmth or affection.

"You know," Grayson said as he held her out from him, "if you were a few years older, I would ask you out on a date, but since you're still a kid, I guess we're going to have to be just friends. But you're an interesting person, Scarlett Wrigley."

"Yeah okay, Grayson. Whatever," she said, laughing and rolling her eyes. While Grayson's good looks intimidated her at first, after getting to know him over the last few months, he had become a good friend. He meant a lot to her. She didn't tell him this; instead, she said, "What makes you think I would say yes if you asked me anyway?" and stuck out her tongue at him.

"Yeah, on second thought, your feet probably smell. Forget I said anything."

She started to laugh but became distracted. Out of the corner of her eye, she saw a man with long gray hair and a long beard that went down to his knees. He wore silvery blue satin robes. Scarlett stared at him, and he stared back at her. A glowing light filled her eyes, and she looked down to see her charm necklace glowing a silvery blue. He appeared to be carrying something that looked like an hourglass or an old-fashioned lantern, but she couldn't make it out from where she stood.

"Scarlett...hello...?" She took her eyes from the man and looked back to Grayson. "Hello? You zoned out."

"What? Oh, sorry. What did you say?"

"I said are you going to play at the variety show at the end of the year?"

"Uhh...yeah for sure. Our band is gonna play."

She scanned the room to look for the man, but he was gone. "Excuse me, Grayson. I'll be back." She hurried out of the ballroom looking for the strange man in the silver robes. She ran down the hall and out onto the balcony, where she saw the trailing ends of his long robes flutter in the wind from over the railing. She looked down five stories to the city street below, but he was gone as if he had vanished into thin air.

"What was that about?" Grayson asked as he ran out onto the snow-covered terrace. He found her leaning over the balcony railing standing in a pile of snow up to her ankles with no coat on.

"I uh…I don't know. I thought I saw someone, but he's gone." She began to shiver as the snow fell on her bare shoulders, her satin slippers soaked through from the wet snow.

Grayson put his tux jacket over her shoulders. "C'mon weirdo, let's get you back inside."

***

The next day Scarlett told Myles about the man in the silver robes as he fixed her a hot cup of cocoa. Myles grimaced and a white line formed around his mouth where he pursed his lips. He handed her the cocoa, tented his fingers beneath his chin, and stared into the fire in silence.

"He looked like he was carrying something—an hourglass or a lantern. I couldn't make it out." She searched his face for a reaction but found only a stone wall. After getting no response from Myles, she continued, "I wonder if it had something to do with the New Year…like Father Time. Is that real? Is time like a person?"

"No more of this conversation right now, Scarlett. Time control is not something to be discussed," Myles said sternly. By his expression, she could tell he was serious and maybe even scared, and she knew there was no point in pushing the subject for now. She looked down at her watch. It had already broken.

SEVENTEEN
TRULUTHU

The day of auditions finally arrived, and Scarlett could almost explode with nerves as she waited in the line up to go backstage. Michelle walked out from the music hall after her audition along with the rest of the drums tryouts with a broad smile across her face. "I made it!"

"Congrats!" Scarlett threw her arms around her. There were two more students ahead of her. She was last in the violin group. With a last name like Wrigley, she was used to being last in line, unless there was an unlucky kid with a last name that started with X or Z. Luke stood in the lineup next to her biting his lip. There were twenty kids in his group and only one piano spot. His face was pale. "Just relax. You'll do fine. You got this," she reassured him.

"Wrigley," Mr. Takistas, the sixth year strings teacher, called her name.

"You're up." Luke squeezed her hand. He met her eyes as he smiled at her. "Good luck."

Scarlett walked into the music hall from the backstage corridor and stepped onto the stage. The lights blinded her, and she blinked to adjust to the brightness. She could faintly make out the silhouette of Ms. Beasle and a dozen other faces she didn't recognize. A million little butterflies pummeled her stomach, causing her breath to come in short gasps. She picked up the violin laid out for her, took a deep breath, closed her eyes, and began to play.

To calm her nerves, she imagined herself practicing with her Juma down by the river, remembering the first time she ever flew. Then she imagined herself enjoying time with the people she loved. She began to relax, and the tension in her shoulders let go. Now, in her mind, she was baking cookies with her mother. She hardly paid attention to the sound that came from her instrument, only focusing on the feelings the sound generated. About three-quarters of the way through, it occurred to her that she had never heard this song before that was coming from her instrument.

She planned on playing Monti's *Csárdás*, but what she played was something else—an unknown melody. It didn't concern her. It was beautiful. Scarlett didn't even care if she could be part of the orchestra anymore; she only cared about her song. All she knew was that playing it made her feel alive and that was enough. Her Juma radiated slightly outside her body, but Scarlett didn't care, too enthralled in her task to pull back. Finally, after several minutes and a thousand joyful feelings, she felt an end coming to her melody. She stayed with it, guiding it until it was through.

The silence remained in the auditorium for several moments after. Then…applause. "Beautiful! Just beautiful, Scarlett." Ms. Beasle skipped onto the stage, her ringlets bouncing. With tears in her eyes, she hugged Scarlett. The stage lights dimmed, and Scarlett could make out the other judges. Some looked like they might be members of the business community while others were famous musicians. *Louzanne's mother is here!* All of them stood clapping for her. Ms. Beasle hugged her again and whispered in her ear, "You'll be first violin."

※※※

It was a cold rainy day in early February down at the riverbank. Scarlett hardly felt like getting out of bed that morning, but with much poking and prodding on the part of Snuke, Precious, and Honeybee, she was up and out the door by mid-morning. She didn't feel the cold as much, but she still felt the dampness despite her waterproof coat and pants.

Myles stood on the riverbank in a yellow slicker. The Romanaskis' many campfires were merely smoldering ashes today as they opted for activities indoors. "I want to show you how to do something new today," he said as he smiled and gestured for her to follow him closer to the forest.

Puffs of steam escaped their mouths and nostrils as they squelched towards the forest line. While Scarlett was still bursting with questions about the strange man she had seen on New Year's, Myles was stern and resolute in not discussing the subject any further. It had been over a month, and she couldn't get an answer from anyone. Even Yadira and Rolph, an endless source of knowledge, were tight-lipped on the subject. She was unable to get any more information from anyone about the man in black she saw on Halloween either, despite months of questioning.

"Okay, so you won't tell me who he is. Can you at least tell me why my necklace lit up when I saw him?"

Myles' lips tightened, and he shot her a reprimanding look. Scarlett sighed. Rather than pressing further, she simply shrugged and said, "Okay, fine," hoping her compliance would lead to a quick lesson so she could at least get out of the rain.

Myles looked toward the forest and said, "Come out, innocent one. I see you through the trees. You don't have to be afraid." He held out his hand, filled with grass and leaves, as he called toward the forest. Scarlett heard rustling and crackling coming from the brush and the sound of hooves. A beautiful large elk emerged from the woods and trotted toward Myles.

Scarlett gasped and took several steps backward. "He's so big!" *And those antlers look like they could spear several men at once.* She instinctively placed her hands over her abdomen as if to protect from an oncoming charge.

Myles stood his ground and held out his hand. The elk approached, put his snout in his hand, and began to eat right out of his palm. As the elk ate, Myles stroked the animal's head. "Yes, yes." When the animal finished eating, he asked, "Any news, old friend?"

Scarlet looked around to see who he was talking to but there wasn't anyone. The elk didn't make a sound, but Myles nodded and spoke to it as if he were having a conversation with the animal. "Mm-hmm, and what of the crows?" Again, she heard nothing from the elk, but Myles appeared to be listening carefully as if it were speaking.

"Very good, gentle one. Could you please assist me in my lesson today?" The elk just batted his soft brown eyes and looked from Myles to Scarlett. "You may want to lie down as our friend here is small and frightened by you." The elk snorted and tucked its long legs beneath its body as it rested on its belly.

"Whoa." Scarlett couldn't believe her eyes. "It understands you?"

"Yes, my dear, and I understand him. Come close. This is Truluthu, king of the forest—king of the forest in these parts anyway." Myles gestured for her to move closer to the giant beast.

"Hello," she said as she gingerly shuffled her feet toward the animal, intimidated by his size and not knowing what to say to a king, "uhh, your highness."

"Animals don't pay any mind to formalities as humans do. Truluthu is fine," Myles said as he stood behind her. "Scarlett, I want you to look into Truluthu's eyes and concentrate on listening to him." As silly as it sounded, after all she had seen, she knew better than to question. "Okay." She moved even closer to the giant beast until she could feel his breath on her face and gazed deeply into his big brown eyes. The animal had long eyelashes and a thick tuft of dark brown fur that trailed from his chin down to his chest. The spread of his antlers was unusually large for an elk and had to be about fifteen feet. He was a magnificent animal. This animal was kind and innocent. She could tell by looking into his eyes.

"Concentrate," Myles instructed.

She focused on listening. She heard the rush of the river, the freezing rain pelting down, and the rustling as the wind whipped through the trees. She heard him inhale and exhale, and felt the animal's warm breath on her face, but nothing that could be described as language. "I don't hear anything," she called back to Myles after several minutes of concentration.

"Keep trying," he encouraged.

The rain beat down on her head as she tried to focus. Steam rose from the beast's body, and warm mist escaped his snout as they remained still, facing one another. After several more minutes, she said, "I still don't hear anything."

"*That's because I haven't said anything,*" said a deep baritone voice.

Scarlett, still inches from the creature's face, looked all around and back at the elk. "You're talking!"

"*Yes, and now you are listening.*"

Scarlett became so excited, she forgot the freezing rain that beat down on her head and ran down her shoulders and back. "Wow, I don't know what to say...hello," she said with a laugh.

"*Hello,*" the creature replied. "*How are you?*"

"I'm good, thank you. How are you?" she asked.

"*I am well. Thank you,*" the elk replied.

"Uhh, do you live in these woods?"

"*Yes, I do, as do many other creatures.*"

"Can you all speak?"

"*Only to those who listen,*" the elk replied.

"I'm listening."

"*Indeed, you are.*"

"How old are you?" she asked.

"*Oh, I'm very old.*"

"So you're a king?" She blew on her hands and rubbed them together to ease the stiffness caused by the cold rain.

"*I look out for all living things in this forest, so if that makes me king, then yes, I am king.*"

"Oh. Do you have a wife or a girlfriend?"

The elk's eyes became glassy. "*I did once.*"

"Did she die?" Scarlett asked. The creature nodded. "How did she die?"

"*She drank water from a poisoned stream. It was many years ago, before you were born.*" His eyes became misty. He still looked heartbroken.

"I'm very sorry to hear that." She reached out to touch his snout then paused. "Is it okay to touch you?"

"*Yes.*" The elk let out a deep sigh. His eyes became less watery.

Rubbing his snout and his ears seemed to ease his melancholy.

"*Ahh, humans. What a confusing species. Some of you are so wonderful—as kind as or kinder than all the animals in the forest—and yet are capable of such horrors. I'll never understand.*" He shook his massive head from side to side. With a sigh and a big stretch, the animal rose to his feet until he towered several feet above her. "*Goodbye, Scarlett Wrigley. Be well.*" He paused as he passed Myles and said, "*The crows are waiting at the crossroads. They haven't decided.*"

"Hmm," Myles rubbed his chin. "Thank you, Truluthu." Silently, Truluthu trotted off back into the forest. Scarlett stood in the rain watching the animal disappear.

"Myles?" she asked after a few minutes of silence.

"Yes?"

"Can you talk to all animals?"

"Yes."

"Can I talk to all animals?"

"Yes, if you try."

"Even Betty and Elvis?"

"Especially Betty and Elvis. They've been with you since you were born. They love you and are fiercely protective of you. You seem to have prolonged their lifespan, especially Betty, who was quite an old dog even before you were born."

"Huh," she said more to herself. "Myles?"

"Yes?"

"Are you ever going to tell about the man I saw on New Year's or the man I saw on Halloween?"

Myles sighed. "Yes, but another time. A few years from now when you're older. Now is not the time. Please accept this and don't ask anymore. Come, let's go inside and warm up for a while." He pointed toward the Winnebago. "You can practice talking to Alfred."

It was Rolph's day to cook, so it was grilled spicy sausages and boxed macaroni and cheese for lunch at the Romanaskis. Scarlett opted out of the sausage but enjoyed the macaroni and cheese. With a bowling alley and an arcade at their disposal inside their living quarters,

Scarlett wondered how they ever managed to get the kids to play outside.

The Romanaskis were modern in many ways and enjoyed modern amenities and comforts, but they were also much more in tune with nature. They gravitated towards the natural world and spent most of their time outside. Which would explain why they chose to camp in caravans by a river in the woods rather than live in a house in the suburbs or in a city.

Alfred was far less refined and majestic in his communication than Truluthu. Amidst snorts and squeals, Scarlett learned that Alfred's favorite foods were cheeseburgers and apples. His favorite place to sleep was underneath Gustaf's bed, and he loved to have his belly rubbed. Overall, he was a very nice pig, and Scarlett liked him much more now that she could converse with him.

***

Later that night, at home when everyone else was sleeping, Scarlett tucked herself into bed with Elvis and Betty at her feet and had her first real conversation with the pets she had loved and cared for all her life. They told her that they loved her and they especially enjoyed their walks together and the cookies and leftovers she gave them. She apologized for any time she may have talked to them as if they were dumb and didn't understand her. They accepted her apology and told her they didn't mind the baby talk as long and she scratched behind their ears and rubbed their bellies, as they particularly liked that.

EIGHTEEN
BANDS OF GRAY

"First years report to the gymnasium for vocation day," Mr. Lechey's voice crackled over the PA system. Scarlett, Michelle, and Luke met up in the gym. Louzanne, being a second year, and Grayson, a third year, they already had their vocational field trip in their first year, so they were spared.

"I don't understand why I have to go to this," Luke groaned as he shuffled along in the lineup with the rest of the group. "All I want is to play piano. I think I might be able to make a living at it."

"Well, just in case you can learn all about being a waiter or a janitor," Michelle teased. Luke put her in a headlock and gave her a noogie, messing up her hair.

"Gerroff," Michelle cried as she shook him off. He stumbled backwards a few steps and fell on his butt. "I hate when you do that." She huffed, but she laughed too as she tried to fix her wild pink and blonde hair that now stuck up in several places. Since her hair was a write off for the day, she took the elastic band Scarlett offered and tied it up. Scarlett always had an extra elastic band around her wrist for backup.

Five different tables loomed before them labeled "Hospitality", "Healthcare", "Finance", "Agriculture", and "Manufacturing".

"Students, if you already know you have a particular interest in any one of these industries you can sign up on this list here," Mr. Lechey directed from behind the table. He wore a pink silk tie and white and black loafers. "You can do a more in-depth tour of your chosen

165

industry rather than tour all of them." Several students began lining up to choose an industry. Scarlett, Luke, and Michelle stood there in the gym, frozen like deer caught in headlights.

"I don't want to work in any of these industries. Do you?" Michelle asked.

"I'm not sure." Scarlett hadn't really thought about what she wanted for a career when she was older. She imagined she would like to do something with music but never really thought about what.

"Nope, definitely not," Luke chimed in, looking at the students lining up at the tables as if he were watching unknowing animals being led to a slaughterhouse.

"Having trouble choosing?" Mr. Lechey drawled. "You're not alone. You don't have to. You can tour all of them today. Follow me." He led them to the parking lot and directed them onto a school bus already filled with Rosemont first years.

"Hi, guys!" Mrs. Goodspeed sat in the front row. She and Mr. Arun, the Math teacher, were chaperones on their bus. When all the seats were taken, they headed off to their first stop point: Smith Farms, an apple farm thirty miles west of Riverstone.

Frost covered the orchards this time of year, and very few workers remained on the farm until the harvest in the fall. Farmer Smith explained that by October the orchards would be teeming with workers who came from the south. He showed the class the various buildings and machinery associated with operating the farm. Scarlett was surprised to find out there were so many chemicals involved in farming. There were pesticides, solutions to wash the apples, chemicals to use on the machines, and when processing the apples and so on.

Finally, he showed them the large storage building that was full of rotting apples. "These here are the apples that fell or didn't meet commercial grade. They were either too small or misshapen. Most of them fall, and we just can't get them in time."

Scarlett raised her hand from the back of the tour group. "What do you do with all those apples?"

"The ones that can be salvaged get sold to various food manufacturers to make juice, pie filling, and other food products. The rest will be left to rot and then sold to make fertilizer," the farmer explained.

While she understood that the rotting apples were at least being used for something, with so many hungry people in the world, it didn't make any sense to Scarlett why someone would let a perfectly good apple go to waste, even it was lying on the ground for a day or so or if it was a little small or had a funny shape.

"Why not give them away before they rot?" she questioned, not satisfied with the farmer's answer. "There are food banks and underfunded schools that would love to have free apples."

Farmer Smith shifted on his feet and rubbed his balding head. "Well, it's not that simple…that's not how the world works," he stammered, his ruddy cheeks turning even redder.

"Everyone, come this way. It's time to sample some Smith Farm applesauce," Mr. Arun interrupted as he gave Scarlett an 'if I hear one more word out of you' look and ushered the students towards the large cafeteria building at the entrance to the property.

They had to walk through the orchard and Scarlett watched the farm workers covering the tree trunks with burlap cloth.

"Apple trees are real hardy," Farmer Smith explained. "These here coverings are just to make sure the frost don't affect the trees."

The sunlight glistened off the frost on the trees and reflected onto her necklace that lay exposed on her chest. Scarlett had forgotten her scarf on the bus, not that the cold bothered her much anymore. It generated rainbows prisms of light that danced in her walking path. Scarlett enjoyed the visual as she walked through the orchard. She watched the workers intently and began to read their auras. Their colors varied from person to person but did a double take when she noticed an unusual common theme. There appeared to be gray bands wrapped around their necks and wrists. Scarlett looked more closely to see if maybe it was a particular creature that might be causing this phenomena, but she saw none. The gray bands seemed to be part of their auras, but they also seemed to block the person's energy flow at their neck and wrists.

She got a chance to take a better look in the cafeteria when one of the workers served her a cup of applesauce. Close up, the gray bands were even more opaque and visible. She blinked and rubbed her eyes. *What are they? Yadira knows a lot about auras. I'll have to find out from her what they could be and why some people have them.*

After enjoying their apple treat, the students piled on the bus and headed north to tour a manufacturing plant. Smoke rose from several stacks as they pulled into the parking lot. Mr. Kurfey, the plant engineer of GMT Industries, ushered them into a room and gave a brief visitor's safety orientation. He was a middle-aged man with thick eyebrows and thinning black fuzzy hair. He wore prescription glasses with plastic side shields. GMT Industries made automotive parts. Mr. Kurfey handed out safety glasses and earplugs and instructed them to stay along the marked paths during the tour.

The noise was deafening when they walked into the industrial area. Scarlett immediately put in her ear plugs, and that seemed to help a little bit. They toured the various areas of the manufacturing facility. The furnace area where parts were hardened was very smoky. Scarlett couldn't imagine anyone wanting to spend all day there. Other areas involved inspecting and testing the products. Various technicians were going about their duties. Some employees worked on machines repairing them while others operated the machines.

"It takes a lot of different trades and various technical expertise to keep the machines running and the manufacturing process going," Mr. Kurfey hollered over the whirring and droning equipment. To Scarlett's surprise, when she focused on the workers, she could see gray bands around their necks and wrists too. Like the farm workers, the bands were deep and opaque. She rubbed her eyes and looked around at everyone who worked there and sucked in her breath. *Is there something wrong with my eyes? Everyone has gray bands!*

They toured the research and development lab and the engineering department and saw the employees working from their desks. They too had gray bands, though some were less visible than others. Even the tour guide, Mr. Kurfey, had traces of them. By late morning, they ended their tour with a talk in the cafeteria given by the human resources manager on the various careers that could be found at GMT Industries. Then it was time to get back on the bus.

Hotel Luxe, located ten miles east, was their next stop. It is a recent trend for some hotels to have a resident pet, usually a low allergen and low energy animal that looked cute and lounged about the front check-in area making the guests feel at home. Hotel Luxe had a resident shih-tzu named Mr. Pickles. As guests arrived, Mr. Pickles wagged his tail and looked cute from his comfy bed secured on a platform off of the front counter.

The guest service attendant smiled and welcomed them, but Scarlett could tell it was forced. She could see dark gray bands around her neck and wrists that seemed to overshadow the rest of her energy.

As they gathered around the front lobby for the welcoming speech given by Ms. Janes, the general manger, Mr. Pickles yawned and wandered over to Scarlett. She couldn't take her eyes off the guest service attendant in awe of her dark gray bands and the remarkable affect they seemed to have on her. The rest of her aura seemed to radiate around her in broken wisps, unlike the usual connected rings of energy she was accustomed to seeing.

"She's going through a messy divorce."

Scarlett looked all around to find who it was that just spoke. The voice continued, *"She can't make ends meet. That's why she's so bummed."* Scarlett looked down to see Mr. Pickles looking up at her through big puppy dog's eyes and a squished in face.

"Did you just say something?" she whispered to the dog.

"Yeah, but I can't believe you're actually listening. I see you looking at Janine, probably wondering why she looks so miserable. She's going through a divorce and can't make ends meet. That's why. This job don't pay her enough to be able to look after her kids, so she gets a friend to look after them at night and when she leaves here, she takes a bus across town and works at a call center 'till midnight. She's gotta work weekends too. She hardly sees her kids anymore. That's why she's so

bummed."

"That's awful," Scarlett whispered and looked at Janine empathetically.

"Yeah, that happens. Too bad. Nice lady. Sometimes it's good to be a cute dog. Good talking to ya." Mr. Pickles stretched and took off back to his bed.

The hotel general manger personally gave them the tour, going over various aspects of running a hotel and the different types of jobs needed to run it. They started in the kitchens; then it was off to guest services and dining, where they had a chance to have lunch. Then they went on to housekeeping services, administrative office, and finally, special services like the spa, banquet, event planning, and hotel maintenance.

Scarlett watched the employees carefully while on the tour, trying to catch glimpses of the new found phenomena. They too sported the gray bands to varying extents. The housekeeping employees seemed to have the most opaque—the same with those in dining service and the bellhops—whereas the lady who ran the spa, the general manager, and the head chef didn't have any traces at all.

The fourth stop of the day was at the corporate office of a large national bank located just across the street from the hotel. The skyscraper towered above the clouds. They all gathered in the lobby where a sophisticated and fashionably dressed woman directed them to a conference room. In the conference room, the human resources manager gave a presentation and discussed various careers in banking and finance. Many of the jobs required a business degree or university certificate in finance.

The human resources manager showed a PowerPoint presentation with images of sharply dressed confident looking young professionals. Each slide had catchphrases like "Driving the promise of tomorrow" or "Investments you can count on from experts you can trust". She then showed a video with more smartly dressed young people who talked about various careers in the field. Then the video went on to discuss briefly about hedge funds, mortgages, bonds, stocks, and futures.

By the end of the presentation, Scarlett's head was spinning like a top. She hardly understood a thing other than the part about mortgages—probably because her parents used to complain about theirs from time to time—and bonds because her grandma had taken out a savings bond for her education when she was born. She also knew about bonds because she learned in history class that American involvement in the Second World War was funded by American people personally supporting the war effort by buying government bonds.

Suzie Matheson seemed to be impressed by how sophisticated the young women looked in the video and whispered to her friend, "I want to be able to dress like that every day. I want to work in finance."

After the presentation, Mrs. Goodspeed and Mr. Arun corralled them back onto the bus. They didn't have time to tour the building or see any of the employees other than the people in the front reception and the human resources manager, so Scarlett didn't get the chance to observe employees in finance to see whether or not they had gray bands. But she did notice them on both ladies—although the receptionist's were much more visible.

As the bus drove off, a helicopter landed on the helipad next to the parking lot. A man dressed in a suit got out. He had varying colors in his aura, but the peculiar thing about this individual was that a thick red band or halo draped over the man's head that seemed to obstruct his energy flow. Scarlett pressed her nose against the window to get a better look, but the bus pulled away so quickly she couldn't quite make it out. Scarlett rubbed her eyes and blinked several times because she thought she saw something dark clinging to the man, writhing around his body like a serpent.

The last stop of the day was right back in Riverstone at the community hospital, where they toured the various occupations one could find there: administration, nursing, nurse's aides, physicians, technicians, and many others. Dr. Blake gave them a quick tour of the prenatal and pediatric ward. Scarlett was happy to see that this wing was cheery and the staff seemed caring and professional since this was where her baby brother would be born this summer. They toured the laundry and kitchen services and the housekeeping service areas. They pretty much toured every location in the hospital except the morgue—which Mrs. Goodspeed thought to be too morbid for first years.

As Scarlett studied the people working, she noticed that while many had gray bands, some didn't have any at all. While some bands were thick and opaque, others were thin and almost transparent. Scarlett looked around at her classmates. *Can kids have gray bands too?* But she couldn't detect any on them. *Maybe it's just an adult thing.* She eyed her teachers. Mr. Arun had faint traces of gray about his neck and wrists, but Mrs. Goodspeed had none; neither did Dr. Blake or some of the ladies that worked in the kitchen and laundry room. It was very strange. *Do most adults have these bands and I just didn't notice before?* She couldn't wait to get down to the river and talk to Yadira about it.

Finally, they finished their day back at Rosemont, where they had to go back into the gymnasium for a final head count before being released for the day. Scarlett scanned the room looking at the other kids, but couldn't see bands on any of them. She scanned the room again looking at the faculty and saw that some had them while others didn't. She couldn't detect a trace of anything on Mr. Lechey, but Mr. Smith, the Biology teacher, had the bands on his neck and wrists, although not nearly as noticeable as some she saw on the vocational tour today.

The bell rang, and the kids and faculty filed out of the building. Scarlett watched Mr. Smith leave. As he stepped over the threshold of the school, the bands began to fade. He turned on his car, loud rock music blaring from his car stereo, and as he pulled away, the bands completely disappeared. *Hmm…how odd,* she thought.

Scarlett raced down to the river on foot to find Yadira—the icy roads prevented her from using her bike this month. She wanted to run, but icy patches covered the path. She had to slow down and be careful where she placed her feet, so she didn't fall. Anxious to get there, she looked around the path to see if anyone was watching. With a bounding leap, she took flight. After only a few seconds, she looked around the trees and caught a glimpse of a sparkle and a flash of blue hair from the corner of her eye. She descended back to the ground. *Better not. I'll never hear the end it from Honeybee if I get caught.* "Snuke, don't tell Honeybee, okay?" Snuke just shrugged.

Yadira sat in her kitchen looking out the window of her caravan as if she had been expecting her. She wore a silk shirt covered with butterflies, and her dark hair was pulled away from her face with a matching hairband. When Scarlett walked into the kitchen, Yadira directed her to the table. "Scarlett, sit." Yadira's crystal ball sat on the table, but she quickly covered it with a cloth when Scarlett sat down. Yadira rubbed her palms together to warm her hands then reached for Scarlett's temples, placing her hands there and closing her eyes.

"How was your day today?" Yadira asked after several minutes.

"Okay. We toured jobs in some industries in the area."

"Something is different today though, isn't it?" Yadira queried.

Scarlett nodded. "I saw what looked like bands around people's necks and wrists. They were gray, almost as if something was covering or blocking their energy in those areas. Not everyone had it, and some were more noticeable than others."

"Aha." Yadira sat back in her chair. "And what do you think they are?"

"I have no idea. That's why I'm asking you. It doesn't make any sense. I've never seen them before."

"Is it possible you just never paid attention before?" Yadira asked.

Scarlett thought for a moment. "Yes, I suppose that's possible. I know it doesn't seem to affect kids—and some adults."

Yadira's dark eyes flashed, and she leaned forward and put her palms on the table. "What else did you notice about the people who had these...bands as you call them?"

Scarlett thought about it carefully. "They seemed like they weren't living in the moment. Their minds were preoccupied with something, like worry, and they seemed to not enjoy what they were doing as much as the others who had less visible bands or none. And...I don't know;

they seemed to be under a lot of stress."

"Hah!" Yadira clapped her hands. "You are much more perceptive than you know, my dear."

"But what are they? What do they mean? Can those bands be harmful?"

"Yes, they can harm if one sacrifices their health and happiness in the process."

"Why do some have it and some don't but they're in the same place doing the same thing?"

Yadira paused for a moment. "One thing is not necessarily for everyone. One person may find fulfillment in one activity while another detests it."

"Then why would somebody do something they don't want to do?"

"Why do you think?"

Scarlett already knew the answer when she thought about it. "Because they need to make money."

Yadira clicked her tongue, wagged her finger at Scarlett, and winked.

"But everyone needs to make money. That's how the world works!"

"Is it, dear?"

Scarlett didn't know what to say. She just looked at her, dumbfounded. Yadira continued, "Some work out of fear—fear of not having enough, fear of not being able to provide for their families, fear of not having stability, or for some, it is simply fear of a lack of opportunity. Then there are others that carry out their day with love. They love what they do because of the task itself, or maybe it allows them more time with their kids, or they love that it allows them to provide for their family. Some people enjoy what they do, but they have stress because what they do doesn't pay enough for them to keep food on the table and pay their bills every month. Or maybe it takes up too much of their time that they really need to spend with their families. You see, life must be in balance. When it is out of balance, there is stress, hardship, and slavery."

"Slavery?" Scarlett could hardly picture a receptionist as a slave, although the bands did bear resemblance to shackles.

"Yes, slavery. Many people are never really free to make the right choices for themselves because they live in constant fear. It is a difficult and complicated balance. There is no easy explanation or solution."

Still confused but trying to follow, Scarlett had never really thought about things in that way before, but it did somewhat make sense to her, although she didn't really fully understand it. "How come you don't have any bands?"

"Because I don't live in fear or worry and because I have faith."

"How come kids don't have gray bands?"

"Some don't, some do. It just depends on their circumstance. Many children go about their days without fear or worry about whether they'll have a place to sleep or enough food to eat. Others live in poverty and have these worries. Some have other stresses. War or abuse, for example. Some may also have the burden of having to work on top of going to school to help their families get by. Or they may have to leave school entirely."

Scarlett hadn't seen any bands on any kids at Rosemont. *Maybe there are and I just never noticed. I wonder if Mom and Dad have gray bands blocking their auras.*

***

Mrs. Wrigley had taken on an energetic glow over the last month. She kept fussing around the house—over setting up the nursery and over Scarlett. The Kroakes were ultra-excited about the prospect of a baby in the house since there hadn't been one in over a half a century. Unbeknownst to Mrs. Wrigley, Mrs. Kroake could be found hovering over her all the time, following her up and down the stairs to make sure she didn't fall while keeping her distance so as not to give her the chills, and fluffing her pillow at night, so she woke well rested.

Scarlett paid special attention to her parents to see if she could spot gray bands blocking their energies but she couldn't see any. Since the proposal had been accepted and there was now additional funding, the Wrigleys were able to hire assistants to help them with their projects. This left Mrs. Wrigley more free time to spend at home resting and with Scarlett. But Scarlett was on her own journey now. Between Juma lessons, symphony practice, and their band, her plate was full. She usually didn't make it home for supper until around eight pm.

While her mother worried she might be taking on too much, Scarlett assured her that she loved what she was doing. Besides, she didn't get hungry until later anyway so she didn't mind her new ritual of late suppers, rushing to get her homework done, and then off to bed. At least the Wrigleys made time for each other on Saturday and Sunday mornings. Scarlett loved the weekends when she could sleep in and have time to catch up with her family over breakfast. They always had some interesting project that they were working on, and they loved hearing about her experiences at school. Of course, they still knew nothing of her activities at the river, but there was enough truth in her other extracurricular activities to keep them distracted from that detail.

***

"Keep stirring, honey. Don't let the wax get cold," Mrs. Wrigley instructed, peering over Scarlett's shoulder.

"Jeez, I didn't think making old-fashioned candles was going to be this much work," Louzanne groaned as sweat poured from her brow. "Next time, Mrs. Wrigley, can we just bake some brownies and watch movies in our pajamas?"

"Of course, hon." Mrs. Wrigley affectionately squeezed Louzanne's shoulder.

Michelle's cheeks turned bright pink, matching the streaks in her hair, as she stood over the hot pot of candle grease, but she seemed to be having a blast. "I love all this crafty stuff. I used to do a lot of these kinds of activities with my mom at the ranch."

"Nuh uhh, not me, girl," Louzanne said. "I think it's cute and I appreciate handcrafted stuff and all that. I'd just rather buy it from a boutique not slave over a hot stove making it."

The girls were having a sleepover at the Wrigleys. They were making homemade old-fashioned candles. Excited about the sleepover, Mrs. Wrigley, with her new found energy, had planned the activity. To

Nick's chagrin, she had been saving the fat drippings from all of their cooking for over a month to make the candles.

Since Mrs. Wrigley kept tabs on the leftover fat drippings, Nick could no longer have his helping of bacon grease that he so enjoyed without raising suspicion.

"I'll be glad when this is over too," Nick grumbled, looking very lean and rather healthier—however, unhappier than before.

Scarlett couldn't help but giggle at his comment. No one else could see or hear Nick, so Scarlett followed up with, "This is fun," so they wouldn't wonder what she was laughing at.

Interested in the activity, Mrs. Kroake kept peering over the girls' shoulders as they worked. She accidentally brushed against Michelle, who turned pale, her body shook with a bout of the chills. Scarlett had to get her another sweater. Poor Michelle didn't warm up until she had been standing over the hot pot of grease for another half hour.

All four of them dipped strings in the fat then pulled them out, letting the fat cool, then dipped them in for another layer, then another and another.

"Are we almost done, Mom?" Scarlett asked, anxious to just relax and watch movies with her friends.

"Just a few more minutes, hon. We have to be patient and allow the grease to cool on the string. The consistency and the temperature have to be just so before you take another dip. Otherwise, the grease on the wick will just melt off back into the pot." Michelle dipped her candle in the grease a little too soon, demonstrating exactly what Mrs. Wrigley had just said. "See what I mean? We need to be patient."

Scarlett sighed but didn't complain further. She knew her mother was enjoying this. "Girl time", she called it, and Scarlett didn't have the heart to ruin her fun. She wondered if Vivian would enjoy making candles. Despite protests from Michelle and Louzanne, Scarlett had invited her to the sleepover, but Vivian said she was too busy planning her fashion show for the year-end variety show and had other plans with Jessica Benner and Alison Mitchell that weekend. "We're going shopping and then attending an art show," Vivian explained haughtily in a tone that really meant: *As if I'd waste my weekend at your house doing nerdy hick stuff when I could be in the city doing something cool and trendy.*

Scarlett imagined Vivian, Jessica, and Alison would go shopping in the city and look down their noses at other people who couldn't afford the stores where they shopped. Vivian was a hard person to be nice to, but for reasons she couldn't even explain herself, Scarlett was still determined to win her over.

"Okay, one last dip and we're done," Mrs. Wrigley said, giving the wax a sniff. Fortunately, Mrs. Wrigley ground up lavender into the grease, so their candles smelled floral and didn't reek like month old animal fat.

When they finished, and the remaining grease cooled, Scarlett brought it out to the compost container in their backyard. From over the fence, she saw Ms. Beasle, Fonso, Pesha, and Bo having a bonfire next door.

"Hi, Scarlett," Ms. Beasle greeted her. "I was just telling Bo about your band. I've listened to you guys a few times now, and you just keep getting better and better. I'd like to record it and show you how to record so you can share it with your friends and family."

Scarlett had never really thought about trying to record their music before. *I guess that would be kind of cool. Mom and Dad and Grandma would probably love a copy.* For a moment, Scarlett grimaced at the mental image of her mom listening to their music through her earbuds while on the train and belting out the lyrics at the top of her lungs. *Ugh. But using the recording equipment would be kinda cool.* Scarlett shrugged. "Okay, that sounds like fun. I'll let the others know."

"Try this." Pesha handed her a skewered stuffed marshmallow over the fence.

Scarlett popped it in her mouth and a burst of amazing flavors dissolved on her tongue. It wasn't just a marshmallow; it was chocolate and marzipan stuffed inside a marshmallow and then caramelized over the fire. Scarlett waved goodnight with a mouth full of the sweet chocolatey goodness and headed back inside to watch a movie with her friends—something about a talking cat. Scarlett laughed the whole way through, empathizing with the cat owner over the awkward predicaments one finds themselves in when they can talk to their pets, and their pets talk back.

***

On Monday, Scarlett told her friends over lunch about Ms. Beasle's offer to show them how to record their music. They loved the idea and agreed to ask Ms. Beasle if they could do it tomorrow afternoon. Even Grayson, while not in the band, got excited for them and offered to design their album cover. They had twelve songs in total, although the twelfth one was choppy and missing the main chorus, so they agreed to leave it off the recording list for now.

They recorded all eleven tracks in an afternoon with very little editing. Ms. Beasle told them she would make several copies so they could give them out to their family and friends.

"I can't wait to send one to my mom," Louzanne said excitedly. Then she turned pale and furrowed her brow. "Do you think she'll like it?"

"Yeah, sure she will," Michelle reassured her.

"If not, who cares, right? *You* like it," Scarlett added.

Louzanne's cheeks colored and she smiled. "Yeah."

NINETEEN
BANDS OF RED

The day of the Washington trip arrived. They had been practicing for months, and they were as ready as they were going to be. The festival was not a competition; rather it was a week-long event where youth symphonies from around the country played at various venues throughout the city. Even though it wasn't a competition, Ms. Beasle wanted everyone to do their best and represent Rosemont as the high-quality school for the arts that it was.

The magnet train glided effortlessly along the terrain. Grayson, while not part of the orchestra had volunteered to photograph the trip for the yearbook. With eyes squeezed shut, Scarlett gripped her armrests for dear life. Even though the train was like her parents' second child and she had heard about it for most of her life, she'd never ridden the train and traveling at such high speeds frightened her.

Michelle and Luke talked excitedly. They lived in the city, but they were allowed to stay in the hotel with the rest of the group so they could feel more involved. It would also be more like a real getaway for them. Louzanne remained silent, not quite used to the train either. Louzanne was chosen as a bass player at the last minute, and some people would argue that she only made it because her mother was one of the judges. But if anyone listened to her play, they would know that wasn't true. She really was a good bass player.

"I wonder if there'll be an indoor pool," Michelle said, clapping her hands.

"Yeah, I think the group that got to go last year stayed in a Holiday

Inn that had a waterslide," Luke said. He looked over at Scarlett, whose face was now sheet white, still gripping her armrests as if she were hanging off a cliff. "Hey, you gonna be sick or what? Cause if you are, can you aim over that way," he said, pointing at Michelle. Luke wasn't nearly as nervous and shy around Scarlett anymore. He was even comfortable joking around with her now.

"If I do, I'll be sure to barf on you," she said and stuck her tongue out at him. That got a smile from Grayson, who had been busy snapping pictures of the blurred landscape outside, distracted from the conversation in the cabin.

The symphony festival was to take place over a five day period. A group of thirty-six orchestras from twenty-seven different states would be playing in the city over the course of the week. The Rosemont orchestra was set to play three venues. One was at the John F. Kennedy Center for Performing Arts, another inside the National Geographic Society building, and the third, daytime outdoor performances in front of the Washington Monument. Being that it was late March, the weather was still a little chilly. Scarlett was relieved that two of the three venues were indoors Even though the cold didn't bother her like it used to, she didn't want her hands getting stiff during the performance.

It was Monday morning. Today, the plan was to get checked into the hotel, do some sightseeing, and check out a performance from one of the fellow visiting orchestras in the evening. Rosemont was scheduled to play on Tuesday, Thursday, and Friday. This left plenty of time to tour the city. Scarlett and her friends were even going to fit in dinner with Michelle's parents on Thursday night.

Despite the fact that her parents' main office was in the city and she had been living in Riverstone for six months now, other than the New Year's gala, Scarlett had never been to the city. Her mom wanted her to come with her a few times over the last several months, but Scarlett was so busy with band practice, orchestra, and lessons at the river that she always had an excuse to not get away.

*Bing...Bing...*the electric chime sounded. A female electronic voice announced, "Arrival: Washington Square."

"Wow, I can't believe we're here already," Grayson said as he crinkled his forehead. "My father always sends a car, and it takes forever to get here. This is great!"

Relieved they were no longer moving, Scarlett felt it was safe enough to pry her hands from the armrests. Her fingertips were whitened from the firm grip.

"Right, this is everyone. That's it. Get in line," Ms. Beasle called out to the students, assembling them for a head count. Bo stood next to her as he volunteered to be a chaperone. His dark hair fell down just above his shoulders tied back in an elastic. He was dressed in jeans and a khaki-green button down that matched his eyes. He stared down at Ms. Beasle like she was the only person on earth and she stole glances up at him with a similar expression. Since the pair couldn't seem to keep their eyes off one another, one could assume he was also there to keep Ms. Beasle company as well.

"Luke…Lukie…over here!" a chubby round-faced woman waved. Luke blushed and pretended he didn't hear her. "Luke…yoo-hoo! Luke!" The woman waddled toward them, dragging a tall skinny man with her. "Honestly, I don't know why you took the train into school this morning since you were coming right back."

"I wanted to ride in with my friends, Mom. Michelle did the same thing too."

Scarlett looked over the short fat woman and the tall skinny man. "These are your parents?" she whispered to Luke. *I don't see the resemblance at all.*

"Yeah. Everyone, these are my parents. Mom and Dad, you know Michelle, but this is Scarlett, Louzanne, and Grayson," he said, pointing out each of them.

Mrs. Peters' face lit up. "Scarlett! We've heard so much about you," the woman said as she vigorously pumped Scarlett's hand. Luke's cheeks turned a bright shade of fuchsia. "So nice to meet you all. I'm Diane, and this is my husband, Keith." She gestured to the tall, thin man with red cheeks and a unibrow. "It's spring break for us at our school. We're both teachers, you see, so we had some free time and volunteered to be chaperones. Now we've finally met our Lukie's friends that we've heard so much about." Mrs. Peters clasped her hands. "Except for you, Grayson. I don't remember Luke talking about you. Are you in the band as well?"

"No, ma'am. I'm just the photographer," Grayson said politely.

"He's our friend too, Mom. Remember I stayed at his place on Halloween?"

"Oh yes...yes, of course." she laughed. "I'm so forgetful." Mrs. Peters threw her hands in the air and gave a little snort.

Luke pulled his mom aside and spoke in a hushed tone, but everyone could still overhear, "Mom, I'm glad you're here but try not to smother us, okay? And don't embarrass me in front of my friends."

Whispering, she said, "Oh I know, honey. We don't want to crowd you. We'll keep our distance. I promise, sweetheart." Mrs. Peters raised her two fingers in the air and crossed them over her heart. "Cross my heart, I promise."

Relief washed over his face as he came to this new understanding with his mother. He paused before rejoining the group. "And don't ever call me Lukie around any of my friends, okay?"

Ms. Beasle assembled everyone for a final headcount. When finished, she ushered them up the stairs and onto the sidewalk above, which was only a few steps from their hotel. The hotel was an impressive old stone building that had been updated several times over the years. It didn't have a pool with a waterslide but the proximity to everything fun more than made up for it. They were given an hour to get themselves settled into their rooms before they had to meet in the lobby for a tour of the Capitol Building.

***

From the moment she stepped off the train, Scarlett could feel the vibration of power emanating from the city. This sense was magnified when their bus dropped them off in front of the Capitol Building. Scanning the passersby, she noticed several people had the gray bands wrapped around their necks and wrists but did a double take when she also saw some people with red halos or energy bands, like what she

183

saw on the man at the bank last month. These red bands radiated over the heads and shoulders of some of the people coming and going from the building.

Scarlett blocked out the chatter from her classmates and focused on observing the people with red bands. Dark shadows surrounded these people. As she observed them, she saw that the shadows seemed to writhe around the individuals as if they were living creatures. Scarlett hadn't seen too many dark creatures in Riverstone. With little or no exposure to them other than Vivian's demon, she couldn't even begin to guess what they might be. *I suppose Myles and the Romanaskis keep these kinds of creatures away from Riverstone. What are they?*

They appeared to be like goblins from what she remembered in fairytales, only more serpent-like. The creatures were foul and dark. Scarlett could sense that no good could come from them. And they smelled even worse than the ghoul she had run across last fall. Scarlett coughed and gagged on the stench coming from the serpent-like creatures and had to cover her nose with her sleeve so she wouldn't puke all over the floor.

The creatures seemed to take notice of her right away and hissed as her unknowing group walked past. She counted thirty in total at the Capitol Building, all attached to humans with red bands or halos around their heads and shoulders. The connection puzzled her. She got the sense that their hosts weren't innocent, friendly people either. She had so many questions for Yadira about the people with the gray bands that she had completely forgotten to ask her about the red halo she saw on the man at the bank. In the end, Scarlett questioned if she really saw it since she was on the bus and it was pulling away. She thought it might have been a trick from the sunlight in her eyes, but now she knew for certain that she hadn't imagined the red band and the dark shadow that clung to the man.

Inside, she inched her way closer to two men with red halos, hoping to glean more information by observing as the tour guide droned on about the architecture of the building. She overheard one of them casually talk about how his company held off on negotiations until the locals were sick and starving and had no choice but to concede and then he chuckled to himself. The other man laughed callously as if he'd heard a funny joke. "That was a smart move, Warren. If only my problem with the Wrigleys would have gone so smoothly."

At the sound of her last name, Scarlett's ears perked up. The man had gray sallow skin, and sparse black hair combed over the middle of his head in an attempt to cover his bald spot. *He had something to do with the attack on my mother!* The red bands radiated around the men's heads and shoulders as they spoke. The creatures that lurked about them were particularly hideous and gave off a terrible stench.

The sallow skinned man continued, "No matter. We're meeting this afternoon to determine the next steps for the train."

At first, she was stunned. Then realization set in. *This man meant for my mother to die and he's disappointed that she didn't!* A storm brewed in her, making her angrier than she'd ever felt before. Scarlett could no longer control her emotions as she set her eyes on him. A fiery rage erupted from the pit of her stomach that consumed her. Her eyes burned into him. The lights in the Capitol Building began to flicker, and the chandeliers shook. Scarlett felt the vibrations beneath her and looked to the ground below her to find that it too was shaking. She looked around and realized that she was no longer in control of her Juma. It had taken on a fiery red color and had been cast out fifteen feet in front of her, wrapping itself around the vile man like a python.

The man reached for his collar, coughing and wheezing violently as if he were choking and couldn't breathe. She trained her eyes on him again. *I hate you,* was the only thought that came to Scarlett's mind. Threatened by the assault, the creatures that clung to these men hissed at her as she stood there glaring at the man with the greasy comb-over. The creatures didn't frighten her. Enraged, her stomach burned and the taste of acid and metal in her mouth only made her angrier.

The hissing turned to screeching as the serpent-like creatures desperately grasped for her, but she wasn't close enough for them to reach. It seemed the creatures couldn't lose contact with their hosts, as if they were to let go, they would disappear back to wherever foul creatures went.

They screeched and wailed louder until the sound was deafening. This drew the attention of the other dark creatures in the Capitol Building, and they too began to screech. The building continued to shake, and the sound of the screeching made her ears ring. She covered them to drown out the sound, but her eyes remained fixed on the man.

"Uggh. What's that hideous noise?" Louzanne said, covering her ears and looking around for its source. She looked down at the floor trembling beneath her.

"I think it's electrical interference of some sort. Maybe from a speaker system," Ms. Beasle explained as she scanned the room frantically. Catching sight of Scarlett standing only a few feet away from the red-banded men and their hideous creatures, she hurried over to her.

Mostly everyone else in the area seemed to be unfazed by the commotion, although some took notice of the vibrations and swaying chandeliers. But Grayson seemed to know better. He had been practicing with his new talents and could almost see the creatures through the veil now. He drew nearer to Scarlett as if to protect her, while Scarlett stood there in a trancelike state, staring at the man who spoke of her parents. Her fiery Juma had completely engulfed the man. Her Juma had such a choke hold on him; he could no longer cough, his face turned purple, and he fell to his knees.

The red haloed man, the greasy comb-over called Warren, reached to help his colleague. "Are you all-right? Should I call an ambulance?"

Ms. Beasle grabbed Scarlett by the arm. "Come with me, dear. I want to make sure you know where the ladies' room is," she said sweetly, as if Scarlett wasn't doing anything wrong. Forcefully, Ms. Beasle dragged her away, breaking the hold her Juma had on the evil man and his creature as she went. As her energy unraveled from his throat, the man coughed and sputtered. "I must have forgotten to take my medication this morning," the greasy comb-over said, and his colleague helped him to his feet.

Scarlett tried to shake free of Ms. Beasle, but she was deceivingly strong for a woman of her size. Ms. Beasle drug her to an empty corridor and held her still.

"Let me go! He's the one who planned the attack on my mother!" she screamed.

She continued to embrace Scarlett. "Shhh now. Killing him won't solve the problem. Everyone has a boss; he didn't act alone. He was merely a henchman. Killing him will only damage your soul. It will serve no other purpose. Someone else, maybe someone even worse, would only pick up where he left off. You need to remain calm."

Her words only served to further enrage Scarlett. "CALM? HOW CAN I BE CALM? He was involved in my mother's shooting. What if I wasn't there to heal her? I would have lost her and my baby brother!"

Ms. Beasle looked around the corridor to make sure no one could overhear their unusual conversation. "I know, hon. I know. We'll get them, but now is not the time to draw attention. Please trust me. All will work out as it should. I know that it's very hard to understand but please let it be for now."

Scarlett never really had a chance to cry after what happened to her mother. The thought of what would have happened if the attack was planned on the train or while Mrs. Wrigley was at work where Scarlett was too far away to help terrified her. Unable to break free of Ms. Beasle, she broke down and cried while Ms. Beasle held her and cooed and stroked her hair. Sobs wracked her ribcage as she wailed uncontrollably. She wept out her fears for her mother. She cried for the poor mother who couldn't afford to spend time with her children and the rest of the people out there with gray bands bringing them down. She even wept for the bad elf Felix McCaan lying in a shallow grave back in Indiana.

After several minutes of sobbing, she found her voice. "Did I really almost kill him?" she asked through sniffles and sobs.

"Yes."

"I didn't know what I was doing. I only knew that I hated him for what he did and I wanted to stop him from hurting anyone again. I didn't know I could kill someone just by getting angry."

"I wasn't sure you could either, dear, but that's why Myles has been working with you to make sure you are safe and to make sure others are safe around you."

Puffy eyed and blotchy faced, Scarlett sniffed and blew her nose on the tissue Ms. Beasle offered. "I don't really want to kill anyone. I wouldn't mind it if that man died but I'll try to control myself better next time."

Ms. Beasle hugged her again. "I know you will. Come, let's go find the group. We're going to a cool restaurant for lunch. They play live jazz music. You'll love it!"

When they returned to the group, the tour guide was still talking about the architecture of the building. Grayson took her hand. "Are you okay?" Scarlett nodded, her eyes still puffy from crying. The ghoulish looking man stood where Scarlett left him, looking shaken, but still talking to his colleague. Scarlett had better control of herself now. She wasn't letting any of her energy out, but she kept her eyes trained on him. The man began to walk away. She knew Ms. Beasle was right, but she couldn't just let it go and trust blindly that justice would be served. Determined to at least find out more about the man, Scarlett excused herself to go to the restroom then snuck past security and took off to follow him.

The greasy haired man walked down a corridor where he took a flight of stairs down to the basement. Then he walked through a set of doors and onto a subway platform. Scarlett kept her distance, scared he would notice her. He got on the train when it stopped at the platform. Scarlett had no idea where he was going, but she wasn't going let him get away—not without knowing his name or who he worked for. She would get in trouble for leaving the group, but it would be worth it. She hopped on the subway car. To avoid being noticed, she sat on the opposite end.

When the train came to a stop, the man got out and took the stairs up two flights and into a hallway lined with offices. He entered one of them. Scarlett, still keeping her distance, heard a man's voice. "Good morning, Mr. Matthews. Your files are ready for you."

"Thank you, Jack," his slithery voice replied.

Scarlett looked at the nameplate on the door: Senator Percival Matthews. She'd heard of this guy on the news and overheard her parents talking about him sometimes. Senator Matthews was among the strongest opposition her parents faced for getting funding and support for the magnet train. She remembered Ms. Beasle's words: *"He works for someone."* She wondered who he worked for and how many other people were involved in the plot to kill her mother. *I need to find out more, but I'm gonna need help.* She made it back just as the students were piling onto the bus.

"Where were you?" Ms. Beasle asked with her hands on her hips. The wind whipped her fluffy blonde hair around her face.

"I...went to look for a restroom but I guess I got lost. Sorry."

Michelle shot her a look with one raised eyebrow. "I'll tell you later," Scarlett mouthed.

The restaurant was noisy, and Scarlett made sure they sat far enough away from the adults. When Michelle, Louzanne, Luke, and Grayson sat down around her, she began, "I need your help. I can't do this by myself. I need to tell you the truth about me. I'm kind of a freak. There are people who live in Riverstone who are like me. Ms. Beasle is one of them."

The music was so loud it drowned out her words. Michelle said, "Scarlett, what are you talking about? I can't understand what you're saying."

Looking around for a quiet place to talk, Scarlett pointed to the back of the restaurant. "Meet me in the alley." Scarlett got up first. She walked through the kitchen and into the back alley. One by one, Louzanne, Michelle, Luke, and Grayson slipped away from the lunch group and joined her. Scarlett stood in front of a dumpster waiting for them.

"Look," Scarlett said. "I've been keeping something from you. I've been keeping it from you because I was told it was safer to keep people in the dark than for them to know the truth, but now I need help. My parents are in danger, and I can't just leave it up to the adults to sort things out. I just can't." She shook her head adamantly.

Scarlett took a deep breath. *Okay, here I go.* "I can do things, and I can make things happen, and I see things that are real that no one else really sees." While Grayson already knew and Louzanne already had a clue because Scarlett could see and communicate with ghosts just like her, she wasn't quite sure how Michelle and Luke were going to react.

"I have a lot of energy," she continued. "I don't mean that I'm hyper. I mean metaphysical energy. This can be used to do things, like make things move or heal someone if they're hurt. They call it Juma. I mean, everybody has it. It's kinda like your life force, but some just have more of it, I guess. So, anyway, the world isn't really how you see it. There's magic in the world and magical creatures only you can't see any of it because there is this veil that separates people from it."

No one said anything. They just stood there with the wind howling through the back alley. Nor did anyone think to bring their coats, by the way they shivered and rubbed their hands together for warmth.

Scarlett continued, "For example, fairies are real. They live beneath the veil."

"Scarlett, are you feeling okay? You were gone a long time at the Capitol. Did you fall and hit your head?" Michelle reached for Scarlett's hand to start pulling her back inside.

But Scarlett put her hand out to stop her. "I'll show you." She concentrated for a minute and slowly let out her Juma, bit by bit, until Snuke, who fluttered behind Scarlett's shoulder, was clearly visible to them all. "See, I have this thing where I can magnify your Juma so you can see beneath the veil."

Grayson stood in awe at her true form. Tiny beautiful Snuke with her long blue hair and delicate features. "Wow. I could only make out an outline before, but now I really see her!" Snuke gasped at the realization that she could be seen and disappeared in a *poof* of green sparkles.

"Snuke, get back here." Snuke's orders were to assist and protect Scarlett in any way. Since she couldn't directly disobey orders from

Scarlett, she reappeared and reluctantly waved at the group.

"Whoa!" Michelle approached the tiny fairy and held out her hand.

Snuke flitted over to Michelle and perched on her finger. "Hello, Michelle."

"You know my name?" Michelle's jaw dropped.

"Yes, you're a good friend of Scarlett's. Of course, I know your name. I see you every day at school."

"So umm...you just follow us to school?" Louzanne asked.

"I follow *Scarlett* to school," Snuke corrected.

"So what are you, like her fairy godmother or something?" Louzanne asked.

"Sort of. I'm one of them."

"How many of you are there?" Louzanne asked.

"There are thousands of us, but not as many as there once was. Three of us look over Scarlett."

"Okay, guys. Like I was saying, I have this energy that has a way of breaking down the veil so other people can see the magic in the world. It also enables me to do other things."

Grayson chimed in, "It's true. I followed Scarlett one weekend, and Mrs. Goodspeed was teaching her how to heal, and there's this hobo who's really like a master of magic, but he disguises himself as this weak old man, and there are these gypsies—Bo is one of them." The rest of the group's eyes began to glaze over, and they crinkled their foreheads. It was hard to follow what Grayson was trying to tell them.

"Anyway," he continued, "I scared her. She thought I was an attacker and she flew at me and knocked me down a ravine, and I hit my head. I was bleeding, and I probably would've died if she hadn't healed me. Only she did a little more than heal me...she improved me. I'm faster, stronger, and I can see through the veil as she describes it, or at least a little bit."

From the looks on her friends' faces, this information was all too much to believe even for Louzanne, a psychic and far more used to the weird and unusual.

Frustrated, Grayson reached for a glass bottle that lay next to the dumpster and smashed it on the concrete, leaving only a sharp and jagged neck. With the end he sliced open the inside of his forearm, creating a giant gash.

"Go on Scarlett, show them. Heal me." His arm spurted blood all over the concrete.

"Grayson!" she began to yell at him for hurting himself, but when she realized how much blood he was losing, she didn't waste another second. She rubbed her palms together to form healing balls of energy and passed them over the wound several times until it closed. When it healed, Scarlett punched him in the arm as hard as she could. "Don't ever do that again!"

Grayson laughed, rubbing his arm. "That's gonna leave a nasty bruise."

"Good."

"Now do you believe her?"

The rest of the group just stood rooted to the spot with their mouths gaping open.

"Okay, anyway," Scarlett continued. "Around Christmas time someone tried to kill my mother. They shot her during dinner. I was home, so I healed her and Mrs. Goodspeed came right away to make sure I did it right—she's a healer by the way—I did, Thank God. But anyway, no one knows about it because Myles—the hobo guy that Grayson told you about—wiped their memory. Yeah, he can do that, but, don't worry, I can't. I least I don't think I can."

"Oh my God, Scarlett!" Finding her ability to move and speak, Michelle rushed to her side. "You must have been so scared."

"I was, and I am. The attack had nothing to do with me or fairies or magic. It was about their work. Someone doesn't want the magnet train to expand across America so badly that they were willing to murder my mother to stop it."

"Do you know who?" Michelle asked.

"Senator Percival Matthews was involved. I overheard him talking to another man today about it."

Michelle sucked in a breath. "My dad can't stand him."

"I followed him today. That's where I went—to find out who he was. But I don't think he's acting alone. He's working for someone or a group of someones that'll do anything to stop my parents' work. This trip is my best chance to find out more, but I can't be sneaking off alone all the time. Michelle, your dad's a senator. You must know your way around the Capitol really well. I was hoping you guys could help me find out more."

"Of course we're going to help," Michelle reassured her. Louzanne, Luke, and Grayson all nodded.

"Good." Scarlett smiled, relieved to know they didn't think she was crazy. "Later today, he's supposed to have a meeting. I overheard him say they were going to meet and determine 'the next steps'. I want to see if I can hang around his office and see who he meets. Snuke, you can go right into the meeting and eavesdrop, can't you?"

"I can, but I can't leave you. Honeybee'll have my wings clipped if I do."

"Well, I can sneak around outside unnoticed while you eavesdrop. I'll be right outside so you're technically not leaving me and you won't get in trouble, and I'll be careful not to get noticed," Scarlett said convincingly.

"But what if someone catches you sneaking around?" Snuke protested.

Michelle grinned. "You won't have to worry about that. My dad's office is down the hall. We can pretend we're visiting him."

"Okay…then we have a plan," Snuke reluctantly agreed.

"Let's go back before we're missed." Scarlett gestured for them to go back inside. She pulled in her Juma, so Snuke became once again invisible, or at least invisible to most.

They each slipped back into the restaurant. Scarlett sat in between Luke and his mom, who tapped her fingers on the table and swayed side to side to the music.

"Luke is such a talented boy. We were amazed to find out what he could do at such a young age."

"Mom, you're embarrassing me," Luke warned.

"Yes, he's an amazing piano player," Scarlett agreed.

Mrs. Peters told them about how the only way they were able to potty train Luke was by parking it in the front of his baby piano. "He would sit there for hours pecking out notes, so eventually, he was bound to need the potty." Mrs. Peters snorted. Luke's face flushed a bright cherry shade of red, and he shot his mother an admonishing glare.

During dessert, when everyone else was distracted, Luke whispered in her ear, "Grayson didn't have to cut his arm for me to believe you. I see things too."

Scarlett just about choked on her strawberry shortcake. "What? Why didn't you ever tell me?"

"I never got the chance, and I didn't know what to say. I knew you were special because I can see your energy but I didn't know how much you were aware of it. I couldn't exactly go up to you and say 'Your energy is strong and I think you're special'. What if you weren't aware of your abilities? You would've thought I was a weirdo and wouldn't have been my friend." He looked down at this shoes.

"Can you do things?" she asked.

Luke thought about her question. "Umm...I'm not sure. I can read people. I mean, I can feel their energy and tell if they're mostly good or bad and I've seen the creatures that lurk about people. I knew you had fairies around you all the time. But other than that, I've never really tried to do anything. I guess I can't do anything else."

"How long have been able to see things?" she asked.

"All my life. But it's definitely intensified since I met you. I used to see things as if through a haze but now I see them much clearer."

"Hmm." *I intensified Grayson's abilities when I healed him, and Louzanne said her abilities became stronger when I came to town, so I guess it's not a stretch that I strengthened Luke's ability to see through the veil too.* Though this shouldn't have come as much of a surprise to Scarlett since Myles, Precious, Snuke, and Honeybee had told her all along she had this effect on people, but it was still hard for her to believe.

"Well, I'm glad you told me. It's lonely keeping things to yourself."

She squeezed his hand, which made him blush even more.

TWENTY
THE MARK OF THE DAMNED

After lunch, the group took the bus back to the hotel. They had free time to hang out or shop or do whatever they wanted—within reason and with the accompaniment of a chaperone—until they had to meet for dinner at seven. After dinner, the entire group was going to a concert performed by the students from Juilliard, and Scarlett thought it was more than a little intimidating that they would be performing in the same festival as Juilliard students. As soon as they made it to the hotel, Scarlett and her friends got on a shuttle bus right back to the Capitol Building.

They managed to get away without a chaperone after Michelle explained to Ms. Beasle that they were going to visit her father at work so he could give them a personal lesson on how laws were passed. "I'm happy to see you kids take an interest in government. Not enough young people do if you ask me," said Ms. Beasle, reluctantly allowing them to go without a chaperone since the shuttle was taking them directly there and back and the number of available chaperones was already stretched thin. She glanced at Snuke, making eye contact.

Snuke placed her hand over her heart. "I'll protect them with my life," she said with a bow.

They made it just in time to see Senator Matthews step out of his office and walk into a conference room down the hall. To their luck, the conference room was located directly across from Michelle's father's office. The view of the people coming and going from the room couldn't get any better if Scarlett had planned it that way. They stood outside of Mr. Newbery's office waiting for his three p.m. meeting to be over. Michelle was a familiar face around here, making it less conspicuous that the senator's daughter may have a bunch of her friends hanging about the hallway.

A few minutes later, another man entered the conference room, then another, then another until eleven men and one woman were gathered. They dressed expensively, and they all had red halos around their heads except for two; they were the last two to enter the room: a tall, thin man and a fashionably dressed woman. Both gave off no energy whatsoever. The man's dark hair and pale skin made him look reptilian. The tall woman was also pale and thin. She wore her hair tucked up inside a scarf that wrapped around her head and fastened in the front with a large ruby brooch. She wore large dark sunglasses, so Scarlett couldn't see her eyes. Scarlett tried to get a read on their energy, but it was as if their life force had gone dark. They emanated nothing but cold. As the man brushed past Scarlett, her breath caught in her throat, and she began to shiver.

Mr. Newbery emerged from his office with another man and walked him to the elevator. Mr. Newbery was a portly man with pink skin and white wispy hair. "Thanks for coming, Bob. We'll pick up where we left off next month. Say 'hi' to Pricilla for me." He shook the man's hand. "Safe flight back!" Mr. Newbery looked down the hall as he waved goodbye to his visitor and saw the various people that were entering the conference room. "Wow, Becky. Did I miss something? Is there a summit in town?" he called back to his administrator.

"No, sir," she replied from her desk.

"Well, some of the wealthiest people in the world just went into that conference room." Mr. Newbery scratched his head and stood there for a moment looking perplexed. Scarlett managed to get a look inside the conference room before they closed the door. It was a small dingy room tucked deep in the bowels of the Capitol, probably used primarily for office staff to hold planning meetings or potluck lunches—certainly not a suitable place to host some the world's most powerful people. Unless, they didn't want to be seen.

Mr. Newbery recognized his daughter from the crowd of teenagers assembled outside his office and a broad smile crossed his face. "Michelle! What are you doing here? Why aren't you in school?"

"My school is performing in the city this week. I'm staying at the hotel with my friends, remember?"

"Er…yes, of course." He cleared his throat. "Your mother and I are going tomorrow night to watch, isn't it?"

Michelle rolled her eyes. "Yes, Dad. Tomorrow and Thursday and Friday. Mom said you're going to them all."

"Oh, okay." Mr. Newbery didn't appear to know that his calendar was already planned out for him but he didn't seem to mind. By the way his eyes softened when he looked at Michelle, Scarlett could tell he really loved his daughter and probably loved spending as much time with his family as possible.

"So uh…what are you doing here?" he asked, looking around at her friends.

"Oh, nothing. We had some free time this afternoon, so I wanted to show my friends where you work. You know, show you off a little…my dad the senator," Michelle said with a nervous laugh and patted her dad on the back. Michelle knew how to stroke her father's ego. Mr. Newbery's chest puffed out with pride.

"Er…ok. Hello there. What's your name?" He reached out to shake Luke's hand.

"Dad, that's Luke, and you've met him before—several times. I ride the train to school with him every morning."

"Of course." Mr. Newbery flushed with embarrassment. "You've gotten taller since I last saw you. Good to see you. And who is this lovely young lady?"

"That's Louzanne. She's a second year. She plays bass and is also in our band."

Then Michelle pointed to Grayson. "This is Grayson. He's a third year. He's just a groupie—he doesn't play any music," she said as she winked at her friend.

"I'm here as the school photographer to document the field trip for the yearbook, sir," he explained.

"Grayson Blackwell, am I right?" Mr. Newbery asked.

"Yes, sir."

"I knew I recognized you. Your father is one of my campaign contributors."

"Yes, I know. Keep up the good work, sir," Grayson said respectfully.

Michelle then introduced Scarlett, "She plays guitar and sings a lot of the songs that we wrote for our band." Mr. Newbery smiled and nodded at Scarlett. She smiled back and waved.

"They have a guitar in the orchestra?" he asked.

"No, she plays violin in the orchestra. She plays guitar in the band we started last fall, Dad."

Mr. Newbery shook his head. "Oh yeah, right. Michelle, you have so much on the go, between you and your sister, I can't keep track. Good thing your mother has a head for all these activities and commitments, otherwise I'd never make an appointment or event on time." He gave Luke a slap on the back. "You know what I mean."

"Dad, maybe you can show us this wing and tell us about the people who work here."

"Oh um…okay." He gestured for them to go into his office. "Well there's Vickey and Mike here, they handle requests from constituents, and then there's Becky who handles my appointments and email."

"Dad, I meant the other senators who keep offices in this hall."

"Well, there are only two in this part. There's me and Percival Matthews." Mr. Newbery said his name as if he were sucking on a lemon.

"Does he spend much time in this office?"

"No, actually, this isn't his main office. He has a secretary down here, and he holds meetings at this location from time to time." Mr. Newbery's eyes drifted to the occupied conference room.

"Dad, who were all those people that went in there?" Michelle asked innocently. "They looked really important."

"Well, honey, I recognized a lot of them. There was Harold Miller who is majority shareholder of Dynatam Corporation, the automotive and energy conglomerate, Sir Lionus Spence of British Royal Petroleum and a major player in finance and banking and his brother Reginald Spence, Prince Abuniabi from Saudi Arabia…I thought I saw Claire Mitchell, the last living relative of the Mitchell family and majority shareholder of the American National Oil Company, Selkirk bank, and NOS Industries. There was Agar and Ignid Hans of the Royal Dutch Petroleum Corporation and a few others. I can't quite name them all right now." Mr. Newbery scratched his head, still looking puzzled as to why so many of them were gathered in the dingy little conference room.

"Oh, so they all own oil companies then?"

"Among other things, from the group I saw, it looks that way, honey. Why?"

"Nothing, Dad. Just curious and making conversation. They looked so interesting, and you seem to know everybody. I thought you might know them all."

Mr. Newbery appeared flattered by her compliment as his chest puffed out again. "I'll have to think of the names of the others that I saw."

They tried to keep him talking until the meeting was over so Snuke could eavesdrop on the whole thing. Scarlett kept her eye on the hallway for any activity. Grayson asked Mr. Newbery some questions on the latest bill he was working on. Mr. Newbery talked excitedly about his latest project to drive down tuition rates so universities could be more accessible for everyone. "It's quite a project. I hope to make some headway with it." Then Mr. Newbery talked on and on about wage freezes and spending cuts for another twenty-five minutes or so.

Scarlett remained in Mr. Newbery's office doorway to keep an eye on anyone coming and going from the conference room. Then people began filing out of the room. None of the participants made polite conversation or even looked at one another as they left. They simply scurried away like rats on a sinking ship.

The woman's high heels clicked on the tile floor as she walked toward the elevator. Scarlett couldn't take her eyes from the thin, pale woman, amazed how she couldn't read anything from her. When the elevator door opened, the woman stepped inside and turned and faced Scarlett. A tendril of hair fell from the woman's scarf. At second glance, Scarlett's jaw dropped in horror. It wasn't a lock of hair at all, rather it was a thin snake, writhing and hissing softly. The woman quickly tucked the serpent back inside her headscarf. She still wore her dark glasses, even though it wasn't bright in the lower level corridor. Scarlett couldn't see her eyes. As the elevator door closed, the ruby brooch on her headscarf glowed brightly for a moment and then the woman was gone.

Snuke returned looking ashen. "Well?" Scarlett asked as she met her out in the hall where no one could overhear.

"They didn't come out and reveal their plans, but they definitely don't want the magnet train to be a success. They kept talking about missing their chance and the approval phase being over and about there being too much public support for it now. They said their only opening was on proving there are safety concerns."

"Safety concerns?" Scarlett knew a lot about the safety features of the train since her parents couldn't stop talking about them. *But the train has so many fail-safes,* she thought. *Obstruction detection, reverse pull, quick stop, and high impact technology—on impact the interior cabin releases a high-density foam to encapsulate passengers while allowing them to breathe.* "What could go wrong?" Then she remembered that these were murderous people. "They plan to sabotage the train! We need to get back." She raced into Mr. Newbery's office. He was still talking about his bill. "Ms. Beasle wants us back early to help her organize before dinner. We need to get back now," she announced to the group breathlessly. "It was so nice meeting you, Mr. Newbery. See you at dinner on Thursday."

"Er yes…yes, of course. Thursday, huh? Thanks for stopping by." Clearly, Mr. Newbery had forgotten about dinner as well. "Bye, kids. Come visit anytime," he said as he walked them out of his office and waved goodbye as they piled into the elevator.

"They're going to sabotage the magnet train," Scarlett told them when the door closed. "We need to tell Ms. Beasle right now. She'll know what to do. I gotta tell Myles." But she was pretty sure Myles didn't have a phone. "Snuke, can you get Precious and Honeybee and tell one of them to get in touch with Myles? Tell them what you overheard." Snuke disappeared in a *poof* of green sparkles and returned minutes later as they were getting on the shuttle bus.

"Myles is on his way."

"Good. Thanks, Snuke." Scarlett turned to her friends. "You guys better make yourselves scarce when he comes. Otherwise, he might wipe your memory, and I need you."

***

"How did you come by this information Scarlett?" Ms. Beasle met her in the hotel lobby along with Precious and Honeybee.

"I had Snuke eavesdrop on a meeting," she explained with downcast eyes, expecting Ms. Beasle to be furious for not listening to her and pursuing Senator Matthews against her direction.

Ms. Beasle sighed, looking pale and stricken. "Good thing you didn't listen to me, Scarlett. I apologize. Sometimes when you try to protect someone, you end up overlooking what's important. We're lucky you found out about this."

"Yadira had not predicted this, nor could I foresee this plan," Myles said from behind her. Scarlett looked around to see what direction he came from. It was as if he appeared out of thin air.

"What are we going to do, Myles?"

"Well, Precious, Snuke, and Honeybee aren't the only fairies in the world. I'll get the Sonoa sisters from Scotland here. They're a bit ornery but very capable. In the meantime, we'll have Pesha and Bioko take jobs on the train and act as lookouts. Bioko's eldest boy is old enough now. He can get a job as an attendant on one of the trains as well. They'll keep an eye on things for now until we have reinforcements. I'll send them at once." Myles disappeared. Scarlett looked all around to see where he went. Then he reappeared moments later with his brow less furrowed.

Scarlett crinkled her forehead, perplexed over how he did that, but too concerned over the current events to ask. "This is just awful. Myles, how do we stop this?"

"Well, the real answer is changing the hearts of people in this world who do evil and will do anything for money and power. But that is a subject for another day." His sparkling blue eyes smiled at her as he patted her hand. "We'll have the trains guarded, my child. Don't fret. You and the people you care about will be kept safe."

Myles looked out of place against the backdrop of the sophisticated bustling city. Scarlett thought of him as her wise old friend who lived by the river and always pictured him outdoors close to nature or sitting in his armchair by the fire in his cabin. But he was many centuries old and must have lived in many places over the years—including big cities. He was probably more sophisticated than anyone else in the world yet he chose to live in Riverstone in a tiny cabin in the woods.

"While I'm in town, may I join you all for dinner and the show?" he asked.

"Of course you can," said Ms. Beasle. "We'd be honored for you to spend your evening with us."

Myles sighed. "Ahh, it's been so long since I've enjoyed a symphony."

***

Dinner was pretty casual, but that was to be expected when you're hosting a group of teenagers. Myles was dressed for a night at the symphony in a tuxedo with his hair pulled back neatly from his face. Scarlett was surprised at how refined he looked when he wasn't dressed like a hobo and hunched over an open fire.

The John F Kennedy Center for Performing Arts was packed. Scarlett looked around the room and recognized some of the faces as the people she saw at the Capitol today. Unfortunately, she didn't see any of the people who were in the clandestine meeting hosted by Senator Matthews. Vickey and Mike, Mr. Newbery's assistants, were there and a few other faces she recognized as members of congress.

There were a few people there that had the red bands emanating from their heads while many others had the usual gray bands around their neck and wrists that she had become accustomed to seeing. And there were some adults that didn't have any bands at all. These people appeared to be particularly at peace. Myles, Ms. Beasle, Bo, and Luke's parents were among these people who didn't appear to have energy blockages.

The lights dimmed, and the symphony began its opening notes. Because Scarlett was usually the one performing, she never really paid attention to the way music affected people, especially since she acquired the ability to read people's energy. The music was moving and powerful. She scanned the crowd to see the changes in auras as the tempo and dynamics changed. She looked over to one woman she had previously seen with thick opaque gray bands around her throat and wrists. Now she saw none. Only a soft white glow moving around the woman's body. Her cheeks were wet; the music had moved her to tears. *Interesting.*

She looked to another person whom she had clearly seen gray bands around, and as the music played, he too was free of them. She then checked out several more people. *The gray bands are gone!* She looked for the people with red halos and ghoulish serpent-like smelly creatures hanging about them. While the red bands were still visible, they were greatly diminished, and the creatures appeared to be subdued. They looked weakened and distressed as if an invisible force was working to remove them. Scarlett could see them writhing and fighting to hang onto their hosts. They clung to the individuals as if at any moment the music was powerful enough to cast them out.

Myles observed her. He leaned in and whispered, "You see how a little bit of beauty and joy can set a person free for a while?" She nodded. Yes, she could see it. She could also tell Myles was straining himself so as not to let his energy out or block anyone else's energy.

"Myles, why do some people have red halos over their heads?"

Myles sighed. "Ahh, so you see it now? That is a deeper and darker form of slavery, my dear. That is the mark of the damned. They have given up a part of their soul in pursuit of their desires."

Scarlett thought about what he said. "What do you mean?"

"They have done terrible deeds or turned their backs on an essential part of their better nature. These people are not like the others. They tend to be very powerful and dangerous."

"Are those snakes or goblins?" She gestured to the serpent-like creatures that clung to the red haloed people.

"Not in their true form. They are the energy force of darklings that have chosen the path of evil."

"Why are there no darklings in Riverstone?"

"We guard Riverstone against the damned and the darklings. For a darkling to roam free in this realm is not easy. The Mother made sure of it before she was put in bondage. They can only survive in this realm by staying close to their energy source—the souls of the damned." Myles pointed to the people with red halos. Many of them were beautiful. They gave the appearance of being happy. Knowing that they had done horrible things to earn their red bands, Scarlett should've felt revulsion and hatred towards these people, but instead, she found herself feeling sad for them.

"Myles?" she whispered.

"Yes?"

"Can the damned be redeemed?"

Myles thought about this for a while. "I suppose anything is possible."

"Who is the Mother? Why was she put in bondage? Who put her there?"

Myles patted her hand. "You're missing the performance." He pointed to the symphony. Scarlett had so many questions, but she knew from the thin white line around his lips and the look on his face that she would get nothing more out of him tonight and resumed watching the concert.

After the performance, Scarlett was convinced that they couldn't possibly outperform Juilliard but felt flattered to even be in the same festival.

***

The next day, it was Rosemont's turn to perform at the Kennedy Center. They had performances scheduled for noon, two p.m., and nine p.m. Preoccupied with the potential threat to the magnet train, Scarlett didn't feel like doing the early morning White House tour with the rest of the group. Rather, she paced the floor of the hotel room worrying a groove into the carpet. Her parents were riding the train this morning for a work meeting then staying in the city until after Scarlett's evening show. She paced the floor until Myles knocked on the door and informed her that the rail lines had been secured. The Sonoa sisters had arrived and were each assigned a rail line, along with Pesha, Bioko, and Franco Romanaski.

"Thirty more have joined security detail. Some will be disguised as passengers, others as train staff. They'll ride the trains day and night looking for potential threats. You can rest your head, young one. Your trains are safe."

With tears in her eyes, Scarlett let out a sigh of relief and wrapped her arms around Myles. "Thank you," she whispered. He still smelled like the woods, like hickory and evergreen. Myles patted her head. He left shortly after, explaining that he had urgent business but would see her when she got back this weekend. Relieved that her parents would be safe, she felt she could eat something. She made her way to the café downstairs to get some breakfast.

Scarlett entered the café to find Luke sipping a cup of coffee and eating a bagel. He was reading the newspaper and brushing away his blond curls that kept falling into his eyes. "You made the paper this morning," he said without even looking up at her. "See?" He pointed out the article.

Page two on the second column read:

Headline: Tremors Erupt in Capitol Building Monday Morning: Mild tremors could be felt in the Capitol at eleven a.m. Monday morning. "Earthquakes can happen anywhere in the world, although highly unusual in this region," explained leading geologist Todd Wampervich. It is not anticipated that DC should expect any that would cause serious damage.

She knew she caused the tremors when she lost control of herself. *How am I gonna explain this without freaking him out?* She opted to ignore the article and his comment completely. "Your parents let you drink coffee?" she asked, changing the subject.

Luke studied her through his forest green eyes. Scarlett had never noticed how intense nor how beautiful they were. Then he laughed and shook his head. "No, they think it will stunt my growth, but they're not here, are they?" He winked at her and took another sip. *I suppose Mom and Dad would never know either, but I keep so much from them already. I don't think I can handle any more lies.*

"Yeah, I guess. Mine don't let me drink it either. What's good here?"

"Uh, I don't know. I had the bagel and fruit cup."

Scarlett eyed the menu. The Belgian waffle served with a side of fruit looked delicious. After she placed her order, she asked, "So, how come you're not with the others?"

"I don't know. I figured you would be too worried about the trains, so I decided to stay back and hang out with you."

Scarlett narrowed her eyes. "How did you know?"

Luke shrugged. "I don't know. I just know."

"Well, I was really worried. I was worried sick, but Myles told me they have extra security now and he assures me the trains are safe. I have no reason not to believe him, but I'm still a little concerned."

"Me too. That's how I get to school every day."

"Did your parents go on the tour?"

"Yeah, they had to; they signed up as chaperones."

"I like your family. They're really sweet. It's funny; you don't look anything like them," she said, examining his features.

Luke smiled sheepishly. "That's because I was adopted."

"Oh, do you know your biological parents?"

"No, they died in a boating accident. I was with them at the time, but I survived somehow. I washed ashore, and some swimmers found me."

"Oh Luke, that's horrible. I'm so sorry."

"It's okay. I was only a baby. I don't even remember them. My adopted parents are great. They love me, and I love them. I'm really lucky."

Not knowing what else to say, Scarlett ate her breakfast in silence. The smell of maple syrup proved to be too much for Snuke and Precious. Scarlett scanned the café for Honeybee, but she was nowhere to be found. *Must be on urgent business with Myles.* The other two kept fluttering over Scarlett's breakfast, sniffing it euphorically until Scarlett gave in and invited them to help themselves. Fairies only had reservations about nicking food when the person could see them doing it. They tended to be rather shy like that. If she didn't have the ability to see fairies, her waffle would have been half gone by now. But Scarlett didn't mind. She delighted in seeing how much they enjoyed sweets. It was a real treat for Scarlett because she knew Luke could also see them. He watched the spectacle with an amused expression.

"They love you, you know."

"Yeah, I think they do. I've only really known them since my birthday last year, but they've known me all my life. I love them too," she said, only now realizing how much they had come to mean to her over the past several months.

Scarlett's phone rang. It was her mother telling her that they arrived in the city and were off to a meeting but would catch up with her later that night. Scarlett checked the time on her phone. They had three hours to kill before they had to be at the concert hall.

"Hey, there's a movie theatre around the corner. I thought I saw they had morning shows. Do you want to catch a movie?" Luke asked.

Scarlett thought that was a perfect idea.

TWENTY-ONE
TREMORS

Preoccupied with her performance, Scarlett couldn't pay attention to what effect the music might have had on people's energy. She had no idea how they compared to last night's show from Juilliard, but based on the applause afterwards, she guessed they did all right. When the lights came on after the last song, she could see her parents giving a standing ovation. Nick stuck to Mrs. Wrigley's side as he had been since December's incident.

By now, Mrs. Wrigley's pregnancy was beginning to show. Her belly wasn't enormous yet and not quite to the point where strangers wanted to come up to touch, but large enough to show that she was visibly pregnant. Scarlett's parents gave her a big hug after the performance and raved about how wonderful everyone did. They introduced themselves to the Peters and Newberys, who were also in attendance. Louzanne's mother was on tour, and her aunt couldn't get the time off work to make the trip from Louisiana, so neither were available. Louzanne didn't seem bothered by it. She was probably used to being on her own, but Scarlett wondered how much of it was just putting on a brave face.

Nick patted Scarlett on the hand—he was too small to reach up and pat her on the back. "Beautiful. Just beautiful, kid," he said and dabbed the corners of his eyes with a handkerchief. She managed to catch up with him while no one was listening to find out that several more people had moved into town over the last two days since she'd been gone. Most were at Myles' request for additional security at the magnet train lines. News of the potential threat of sabotage made Nick even more desperate to protect Mrs. Wrigley and Scarlett could tell he was anxious and extra emotional. She gave his hand a little squeeze to reassure him before turning her attention back to the parents.

After a brief get together in the hotel café with the Peters and the Newberys, the Wrigleys left to go home to Riverstone. Scarlett watched them leave and prayed they would be safe on the train. She headed to the hotel room she shared with Michelle and Louzanne and waited for her mother to call to tell her they arrived safe. After she hung up, exhausted from a long day, she pulled back the covers and climbed into bed looking forward to having a free day tomorrow so she could find out more about Senator Matthews and his mysterious conspirators.

***

The next morning, Scarlett, Michelle, Louzanne, Luke, and Grayson went to the Capital Building. Scarlett wanted to make a list of the people who were in attendance and pick Mr. Newbery's brain. She didn't tell her friends about the snake she saw slither out of the woman's headscarf—mostly because she couldn't quite believe it herself and questioned whether she really saw it.

"Sorry, Michelle. Your dad's in meetings all day," Vickey informed them when they arrived at Mr. Newbery's office.

Louzanne threw her hands up. "What are we gonna to do now?"

Scarlett had made note of the people Mr. Newbery mentioned yesterday. A quick Google search didn't turn up much other than their names, countries of origin, and the fact that they were all major stakeholders in the energy and automotive industries.

We're running out of time. It's Wednesday already. I have to find out as much as I can before we leave on Friday. Scarlett ran her fingers through her hair in desperation when a thought occurred to her. "Hey, we had to sign-in and get approval before we could get down here, right?"

"Yeah, so?" said Grayson.

"Well, the people who met with Senator Matthews, they all came down in the elevator. That means they had to have gone through security upstairs."

"Which means they would be in the guest log," Michelle finished Scarlett's thought for her. "I have an idea. Follow me."

In front of security, Grayson pretended to slip, and he threw himself onto the tile with an impact that would have broken the bones of a frailer person. Grayson rolled around on the floor wailing while Michelle and Louzanne screamed frantically for help.

"I think he broke his neck!" Louzanne screamed.

The security guard rushed over to help the flailing Grayson.

Scarlett and Luke had their opening; they rushed behind the counter, grabbed the guest log, and flipped back the pages to yesterday's visitors. Scarlett felt like she'd been kicked in the stomach when she saw that the log showed visits right up until three p.m., but the remainder of the page had been torn out.

With shoulders slumped, Scarlett and Luke rejoined the spectacle in the lobby. Grayson was still groaning in agony.

The security guard knelt over Grayson, encouraging him to stay still until help arrived while Louzanne shouted in his ear, "Oh sweet Lord Jesus, help him. Be careful. I think he has a bad heart."

At the sight of Luke and Scarlett's return, Grayson stopped groaning and said, "You know, I actually think I'll be okay. Yeah, help me up." Luke grabbed Grayson and pulled him to his feet before the security guard could protest.

"Are you sure you're okay?" asked the security guard.

"Yeah, thanks for your help but I think I'm gonna walk it off."

***

Discouraged by the lack of progress, Scarlett and her friends resigned themselves to spending the rest of the day with their class touring the Lincoln Memorial, the Smithsonian Art Museum, and the zoo. She ended up having a great time; especially at the zoo where Luke and Grayson made fools of themselves imitating the gorillas. After all the angst of the past twenty-four hours, it was nice to take a break from worrying and just be a kid and goof off with her friends.

Later on, their tour bus took them to a restaurant outside the city that was also a huge indoor activity center. There were arcade games and several other interactive games where kids could play for tickets that could be traded in for prizes.

Scarlett ended her evening back in the hotel room laughing with Michelle and Louzanne about the fun things they did that day. She fell fast asleep with a belly full of pizza and a stuffed bunny rabbit tucked under her arm she had won playing whack-a-mole.

***

The next day was Thursday. Rosemont was scheduled for a smaller, more casual performance in the National Geographic Society Museum. There were two p.m. and four p.m. performances. They didn't have as large a crowd as they did on Tuesday at the John F Kennedy Center but Scarlett was too enthralled in her music to pay attention. About three-quarters of the way through the four p.m. performance, a glowing turquoise-green light filled Scarlett's eyes. She looked down to see that it radiated from her crystal pendant. *Could it just be light reflecting?* Tiny vibrations shook the floor beneath her. She glanced around the room to see if others noticed but no one seemed to be concerned. *Are there rail lines beneath us? Maybe it's just a rail car passing through.*

As the music became more fervent, the pendant glowed even more brightly, and the vibrations turned into trembling. The walls began to shake. On the final notes of their last piece, the shaking became yet even more forceful. The concert-goers could no longer ignore it as they sought the cover of interior walls. When the last note sounded, and there was silence in the hall, the tremors stopped completely. Scarlett looked down at her pendant. It had gone dark. She glanced at Luke, who eyed her suspiciously. She shrugged as if to say, *It wasn't me.*

After the performance, they had dinner with Michelle's parents and her little sister Rebecca. The Newberys invited the kids to spend a few weeks this summer at their family ranch in Iowa. Mrs. Newbery was a sweet, down-to-earth woman with a pixie cut and smiling hazel eyes. Michelle looked a lot like her. Scarlett could tell she kept everyone in the family grounded and on track.

"I was getting a little worried when the shaking started," Mrs.

Newbery said. "But I read that this area can get minor earthquakes from time to time. Thank goodness it was nothing serious."

Scarlett looked down at her charm necklace. *Yeah, thank goodness. What could have caused it? I was holding in my Juma so it couldn't have been me. Maybe it was just an earthquake. But why did my necklace glow?*

"So, Mrs. Newbery, how have you taken to city life?" Grayson asked.

"The city is great, but I'm not much of a socialite. I actually preferred to spend time at the ranch homeschooling Rebecca, but with Michelle about to attend school just outside the city and my husband's work causing him to spend much of his time in the Capitol, I found myself spending more and more time in DC. I got sick of traveling all the time, so I finally packed up the kids and made the move over the summer. We still have the family ranch in Iowa, but we'll only visit during holidays now."

"So, Dad, did you get a chance to think about any more names of the people we saw go into that conference room yesterday?" Michelle asked.

Mr. Newbery wiped his mouth with the napkin on his lap. "Err, I don't know. I completely forgot about that, honey. I can't remember. Claire Mitchell, isn't that what I said? And the Spence brothers, I think. I don't know. Who's having dessert?"

Scarlett's heart sank. *My only hope in finding out who they are can't even remember the people he named yesterday!*

***

The next day was Friday—their last day in the city. Scarlett had a lot of fun this week despite the lack of progress with the mysterious saboteurs. Now that her friends knew her secret, she didn't feel so alone. It was also a relief to know that she wouldn't have to weave so many lies. At least with her friends, she could just be herself. She felt closer to them now and would be forever grateful for how easily they accepted her. *Despite being a freak.* Scarlett was also looking forward to getting back to her home and sleeping in her own bed. She missed her parents, Nick, Honeybee, and the Kroakes. She even missed the creaks and groans of the old house. She had so much to catch up on with the Romanaskis and Myles. She knew she would get nothing more from Myles on the people with the red bands or "the Mother" that he so casually mentioned during Juilliard's performance, but maybe she could weed a little more information from Yadira.

By breakfast, their bags were already packed and waiting for them on the bus. They all sat down for breakfast together at the hotel café. They were scheduled to spend their day outside by giving three thirty-minute-long performances in front of the Washington Monument. Luckily it was during the warmest part of the day, and the last performance would be over by three p.m.

There was an article on the second page of the morning newspaper about yesterday's earthquake around the National Geographic Society Museum. Luke made sure to point it out to Scarlett over breakfast.

"Okay, I admit it. I caused the shaking in the Capitol Building on Monday. But I've been holding everything in so tight ever since. I don't know what caused them yesterday, but I promise it wasn't me."

"What wasn't you?" Grayson asked as he joined them at the breakfast table.

"The tremors. I admit I got really mad at Senator Matthews when I realized he had something to do with my mother's shooting and I lost control of myself. I caused the building to shake, and Ms. Beasle said I almost killed him, although I didn't realize what I was doing." Scarlett put her head down. *This is it. This going to really freak them out. They'll probably be scared of me now and not want me around. I don't blame them. I'd be scared of me too.* "But the tremors yesterday, they weren't me...I...I don't know what—"

"Wait a minute," Grayson interrupted. "You mean you almost killed that guy just by getting mad at him?"

Scarlett wanted to curl up in a ball and die. "Umm, yes," she said, not meeting his gaze.

"Whoa!" Luke's mouth gaped open, causing the strawberry he was eating to roll onto the table.

Grayson rushed Scarlett and picked her up from her seat, swinging her around and laughing. "That is the coolest thing ever!" Luke looked uncomfortable, but his expression became less rigid when Grayson put her back down again.

Michelle and Louzanne looked at her with their eyebrows raised, but by their expressions, they weren't horrified. Rather, they seemed amused. "So you're not afraid of me?" Scarlett asked. "You still want to be my friend?"

"Yeah of course...duh," said Louzanne.

"It's like, you could be a bodyguard. That's totally cool," Michelle added.

"Of course, weirdo. Uhh...just don't get mad at me, okay?" Grayson feigned choking and falling to his knees until she punched him in the arm. "Ouch! Well, at least you didn't try to kill me."

"But seriously, guys. The tremors on Thursday, that wasn't me!"

"Hmm. Maybe it's just a natural occurrence just like the geologist said in the newspaper," Louzanne suggested as she picked the chunks of green pepper from her omelet.

"Yeah maybe." Scarlett hoped that was all it was.

***

The weather wasn't as cold as she expected but the monument cast a shadow over the ground where they performed, blocking out the warming rays of sunlight so, despite the warmer weather, they still needed to bundle up in their jackets. But, at least their fingers weren't frozen, and the cold didn't hinder their performance.

Scarlett felt subtle vibrations coming from the stone tile below their feet. Unfamiliar with the city schematics, she chalked it up to it likely being an underground railcar nearby. *At least, I hope that's all it is.* The vibrations grew stronger as the music became louder and more fervent. Then it would stop immediately after each performance. Halfway through the final song, the vibrations turned into tremors. The orchestra continued to play through it until the shaking became violent. Scarlett looked down to see glowing red embers radiating from her pendant. The glow became so vibrant that it beamed through the fabric of her tightly woven jacket. *Something's going to happen!*

Just then, the stone tile directly in front of the monument cracked and split open, creating a one-foot chasm. The audience scrambled from the area in a panic. Ms. Beasle, as their maestro, stopped the performance immediately.

When the music stopped, the tremors abruptly halted as well. Frozen in shock, Scarlett remained seated. She surveyed the damage, allowing her eyes to travel to the base of the monument then upwards. She swore she saw the monument glow red for a moment. It reminded her of how the stone in Yeeta and Yaw-Yaw's caravan glowed before something reached out and grabbed her. She shivered.

Grayson roamed around snapping photos of the damage and of the shaken crowd. Ms. Beasle directed the students to pack up their instruments and to begin filing onto the bus that would take them to the train station.

"Did you see that earthquake? That was so cool!" Jordon Nathanson, one of the fifth years who played trombone, said while other kids were on their phones telling their friends and family about it. The bus ride to the train station was short but filled with excited talk about the earthquake they had just witnessed. Scarlett kept to herself, replaying the event in her mind. *I'm sure I had my Juma under control. I couldn't have caused that. Could I?*

***

"Good afternoon, Miss," Pesha greeted Scarlett dressed in a magnet train attendant's uniform. He winked at her and put his finger to his lips.

"Good afternoon," she replied formally so as not to unmask his ruse and found herself a seat in the same car as Grayson and Louzanne. It was late Friday afternoon, so Michelle and Luke went home and wouldn't be riding the train into Riverstone until Monday morning for classes. Since the Romanaskis worked a lot with Grayson, teaching him sword fighting and other ways to use his Juma, Grayson would have recognized Pesha right away, but he didn't say anything to blow his cover. Louzanne didn't know Pesha since she had never been down to the river with Scarlett or been introduced to the Romanaski clan.

"This breaking news comes to you now," the TV monitor in the car flashed images of the crevice in the ground surrounding the monument caused by the earthquake. The headline on the screen read "Earthquake Rocks Monument" in bold font. The volume was turned down, making the commentary impossible to make out, but Scarlett could read the script on the news ticker. More images flashed across the screen of people fleeing the area. Below the images in tiny type read: *Courtesy of Grayson Blackwell*.

"Grayson!" Scarlett hissed and shot him a reprimanding look.

"What? I freelance sometimes. It's good money. If not me then somebody else would have sold them their pictures and they wouldn't be as good. So really, I *improved* the news," Grayson explained indignantly.

The glowing monument and the glowing pendant that seemed to signal the oncoming tremors was too much of a coincidence for Scarlett to continue to believe this was a natural occurrence. But since these events weren't exactly a secret—they were right there on *CNN* for the world to see—she cooled her temper with Grayson.

"I guess you're probably right. It happened in broad daylight in plain view of everyone. Otherwise, Myles would be very upset," she said. Scarlett saw a flash of light and green sparkles over Louzanne's shoulder before a tiny fairy appeared. She had long red hair and large green eyes. She bowed her head to Scarlett but looked perfectly miffed to be spending her time on the train. She sniffed the air haughtily then disappeared before Scarlett could even say hello. Scarlett could only guess that this was one of the Sonoa sisters, that Myles had mentioned, patrolling the cars for any suspicious characters.

They arrived at Riverstone station safely and without incident. Scarlett said goodbye to her friends and walked off the platform to where her parents were waiting for her in the parking lot. Mrs. Wrigley ran to her daughter and pulled her into a hug. "We just heard on the news about the earthquake. Thank goodness you're ok."

***

It was nice to catch up with them about their week over supper.

Mrs. Wrigley had a craving for pancakes, so they went to a diner that served all day breakfast. Nick sat beside Mrs. Wrigley in the booth while Scarlett sat next to her father. Snuke and Precious enjoyed the pancake breakfast, and Scarlett made sure to inconspicuously slip some of her meal over to Nick while she distracted her parents with conversation. Scarlett hadn't seen Honeybee all week. "She's away on business for Myles, love," Precious told her when she asked.

By the time they came back from dinner, it was late. All Scarlett wanted to do was have a bath and go to bed, so she kissed her parents goodnight. Mr. and Mrs. Kroake welcomed her in the hallway upstairs. Scarlett greeted them warmly and told them about her trip while she got the water ready for her bath. Finally, she was clean and in a fresh pair of pajamas. She pulled the covers back and slipped into her nice warm bed with a sigh of relief. *It's so good to be home.*

TWENTY-TWO
SIDHE, BEYOND, AND BACK

Rap...rap...rap...ooohhh whooo...rap...rap...rap...oooh whooo. Scarlett woke to find a tiny burrowing owl rapping at her window. The room was dark except for the rays cast by the moonlight. *Rap...rap...rap...oooh whoo.* The bird seemed to be gesturing for her to open the window. Groggy and still half asleep she opened her window, and the tiny owl flew inside. *Oooh whoo oooh whoo.* It flew around her bedroom ruffling up papers and knocking down books and some of her old stuffed animals from shelves, making a ruckus until Scarlett was fully awake. Then, it flew out the window towards the woods in the back of her house.

Looking out her bedroom window, Scarlett could see sparkling green lights flashing in the grassy clearing just before the woods. She blinked and rubbed her eyes. The lights were still there, moving around the grass, sparkling and flashing in the moonlight. *Oooh whoo.* The tiny owl flew back in then out again. It flapped its wings and hovered outside her window for a while before it flew back in as if it were gesturing for her to follow.

Scarlett put on her slippers and pulled on her bathrobe over her pajamas. She tried to sneak down the back stairs without a sound, which was difficult to do in an old house. She opened the kitchen door leading to the back steps and then wandered out into the field behind her house. *Oooh whoo.* The owl continued to hoot as she followed it towards the flashing green lights.

In the clearing in front of a large oak tree was a circular mound where dozens of green lights danced around. As she drew nearer, she recognized the creatures. They appeared to be some sort of fairies. They were a bit smaller than the fairies she was accustomed to and rather than each having unique skin tones, hair, and features, these fairies all appeared to look very similar. They had pale green skin and dark green hair. Their wings were smaller than Precious, Snuke, and Honeybee's, but she could tell that they were definitely fairies.

As she drew even nearer, Scarlett could see that they were dancing and could hear their tiny voices singing. They danced around and around in a circle in the front of a tree. Several more tiny owls danced around with them while some fairies rode on their backs. Scarlett could make out the face of a man carved in the tree. His face and hair were also green, and he appeared to be wearing a wreath of flowers over his brow.

At first glance, Scarlett thought the fairies might have carved this image into the tree but took a step back when she realized that the face was animated, smiling and singing along.

"Come, Scarlett. Join us. Come celebrate!" the fairies beckoned.

"What are we celebrating?"

"Why, it is the eve of the spring equinox, silly," a male fairy said.

"A fresh new season. So much to rejoice!" another cried.

Some beat tiny drums while others played what looked and sounded like tiny flutes. Their music was beautiful and hypnotic; it was difficult to not want to dance and rejoice after hearing it. It wasn't long before Scarlett was dancing around and singing along with the fairies in the circle. She sang and danced around and around for what felt like hours. The music and movement filled her with joy. She was having so much fun it was difficult to keep track of how much time had passed. Scarlett closed her eyes for a moment, and when she opened them, she was no longer in the clearing in front of her house but in front of a crystal clear pond, deep in the woods.

She looked all around but could no longer see her house or the tree with the face of the man. Nor could she see the green fairies. She looked down at her feet and found she was standing on the same grassy mound where she danced with the fairies only moments ago but now she was in a completely different place. She looked in all directions. Over the horizon, toward the north, she saw a dark plane. To the west, she saw hills. The moonlight on the pond made the water appear like glass, and tiny tadpoles created ripples in the crystal clear water. Intrigued by its beauty, she drew nearer until she found herself standing over the pool and peering down at her own reflection.

Scarlett saw her blue eyes, her messy golden hair, her pink fuzzy bathrobe…and she saw something else she couldn't quite make out. She kneeled down on the water's edge to look closer until her face was inches from the surface. There was something else in her reflection— a flash of gold light or maybe it was her Juma taking form outside her body. Without thinking much about it, she leaned forward and dove into the pool headfirst. She swam deeper and deeper looking for the golden glimmer.

It was dark down there, but she could make out its flashes of gold in the dark water. She swam deeper and deeper until she reached the bottom. A large gilded mirror lay at the bottom of the pond. She looked into the mirror to see her own reflection, but it wasn't a true reflection. The person staring back was much older, and she was beautifully dressed as if she were a queen for a costume ball. But there was more in the reflection than her older self. Again, there was the image of something else, but she couldn't tell what it was. Its image was shrouded from her, and the otherness beckoned. She grabbed each side of the mirror's frame to keep herself from floating upward. She pressed her face against the glass to get a better look and found no barrier where the glass should be.

Headfirst, Scarlett pulled her entire body through the mirror frame and found herself standing in a great marble hall. "Hello!" she cried out, but only the sound of her own voice echoed off the marble pillars. It was dark, lit only by a dim light at the end of the hall. She began walking towards it, her footsteps reverberating. When she reached the end, she found another great room, like a large ballroom or a throne room for kings and queens. Two figures sat on thrones tucked into a circular table lit by candlelight. There were four thrones in all. Two sat empty. As Scarlett drew nearer, she realized that the two figures were women—both very beautiful. One had large feathery wings as white as snow, the other with fin and tail like a mermaid. Their heads were bent over a board game, and they moved pieces around the board in silence.

"Come sit with us a while, sister," called the woman with fin and tail without lifting her head. Scarlett reluctantly approached the round table.

"Please sit." The beautiful winged woman gestured for her to take a seat on one of the empty thrones. One was made of wood, the other metal. Reluctantly, Scarlett took a seat between them on the wooden throne.

The women sucked in their breath as she made her choice of thrones.

"So many choices for you to make, my young one. So many," said the winged woman.

"Fancy a game of Magpie?" the mermaid-like woman asked.

"I don't know how to play," Scarlett replied nervously.

"It is very simple," the woman with fin and tail explained. "A few friends and too many foes. You must do your best to come safely home."

Scarlett raised her eyebrows. She looked back and forth to both women hoping for more of an explanation.

"This is your piece, sister." The winged woman pointed to a glass figurine on the board. It looked like her. Rather, it looked like the older version of herself that she saw in the reflection at the bottom of the pond. "You must make a choice and move North, South, East, or West; the choice is yours."

"How do I know what's the best choice? I don't know the rules. I don't know the consequences of my move." She'd never played a game without someone explaining the rules before. *Who are these women and where am I? This is all so strange.*

"One can never fully foresee the path ahead," the winged woman said.

"You can choose to do nothing," the mermaid-like woman added.

"What will happen if I choose to do nothing?"

The woman with fin and tail answered, "Things may stay as they are or they may change. That too is uncertain."

"What is certain is that the choice is yours and you must choose," the winged woman said.

"Okay, whatever." Scarlett sighed, frustrated by the riddle-speak. She studied the board.

There were seven rows of seven squares. There were figurines positioned about the board, each with unique features. One was the likeness of the winged woman, another like the woman with fin and tail, one looked like a prince but his face was blackened out, another was a woman with Snakes for hair. Scarlett shivered when she saw this figurine because it looked exactly like the woman she'd seen at the Capitol. There were several other vile looking figures. Scarlett began taking turns with the women, making moves around the board. She didn't have a strategy; she just tried to keep her pawn close to the ones that looked friendly and away from the ones that looked foul.

"It is so nice to have another player. We've grown so tired of this game over and over back and forth we wager for turf of air and sea. The land is forbidden to us now," the winged woman sighed.

Scarlett was getting more adept at making moves, although she still didn't understand the objective; something kept calling her to remember there was somewhere she needed to be. "I...I need to go home."

"Sit with us a while, sister. It has been so long." The winged woman paused, looking out into nothing as if caught deep in memory. "So long, I've forgotten her countenance. Perhaps she wears a new face?"

"Perhaps," said the woman with the fin and tail. "Brother has taken our sister away. She is shrouded from us now and we from her. Forgotten, buried, left to wither and die while his fire grows stronger. The flames rage out of control over her head, and we are here helpless except to call to those who listen."

"I miss brother too. So different now. We sit together no more."

The winged woman sighed. Both women looked solemn.

"This is all gobbledygook. It doesn't make any sense!" Scarlett cried. "Where are your sister and brother?"

"Ahhh...song bird play us a song." The winged woman clapped her hands, and a harp appeared before Scarlett from nowhere. She gestured for Scarlett to play for them. Intrigued by the beautiful instrument and somehow unable to resist her request, Scarlett did her best to play the harp in a pleasing manner. The women began to sing along to her melody.

"In the crossroads comes the light.
Choices to make, a dark master or set the world alight.
With power to heal and take flight.
Until time stands still in Old Dominion, dark master sleeps sound.
Call the sister and brother back home.
Forgive old wrongs or let vengeance take flight?
In the crossroads lies the choice, serve darkness or the light."

When the song finished, the mermaid-like woman sighed. "We long for our sister. Could she be you?" She grasped for Scarlett's hand and pulled her near. "It is hard to tell. Nothing is for certain, only whispers in the wind telling of a new future. You feel like her but like something else. Her aquamarine eyes bore into her. It felt like they could lay her soul bare. No...not her," she said after studying Scarlett's face for what seemed like hours.

"Play us another song, sister. Choose your instrument," said the winged woman, gesturing to the rows of instruments that appeared before them in the great hall.

As if unable to resist, Scarlett instinctively walked toward the guitar, picked it up, and began to play. It was the song that she and her friends had been working on before they left for their trip to Washington, but they couldn't quite get the chorus right. She played as the women listened intently. *This is a strange place*, Scarlett thought. *Where am I? Who are these women?* She couldn't tell how long she had been there playing music and games. When she reached the chorus, she strummed out the tune, and she knew that was it—that was the chorus they were missing.

I have to take this back for Michelle, Louzanne, and Luke to hear!

"I have to go," she whispered to herself. Scarlett stopped playing and put the guitar back on its stand. "I'm sorry. I can't stay any longer," she said to the women and ran from the hall before they could raise any protest. She came to the end of the hall where the large gilded mirror stood before her. She walked up to it, took one long look at herself with her messy hair and her pajamas and bathrobe, and jumped headfirst through the mirror to the other side.

The frigid water in the pond bit into her flesh as she swam her way back to the surface. The water felt heavy as if something was trying to keep her underwater. She was running out of air as she struggled with her ascent. Finally, she broke the surface and gasped for air, her arms and legs exhausted from paddling and kicking. Soaking wet and full of goosebumps, she padded back up to the tiny circular hill. She looked around from the North, East, South, and West, turning around and around searching for a familiar landmark. She closed her eyes, wishing she was home, warm in her bed. When she opened them, she stood in the grassy clearing in her backyard.

***

Six pairs of glowing eyes watched as a young girl emerged from the pond, trod onto the grassy knoll, and disappeared.

***

When she stepped outside the grassy circle, the weather felt warmer than it had when she entered, and the light was different. It must have been after midnight when she crept up the back stairs and into her bedroom. Without turning on the light, she changed out of her soaked clothes and climbed into bed. She heard the sound of someone breathing softly next to her and rolled over to see her own likeness staring back at her. Her eyes widened in shock. Like looking at a reflection, the doppelganger's eyes widened at the same time. The likeness to Scarlett was uncanny. She opened her mouth to scream, and it too opened its mouth and let out a bone-chilling shriek. Then it turned into an ugly misshapen fairy and disappeared, leaving only a plume of sparkles over her pillow. Exhausted from the events, she glanced around for Snuke, or Precious or Honeybee to question what it was but she could no longer keep her eyelids open, and she rolled over and fell fast asleep.

***

Knock...knock...knock. "Scarlett, honey. Breakfast," her mother's voice called from outside her bedroom door. The sun shone brightly through her window, its golden rays warming her in bed. She rolled over and stretched, still groggy from last night's weird events. She went to pull on her bathrobe but remembered it was still soaked from the pond last night, so she decided to shower and get dressed for the day instead. As she descended the staircase, she felt overheated. The fleece shirt she put on was too much for the temperature inside the house, and the sun blazed outside the window making her feel even hotter.

"Good morning, sweetheart," her father said as he kissed her on the forehead.

"Morning!" her mother called to her over her shoulder. She slid a pancake onto a plate and handed it to her. When she turned to face Scarlett completely she saw that her mother's belly was enormous; it had doubled in size overnight.

"It's good to have you back, kid. We didn't know how long it was going to take to find you," Nick said as he sat next to her at the breakfast table, chewing on a piece of bacon. Scarlett looked at him confused but couldn't say anything without her parents thinking she was talking to herself. The calendar on the wall showed wildflowers blooming in a meadow with a brook running through it and read "May". There was a red circle marked on May the twenty-first, the day of Scarlett's end of year variety show. She quickly checked her phone. The calendar there read May twenty-first as well. Scarlett began to panic. *Today is the variety show. I've been gone for months!*

Honeybee appeared in a poof of sparkles. "So glad you're back! I'll explain everything—or at least what I know. Eat your breakfast, love-dove, and meet me at the river."

Scarlett wolfed down her breakfast, kissed her mom and dad on the cheek, and rubbed her mom's tummy to say goodbye to her baby brother. Then she gave her beagles' ears a little scratch, not wanting to leave them out.

"I'm going to go practice; I'll be back later," she called out behind her as she ran out the back door and set off for the river.

***

Myles met her on the riverbank. "What happened?"

"All I know is I was dancing around with green fairies in front of the man in the tree and next thing I know I'm in a pond, and then I'm playing a game called Magpie with an angel and a mermaid."

Myles gasped. "You sat with them? You...*played* with them?" he questioned as if she had done something unheard of.

"Yeah. They were weird but nice. Mostly, they were sad and lonely."

"Ahh." Myles closed his shiny blue eyes. A tear fell from the corner of one and rolled down his face. He took a deep breath. "You are back now!" he said cheerfully as he wiped his cheek.

"Scarlett, we looked everywhere for you. Snuke scouted the faery realm for you for months. We kept calling for you. We didn't know what to do, and we didn't want to alarm anyone, so we had a changeling take your place for a while," said Honeybee.

"A what?"

"We planted a fairy—a changeling—to look like you and act like you, or at least try to act like you, to take your place so no one would notice." Scarlett shook her head, giving them a bewildered look.

"You know, go to school spend time with your friends and family," Honeybee explained.

"So, someone has been living my life for me for the last two months?"

"Yes. School is finished now; final exams were yesterday."

Maybe being gone wasn't all that bad.

"How did I do?"

"You did well. We made sure of that," Honeybee reassured her. "Although I think you could've scored higher in music if it were really you. Ms. Beasle was aware of the situation and made adjustments accordingly."

"What about my friends, my family? Didn't they notice that I wasn't...me?"

"I think they suspected something was different, love-dove. Luke and Grayson appeared to be particularly upset with the change, but you're back now! You can call them now and make that right."

"Okay, but first tell me what happened."

"You crossed over to Sidhe—the faery realm, love," Precious explained. "We could trace your path to the pond, but then you went farther, you were among the elementals. We had no way to reach you. We would've never dreamed you could get there so easily. They must have set up some sort of a gateway for you to come through."

Scarlett remembered the mirror. "They did." She sat down on a log and put her face in her hands. "Two months! I feel like I've missed so much. I don't like this feeling of missing time. I wish I could take it back."

"Time is a dangerous thing to play with, my dear," Myles said warningly.

"Since you've been gone, there have been stirrings in the faery realm and talk of goblins trying to break through the plane unbridled," Precious said wringing her hands, her eyes becoming wide.

"Not to worry. They can only exist here as shadows of their true form. They can't do too much harm in this realm," Honeybee reassured her and patted her shoulder. "But it is unusual to see so many teeming at the gates," she added, staring off into space with a furrowed brow.

"Strange indeed," Myles agreed.

"On a happier note, tonight is your show, love!" Snuke clapped her hands excitedly. "You still have time to practice with your friends before tonight. Why don't you call them?"

TWENTY-THREE
SOMETIMES ALL YOU NEED IS A HUG

Scarlett called her friends and made arrangements for them to meet in the Rosemont music hall after lunch. That would give them enough time to practice. Then they could all go out for a bite to eat before the show. She also called Grayson and asked him to join them for dinner after practice. His tone sounded reluctant, but he agreed to join them.

"Scarlett, you're back!" Ms. Beasle was in the hall early on Saturday afternoon getting things ready for the variety show. She rushed over and hugged her. "So glad you're back. Honeybee told me. I'm just so happy you're okay." Scarlett smiled. She was glad to be home too.

She walked into music room 101 to find Luke, Michelle, and Louzanne already there and waiting for her. Scarlett ran to them and threw her arms around each of her friends. They hugged her back but with only a lukewarm reception.

"Look, I have some explaining to do. I haven't been myself since the Washington trip."

"*Pff,* you can say that again." Louzanne rolled her eyes. "You've been like a robot, a weird robot that laughs at the weirdest things like the electric pencil sharpener and shiny things."

Michelle chimed in, "And you kept chugging gallons of milk and sniffing and wiggling your nose anytime you smelled something sweet."

"Your energy was different too; it wasn't your usual warm colors. You just…felt different. I felt different being around you," Luke

229

added.

"No offense, girl, you've been sweet but…weird," Louzanne said.

"And your rhythm has been off," Michelle said. "Technically, there was nothing wrong with your playing, but it was like you were missing something. Like you were lacking soul—*your* soul. What happened to you?"

"No, you guys, you don't understand. I literally wasn't me. I got lost for a few months. The fairies couldn't find me, so they planted a double—a fairy made to look like me, but it wasn't me. I'm sorry."

Her friends just stared at her blankly. Then, Michelle spoke up, "As weird as that is, it doesn't sound so weird to me anymore. Your double told us so much about the world beneath the veil over the last two months that I'm willing to believe anything at this point," she said wryly.

"Yeah, your double even had me leaving out saucers of milk and cream in my window for the little people," Louzanne added.

"But you're back now!" Luke wrapped his arms around her and pulled her into a hug. He smelled like fresh grains and honey. "It's really you, I know," he whispered in her ear.

"So what happened?" Michelle asked.

"I can't explain it. I don't understand it myself. I followed an owl to the field in my backyard where I saw fairies. I started to dance with them, and next thing I know I was in a different place and I couldn't tell how long I was gone or where I needed to be. I'm so glad to be back."

"So are we," Louzanne said.

"Oh…one good part about my trip…" Scarlett pulled out her guitar and banged out the tune she played for the women in the great hall. When she got to the chorus, her friends started to nod and tap their feet to the beat.

"Yeah, that's it!" Luke shouted.

Then they all started to play. They practiced for a few hours until it was time to meet up with everyone for dinner. The Peters and Newberys were making the trip in from the city to watch the show.

Along with Scarlett's parents, they were going to meet them at the restaurant so they could all have dinner together before the show.

***

Grayson swooped her up and swung her around like a rag doll. "You're you again. I could tell the minute you walked into the restaurant. Where did you go?" he whispered.

Unable to get into it while her parents were in earshot, Scarlett just smiled and said, "I'll explain later."

Luke sat down quietly at the table with his parents and shot Grayson a nasty look.

Scarlett ordered veggie soup hoping it would ease the butterflies in her stomach. By the end of dinner, everyone was laughing and having a good time. Mrs. Wrigley exchanged numbers with Mrs. Peters and Mrs. Newbery, agreeing that they would have to make plans to get together soon. Scarlett's friends seemed relieved to see that she was herself again and even her parents took notice of the change in her.

Her mom hugged her after dinner. "I'm so glad finals are over, and you're acting like yourself again. Honey, between the finals and the extracurricular activities, I think you wore yourself out the last few months."

If she only knew. Scarlett giggled to herself, wondering what her mother would think if she knew she had a leprechaun that followed her around twenty-four hours a day and had taken up sleeping at the foot of her bed for the last six months. Scarlett was sure her mother would be horrified if she woke up one morning to see ugly little Nick asleep at her feet.

***

"Ladies and gentlemen, welcome to Rosemont's one hundred and eighty-sixth year-end variety show!" Mr. Lechey announced as he stood at the front of the stage with the curtain drawn behind him. The spotlight was the only illumination in the auditorium. He dressed as a 1930's style circus barker with his striped pants and purple velvet coat and top hat. Then the curtains opened, fireworks exploded on stage, and the music began playing from the orchestra box below. Sixth years banged on large drums on the edges of the stage, dressed as if drumming for a tribal ritual. Then the stage expanded out to become a catwalk, and a parade of students sporting unique and fashionable clothing began to walk down in synchronization with the beating drums. *This must be Vivian's fashion show*, Scarlett thought. The designs were eye-catching, and the theatrics were as good as or better than what could be seen in Paris or Milan or least as far as what Scarlett could tell, given her limited knowledge of the fashion industry.

The next act was an acapella group of fifth years singing songs from the Be-bop and Motown era, followed by a dance act that combined ballet with Celtic dancing. Scarlett bit her lip. She was getting nervous. Everyone's performances were top notch. They were so talented and theatrical that she was scared how her band would be received. She and her friends never even gave a thought about costumes or pyrotechnics or visual images. They only focused on playing their songs well. She was glad they were the second to last act of the night. Hopefully by then, people would be tired of all the visual stimulation and would just want to sit down and listen to music, but she somehow doubted it after what she had seen so far.

Scarlett particularly enjoyed Vivian's fashion show, impressed by all the colors and patterns and not to mention the amount of coordination that had to be involved. She knew that it was something she could never pull off herself and admired Vivian's ability to orchestrate such a show. *I should go find Vivian to tell her what a great job she did.* She looked around the auditorium but couldn't find her.

She checked the hallway and the staging rooms, then the girls' locker room. She could faintly hear sniffling and sobs coming from the back. The sound became louder as she approached the showers. Scarlett pulled back the curtain on one of the stalls and found Vivian slumped on the shower floor with her knees hugged tightly to her chest. The water beat down on her head, and black smudges from her eye makeup ran down her face. She was sobbing uncontrollably and gasping for air.

Vivian looked up at Scarlett through bloodshot eyes which

magnified the green of her irises, so they looked like they were glowing. "She never came—"*gasp*. "All the planning and she never came." *Gasp*. "Said she had an early breakfast meeting and didn't want to be out late. She had no idea how important," *gasp*, "this was to me." Scarlett didn't see Mrs. Patterson in the audience. *That must be who Vivian is talking about.*

The demon seemed to have gained new strength in Vivian's misery and had her in a death grip as she struggled to breathe. It glowered at Scarlett as if daring her to try and stop it. She could see Vivian's life force draining from her and a black mass radiated over Vivian's heart. The image frightened her. *Is this what dying of a broken heart looks like?*

"Vivian, you did an amazing job. I'm not even a fashionista, and I want to buy your clothes. They're awesome."

Vivian wasn't listening. *Gasp* "She doesn't love me. Why can't anyone love me, Scarlett?" Then talking became too much for Vivian. She broke into heart-wrenching sobs. Her body shook as she gave way to the terrible hopelessness she felt inside. The water had run cold, causing her shaking to become more violent. Her lips turned even bluer.

Scarlett turned off the running water and stared deeply into the demon's eyes. Its fiery gaze burned into her. There was nothing there but pure evil. She had seen eyes like this before; it gave Scarlett the chills, but this time, she was not afraid. Vivian's life force was weak. It hung around her in thin white wisps as if at any moment a wind could take it and blow it away forever.

The demon had become almost solid in form. It radiated strength and gloated in its newfound power. Its gestures taunted Scarlett as if daring her to stop it. *This parasite is a sickness!*

Not knowing if it would work, she began to rub her palms together as if preparing to heal a wound. She concentrated on generating a large ball of healing light and created a ball so big it was taller and wider than her. Then she let it go. She allowed it to radiate outside her then stepped inside the orb, so her entire body was a ball of white light. Scarlett pulled the sobbing Vivian into an embrace, patted her hair, and whispered, "Shhhh, you are loved. God loves you, and that's all that will ever matter."

She held onto Vivian for what seemed like an eternity. She concentrated on sending her Juma into Vivian to heal all the hurt and pain she had pent up inside. She could see the demon fading and Vivian's life force returning. The thin wispy lines became thicker, more connected. Scarlett held on. Determined, she wasn't letting go until the demon was gone and didn't care if it took a year and team of firefighters to pry her off. The demon had to go.

The demon hissed and screeched. It was losing its foothold on Vivian. It clawed and scratched at her throat in desperation, trying to preserve its lifeline. Scarlett concentrated with even more intention. The demon dug its claws into Vivian, leaving visible bloody gashes on her shoulders. It lashed out at Scarlett, clawing her face, blood ran down her cheeks, but she continued. Unable to hang on any longer, it gave one final blood-curdling cry and disappeared. Vivian gasped and gave a faint smile as the air filled her lungs and she could once again breathe without restriction. The gashes on Vivian's shoulders healed as Scarlett held onto her. She breathed in and out for several minutes as if enjoying the simple sensation before looking to Scarlett. "I don't feel bad...you...made me feel better."

"Yeah, sometimes all you need is a hug," Scarlett said casually and laughed. She touched her cheek to find the gashes left by the demon had healed. She became serious. "Vivian, I loved your show and so did everyone else. Don't worry about your mom. I know it really sucks, but it's her loss, not yours. Don't waste another minute. There are so many people right here that would love to be your friend. Let's focus on that. You can't choose your family, but you can choose your friends, right? You're going to be okay now. I promise." She reached out her hand and pulled Vivian off the floor. "Come on; my band is playing in ten minutes. I want you to be there."

Vivian still had a dazed look, but the color had returned to her cheeks, and she was visibly less shaken. She managed to give Scarlett a smile and went to her locker, changed into some dry clothes, and followed Scarlett out to the auditorium.

TWENTY-FOUR
GENERAL KWON'S ARMY

It had been two months since Gwork saw the child pass into the pond. It took almost two fortnights to convince anyone to believe him, but after telling his story in every town and village he visited, it was brought to the attention of General Kwon, who was under strict orders to pursue any leads. Kwon reluctantly assigned five of his most vile foot soldiers to accompany Gwork to the location where the child was last seen to observe for unusual activity.

Manark was the leader of this surly group—a particularly foul goblin with a temper and a taste for living flesh. He wore a bone through his nose and always had rotting meat stuck in his teeth. Gwork, while still a darkling, was more on the timid side. He stuck to frightening brownie children and livestock but had never dared or even had the desire to lay a finger on them.

"Another day in this muck," Manark hissed and spat on the ground as he eyed the field of fragrant wildflowers that had recently blossomed where they camped. They had been posted at the Reflection Pond for eleven days, and his men were getting rowdier and surlier by the day. With close proximity to Cobblersville, it was only a matter of time before the men became unmanageable and would turn up in town causing trouble and looking to eat a bit of brownie flesh. He hoped they would get a lead before then. Otherwise, he would have to explain himself to General Kwon and face having another of his fingers flayed

236

for not keeping his men in line.

Another day passed, and the sun had long since set. The pond gave off a ripple in the moonlight, then a splash. All six goblins watched a young girl wade out from the pond and pad softly onto the grassy circle that now bloomed with wildflowers.

"Yum," Ifik hissed, his mouth watering at the sight of a human girl. "I've never tasted one before." His eyes wild with hunger, he bared his worm-ridden teeth.

He lunged after the girl, but Manark grabbed Ifik by the throat and slammed him to the ground. "Our orders are to observe," he snarled.

Gwork sat back timidly. All six creatures, with their glowing eyes, watched the girl enter the grassy circle and disappear.

"It is her! It is she!" Gwork squeaked as she disappeared.

They packed up and headed north for General Kwon's camp immediately, which had been assembled outside Borg County for over a year.

***

General Kwon, commander of Prince Razul's Royal Army, had ambitions outside his station. Goblins were of the darkling kingdom but unlike demons, being a darkling did not necessarily qualify as being evil. Rather, darklings, like humans, had free will but tended to gravitate toward the dark side. While some had a history of being quite noble, more often than not, they could be found keeping company with evil and acted as willing hosts and bedfellows to such creatures. Kwon had done his fair share of evil deeds in his day to gain his powerful position. While all darklings served under the reign of Prince Razul, Prince Razul, too, had a master.

The master had not been seen for many a year. Some whispered that he was dead, others that he had been imprisoned. If one believed the wheezing of the crones and oracles, the dark master slept under a spell while his servants remained to carry out his work. While the scales still tipped to the master's side, the veil brought a balance with a trade-off of diminished abilities and a paler existence for all. Goblins could no longer walk among the world of humans—at least not in their true form. There were also foretellings of simple born humans that could tip the scales. Kwon, had acquired, corrupted, or simply had many of these children killed over the years. It was suspected that some still managed to elude him.

Many no longer believed the oracles, but Kwon believed. Thirteen years ago, in a flash of white light, the sky lit up as bright as the day but only for a brief moment. Then it was gone. This had happened many times before. Each was a telling of a light coming into the world. Kwon dispatched his army of shadows in search of the light. It took months, and while the shadows got close, the light was almost in their reach but vanished before they could grasp it. Its presence undetectable, it was believed the child might have died in infancy.

But Kwon suspected the child to be alive and was being protected, and every now and then, there were rumors that fueled his suspicions. He longed for power and wanted the children under his control. Unbeknownst to Prince Razul, he pursued many leads over the years— leads that led nowhere until now.

The remaining member of the group General Kwon dispatched last year recently returned to him after a long journey through the Seven Paths of Redemption. The goblin had since redeemed himself of his wicked deed along the path but spoke freely while under torture. He told his tale of how he had gotten close to a girl with Juma so strong it was blinding but was banished by a group of powerful fairies and a leprechaun.

It was General Kwon's good fortune that the addled fool Gwork had come around telling his tale of a young girl matching the description. He needed more confirmation and the final piece: the ability to dispatch troops through the veil. It was possible with several powerful spells and incantations to get a small number of goblins through but never in their true form. Even then, they were often detected by lightworkers and dispatched back through the veil or killed before they could accomplish their mission. They didn't have the ability to pass through freely as light faery folk do and especially not in large numbers.

Kwon's sorcerers and apothecaries worked around the clock searching for something to allow them passage. Prince Razul would reward him handsomely for acquiring the girl, but General Kwon's ambitions far exceeded monetary reward. If the sorcerers and apothecaries came through, he would be revered as the one who restored the goblin race back to their full power. They would pass through the veil once again and live among humans—feast upon their flesh if they so desired. And when the dark master returned, he would have to agree that Kwon was far worthier of holding the title "Goblin Prince" or perhaps even "Goblin King". The return of Manark and his account of seeing the child with his own eyes was all Kwon needed to be convinced. He immediately dispatched an army of three hundred thousand to the gates to await for passage to be granted. Now all Kwon needed was one final ingredient for the apothecaries: the heart of a noble man.

***

The stage lights were blinding. Butterflies fluttered in Scarlett's stomach, but she wasn't going to let that affect her performance tonight. She closed her eyes. *It's so good to be back playing in my band.*

"One...two...three...four." Michelle counted it down, and they struck out their first song. It wasn't long before they had the crowd tapping their feet and swaying to the music. Scarlett could make out Grayson in the crowd flashing pictures for the yearbook.

BRRRRRAHHHH....WHOOSH....WHOOSH...WHOOSH...B RRRRRAHHHH...WHOOSH...WHOOSH...WHOOSH. The shrieks and sounds of chaos overpowered the music. Then Scarlett heard someone scream, "GOBLINS." Hundreds of large hideous humanlike creatures stormed the auditorium. Dozens of them rode small fire-breathing dragons the size of horses. The dragons were emaciated, resembling the skeletons of dragons more than anything else. Their ribs poked through their black scaly flesh and they made the most hideous sound. *BRRRRRAHHHH.* They breathed fire as they flapped their grotesque leathery wings, setting the seats and tapestries on fire. The flapping of the wings served to fan the flames, and the auditorium ignited in wildfire.

The Romanaskis stormed into the auditorium, fighting their way through the crowd as people ran screaming for the exits. Scarlett stood on stage in horror, rooted to the floor. The goblins looked nothing like she'd imagined from fairytales. She'd envisioned tiny elf-like creatures with green skin and pointy ears, but these creatures were large—as large as or larger than men. Their greenish black mottled flesh stood out against their hideous features and misshapen heads. Her heart thumped in her chest. Out of the corner of her eye, she caught glimpses of Mr. Lechey, Ms. Beasle, Myles—*I had no idea he would be here*— and the Romanaskis fighting the goblins. Parents and students piled up at the exits, but the goblins had every exit barricaded.

For a moment, Scarlett stood in awe at the Romanaskis' grace as if she were watching a beautiful, violent ballet. Their swords zinged through the air, taking out dozens of goblins with each stroke. It was a graceful and intricate dance. With jumps and backflips, they leaped and pirouetted around the creatures only to appear behind, above, or below them where they delivered the final strokes, and each goblin met their end.

Many goblins were bent on terrorizing the crowd, but the bulk of them headed straight for Scarlett, who still stood on stage frozen in fear along with her friends. Grayson dropped his camera and caught the sword that Bo threw to him. To Scarlett's surprise, he began fighting alongside Rolph, Pesha, Fonso, and Bo and was doing a pretty good job of holding off the goblins. *All those sword play lessons at the river are really paying off.* The dragons were doing their fair share of damage. The auditorium was ablaze, filling the air with smoke. People began to cough and choke.

Among the chaos, the Wrigleys made their way to the corner of the stage, desperately trying to get to their daughter but a group of five goblins had them cornered, brandishing their swords. The meanest looking one, the leader of the group with a bone through his nose, flashed a wicked smile at Mrs. Wrigley's enormous belly.

"Have you ever eaten baby before, boys? Delicious." He smacked his lips, revealing his rotten black pointy teeth that looked like they still had pieces of flesh in them from his last meal. The foul group charged at the Wrigleys. Nick stood staunchly in front of Mrs. Wrigley, ready to fight to the death. Terror had taken over Scarlett's entire body, and she shook to the core.

She reached out to her family and let out a blood-curdling scream, "NOOOO!" She felt a whoosh of air rush across her face, and then the room went silent and still.

Nothing moved. Bo hung suspended in the air halfway through a backflip over a group of goblins who had their daggers pointed up at him, but they too were stuck in place. The Wrigleys were frozen still with a look of sheer horror on their faces as the small group of goblins stood before them with their teeth bared mid-charge. Scarlett stepped down from the stage. *I have to get my family out of here.* She began dragging her parents and Nick like statues into the alcove that led to a backstage door.

When she had them hidden from sight, she walked around the auditorium observing her classmates, still and with terror on their faces. Then she looked over the hideous creatures who pursued them. Black and green veins were visible beneath their flesh, and they smelled even worse up close.

Are these what real goblins look like? Are they frozen in time? Did I do this? Did I make time stand still? Where's Myles? She frantically scanned the room. She spotted him and ran over. Myles held both arms outstretched, bolts of green light emanating from his hands. But the light didn't move. It hung in the air, frozen in time. "Myles," she sobbed, throwing her arms around him, "I need you more than ever. What am I gonna do?" Tears spilled down her cheeks and soaked his shirt. As she clung to him, he began to move. He looked around, disoriented for a moment.

"I think I did this, Myles," Scarlett said desperately.

Myles closed his eyes in resignation as if his worst fears had come true.

Just then, the ground shook violently. Scarlett heard a buzzing in her ears, and the vision of red burning eyes flashed across her mind. She looked to Myles. He cast her a worried look. He felt the vibrations too.

Scarlett closed her eyes and put her hands over her ears. The buzzing was torture and the red eyes she saw behind her eyelids seared into her. Overcome by the excruciating pain, she fell to her knees. When Myles collected his thoughts, he resumed his usual steadfast demeanor. "Not a concern for the moment. Help me dispose of these vile creatures." He turned to Scarlett and pulled her to her feet. "Now is not the time to hold in your Juma, my girl. Send it out at them and repeat after me: *Fugair.*" As he spoke the word, green bolts of light blasted from his hands and struck the group of goblins that had cornered the Wrigleys, disintegrating them into nothing but ash. She staggered through the pain and repeated his instructions with another group of goblins and watched them too disintegrate.

"This will go a little faster if we have help," he said, pointing to Snuke, Precious, and Honeybee. They were frozen mid-air, fighting off one of the dragons that also hung still in the air.

"Myles, it hurts. There's a buzzing in my ears, and I see red eyes that burn me whenever I look at them."

"Concentrate. Block it out and work through the pain. You can do it. You must."

She concentrated for a moment. The buzzing deafened her. The sound reverberated against the insides of her skull, scrambling her thoughts and causing tiny lines in her vision. She met the red eyes for a moment, and a flash of searing pain doubled her over. Her nose began to bleed. Scarlett touched the blood that dribbled from her nostrils and looked at it. Then she looked all around at the unsightly creatures that threatened her school and all the people she cared about. *I need to do something before those goblins figure out how to unfreeze.* She closed her eyes tight and fought through the searing pain, through the buzzing in her ears, and through the image of the burning red eyes and replaced it all with the image of the riverbank and the quiet meadow where she had learned to use her energy. The sounds of the rushing water and the wind rustling through the grass were almost real. It was enough for her to reconnect with her Juma. Then she floated up and touched the fairies as if willing them to reanimate by her sheer intention.

Precious and Honeybee looked around and gasped at the scene before them but quickly joined Scarlett and Myles in banishing the goblins. Scarlett reanimated Ms. Beasle, Mr. Lechey, Grayson, Michelle, Luke, Louzanne, and the Romanaskis.

The floor and walls continued to vibrate as they cleared the hall of goblins and dragons. Michelle and Louzanne had each taken broken pieces of wooden chairs that the goblins and their dragons managed to destroy, using the pointy ends and driving them into the goblins' hearts. Myles gave Luke a dagger and Luke set about stabbing it into the goblins. The red eyes continued to flash across Scarlett's mind, and the buzzing made it difficult to focus. Each flash caused brief seconds of searing pain as if her bones were being torched from the inside out. She tried her best to ignore it as she helped clear the room but still found herself stumbling and covering her eyes as the pain intensified.

When the room was clear of goblins and dragons, and the fires all put out, Honeybee spoke. "Myles, she must be hidden for a while."

Myles sighed. "I think you might be right. For tonight we'll bind her. That might release the hold she has on time and stop any trackers for the night."

"I can't see it holding for longer than a day or so but by then we'll know more and can decide what to do," Precious agreed.

They all nodded and gathered around Scarlett and said, "*Ceangail.*"

A cold sensation traveled along the surface of her skin. Then she felt her Juma travel back inside her body and wrap itself there tightly. The searing pain and the buzzing subsided. Scarlett took a few deep breaths. She felt like a large bird that had been stuffed into too small of a cage and couldn't get free. She could tell that she couldn't let out her energy even if she tried.

Suddenly, everyone in the auditorium reanimated and began clambering for the door, still under the impression they were being pursued by monsters. This was going to be a long night of muddling memories and setting things right for Myles and the Romanaskis.

"Take her to the cabin with the fairies and wait for me there," Myles instructed Yadira.

"Come on, darling. We need to go." Yadira pulled on Scarlett's arm.

Scarlett resisted. "No, what about my parents? My friends?"

"Ms. Beasle and Bo will watch over them. They are safe now. You are not. Come." Scarlett reluctantly allowed Yadira to drag her from the auditorium as she looked back at her friends and family.

"Where are you taking her?" Grayson shouted.

"To the river where she'll be safe," Yadira called back.

Grayson ran towards them. "I'm coming too."

But Myles placed a hand out to stop him. "No, you are needed here."

***

It was one a.m. when Myles entered the cabin. Scarlett couldn't sleep. Honeybee and Snuke had brought some of her things from the house to make her feel more comfortable, but she kept getting up and checking the door to see if he had returned. It was too warm for a fire, but Scarlett sat in the dark in one of Myles' armchairs, staring into the empty fireplace waiting for him. The red eyes and the pain had disappeared ever since Myles and the fairies bound her Juma.

Myles looked worn out when he came through the door and sat down on the chair across from her. He sighed deeply. He looked exhausted as he rubbed his eyes and face. It was as if he had aged a hundred years in one night.

"Your parents believe you have left for Iowa with your friend Michelle to spend time at their family ranch for a few weeks. To avoid any excess mind-muddling, it is important that you are not seen. I would appreciate if you remained here until we decide what to do next."

Scarlett nodded. "I thought goblins couldn't come through on their own."

"It is not easy to break the planes. The Mother made sure of that before she was diminished. Individually, with a good sorcerer, they can sneak in. Good faery folk and people like myself and the Romanaskis usually catch them and send them back before they can cause too much harm, but sometimes we don't get there in time."

Myles sat back in his chair and started to unlace his boots. "Sometimes the bad things you hear about in the news are not always caused by humans. Goblins can have the darkest of souls. While it is difficult for them to cross through the plane, it is not impossible. They often get other faery folk such as elves or brownies to do their bidding in this realm. Despite their villainous deeds, their hearts are not always black or least they do not start out that way. What happened here tonight—walking the earth in their full form—has not happened for many, many years. We must find out how and why."

"Myles…what about demons? I think I might have killed one or—at least I think I sent it away."

"Ahh, demons. Unlike faery folk and darklings, they are of another realm. They are pure manifestations of evil. They do not have free will. Their sole purpose is to cause suffering. Demons rarely take on form until they attach to a human, so it is much easier for them to break planes."

Scarlett didn't say anything for a while. She just stared into the darkened fireplace thinking about the horrible demon that had tormented Vivian for so long. Then she thought about how she made time stand still tonight in the auditorium and about the man who visited her on New Years. "Is what I did really bad, Myles? Why is freezing time so dangerous?"

Myles rubbed the creases on his forehead. "Time…is beyond the realm of living creatures, even beyond that of the elements. Any minor change, however insignificant, causes ripples which can very well change the course of history. This is why it is forbidden to living creatures, and the ability is out of our reach. One can control the effect time has on them. For example, someone like myself or Yadira or Rolph have learned how to significantly slow the affects that time has on us. However, we have no power or authority over time itself. What you did in the auditorium defies the current laws of the universe and confirms my suspicions."

"Suspicions? The man I saw at New Years...Myles?"

Letting out another deep sigh, Myles continued, "There is no point in keeping it from you any longer. I believe Time itself took human form and paid you a visit. I believe it graced you with power that night."

"What? Why? Why me?" *I'm just a kid from Indiana what would Time want with me?*

"The reason is not clear to me, my dear. There is much more that we must learn." Myles didn't look his usual easy going self; rather he looked very concerned.

"Oh...well...I promise I'll learn to control it. I'll never so much as *look* at a clock again. I'm sure you can teach me...right?"

Myles forced a weak smile. "I know you will try, my dear. You are a good girl. It is more the chain of events to come that I fear. I suspected—we have always suspected ever since you were born and before then, but I thought I had more time. I thought I could protect you and teach you at least until adulthood. By then you would be ready."

"Ready? Myles? I don't understand."

"There have been whispers through the years that a human controlling time was a marker of a significant shift in the powers that govern the realms. Outcomes are never clear when talking of shifts in the laws of the universe. Many will suffer in the process."

Scarlett shook with anxiety despite her exhaustion. "I don't understand, Myles. Why are you talking so doom and gloom?"

Myles patted her hand. "That's enough talk for now, my dear. It is time to rest and I must think. Everything will be clearer after a rest, and in the light of day."

From the door, Scarlett watched Myles leave the cabin and walk into the woods where he lay down to ponder his questions beneath the stars.

"No more of this worry tonight, my love. It will do you no good," Precious said soothingly as she coaxed Scarlett to bed. Precious waved her hands and sprinkled some sparkly powder over Scarlett's head which caused her to sneeze. Suddenly, she felt sleepy. Scarlett barely made it into the guest bedroom and climbed into the bed before she fell fast asleep.

TWENTY-FIVE
SWEETIE PIE RETURNS

"*Hmmff...oooch.*" A gruff voice cursed under his breath. Scarlett flicked on the bedside lamp to find a black hairy monster rubbing his toe. Her bag and her guitar had been knocked over on the floor. She screamed before she took a second glance and recognized the creature.

"Sweetie Pie!" she cried and reached out to hug him. He made hacking noises and stuck out his tongue as if he had eaten something rotten, but it was all an act. He held onto her tightly and hugged her back, making what could only be described as a purring sound, like a kitten when you rub its ears.

"So glad you've returned, deary, and none too soon," Honeybee greeted as she appeared over the bedside table along with Snuke and Precious. "There has been trouble here."

Sweetie Pie crinkled his nose. "I know. That's why I'm back," he gruffed. Then he whispered something in Honeybee's ear.

"I'll get Myles and the others at once." Honeybee disappeared, leaving a trail of sparkles in the air. Sweetie Pie disappeared too, which left Precious and Snuke to keep Scarlett company. Scarlett could tell by their wary expressions and the energy in the room that Sweetie Pie hadn't returned with good news. She knew the fairies were upset and frightened—more frightened than she'd ever seen them.

The hauntingly beautiful sound of a lone flute played outside the cabin. The melody reverberated off the rocks and the trees. After waiting inside the cabin for Honeybee to return for what felt like forever, Scarlett couldn't stand the anticipation any longer. She pulled on some warmer clothes and ran out to the field to find Honeybee, Myles, and the Romanaskis.

Dawn was breaking and the morning light slowly cast its rays along the riverfront as Scarlett emerged from the cabin. Despite the early hour, the Romanaskis were all awake and assembled outside their caravans. Even Yeeta and Yaw-Yaw were up and sitting out in the field with their shawls pulled tightly around their shoulders to stave off the chilly morning breeze. Scarlett stopped in her tracks at what she saw.

The riverbank was teeming with people and creatures. Ms. Beasle, Mrs. Goodspeed, Mr. Lechey, the Kaldife sisters, the Sonoa sisters, the warlock Frank, thirteen other Rosemont teachers, Lulu the esthetician, the local innkeeper, Mike the grocery store clerk, the owner of the Chinese restaurant, eleven miniature men, Sweetie Pie and what looked like another bogey, dozens of winged fairies of various shapes sizes and colors, six pint-sized creatures that looked like brownies and seven creatures that resembled leprechauns, Melintha—Mr. Lechey's pegasus, several other mythical creatures that Scarlett could not name, the mailman, Dr. Blake and four of the nurses she recognized from the hospital tour, and countless others that she didn't know were assembled in the clearing along the river. There were animals as well, including large wolves and bears.

All stood behind Truluthu, except the owls and birds that flew overhead and the many fish that popped their heads up from the river. There were hundreds of people and countless earthen animals and mythical creatures. There was barely room in the clearing, and the energy in the air crackled like lighting as all stood still in anticipation.

Myles was in the back of the ranks next to the river, walking through the groups of people and creatures like a general assembling his troops. His wizened eyes sparkled, and he smiled at Scarlett from across the field. He began walking toward her and she toward him. The assembled groups parted to allow both Scarlett and Myles passage.

As Scarlett and Myles drew nearer one another, she could see he still had dew on his face and hair from sleeping outside in the forest all night. He carried a wooden flute in his hand. When they stood face to face, the group assembled around them in a perfect circle. Then they solemnly bowed their heads.

TWENTY-SIX
THE CHOICE

Myles took Scarlett's hand. "My dear, I am afraid it has begun. I wish you had more time to learn and grow, but that is not to be. I am very sorry, but now you must be brave. The darkness has awakened, and now you must choose."

Shaking her head, Scarlett asked, "Choose? Myles, I don't understand." She searched his face for answers.

"There is a war being fought beneath the veil. You have awakened what has slept for many a year. When it finds out who you are, it will come for you."

"The red-eyed man," Scarlett whispered.

"Yes. What you have encountered was merely a shadow of its true self. When it gathers full strength, there will be very little in this world that can stop it."

The blood drained from her face, and Scarlett shook with the gravity of what Myles just said. "We have to stop it before it gains full strength."

"There's more, three hundred thousand goblins broke the planes last night. Only a few hundred managed to get through in Riverstone. By the looks of them, they were General Kwon's elite force. The rest came through in California, Peru, Australia, England, Egypt, Jerusalem, and Tibet. Some of them went on a flesh-eating frenzy but were killed by the humans. Man's capacity for destruction is far greater since the last time goblins roamed the earth. The rest appear to be hiding around the energy vortices."

251

The hair on the back of Scarlett's neck stood up. "What do I do, Myles?"

"You have the choice to join us in the fight against darkness, or you can choose to do nothing. If you choose to fight, you will be thrown into this battle. We will train you, and we will try our best to protect you. This is a dangerous path, and we cannot guarantee your safety. If you choose to do nothing, we will bind your Juma permanently and protect you and your family until the darkness can no longer sense your presence. You will have no memory of any of us or anything that has transpired over the past year. If you choose this path, don't feel that you owe us anything. You are not the only human with your abilities, and you would not be the first to make this choice. In fact, other than those murdered before they had the chance to choose, the rest have all let their light go dark." Myles patted her hand. "We will get by as we always do. And you will get to go on with a normal life. Perhaps you can become a music teacher, maybe even here at Rosemont and have a husband and children and a nice home."

Scarlett couldn't believe what she was hearing. It felt like she'd had the wind knocked out of her. "Why me, Myles?"

"Your Juma is powerful, no doubt, but unlike the others who came before you, my dear, you just keep on stepping up to the challenge, time and again. After everything that has happened this past year you have managed to accept it with open arms, and you just keep soldiering on. The gravity of it would have driven many mad."

Scarlett shrugged. She never really thought about how she was reacting to her new world. She didn't realize she had a *choice* in how she reacted to it. Accepting it and moving on and trying to make the best of things seemed like the only rational decision.

Myles continued, "Many people like you have been kidnapped or murdered by those who serve the darkness, while others were given a choice—just like you are being given a choice here today."

"And?" Scarlett prodded.

"They chose the path that was right for them."

"The path of safety?"

Myles nodded. "Many have gone on to do great things for the world in other ways, discovering antibiotics, vaccines, curing diseases, and so on. Only you can decide what is right for you and no one here can judge you because they have also been given the choice."

Scarlett thought about her options. *Choose to fight, and I get thrown into a war where I'll probably get killed and put my friends and family in danger in the process. The path of safety seems like a no-brainer. The otherworldly creatures will be out of my life forever. I won't even know what Juma is and my family will be safe. And I can go on with a normal life.* Scarlett twisted the ends of her hair. *But if I choose to leave this world, how can Myles and the Romanaskis keep my family safe? After all, it wasn't goblins who shot my mother; it was people. And it was* me *who could save her. If I let my Juma go, I'll never be able to heal someone or cast out a demon like I did for Vivian. And what about my friends? I won't even know them anymore.*

Scarlett had grown to love the friends she'd made, and they accepted her and her abilities, despite it being weird and a little bit scary. Her heart ached at the thought of no longer waking up to see Precious and Snuke fighting over their share of the sugar dish and Nick with his adorable antics or Honeybee and her motherly ways. She would no longer spend Saturday afternoons with Yadira and the Romanaskis or Myles. She would learn no more lessons from him if she let her Juma go. Her eyes teared up.

"What about the goblins? What about the demons who ruin people's lives? Who will help you fight the goblins and demons?"

"We will always fight the goblins and the demons," Myles reassured her.

She thought about how miserable the people with the gray bands seemed to be whenever their energy became blocked. "If the darkness is awake, it will grow stronger. Wouldn't that be bad for all living things?"

"Yes, but perhaps there's some sort of a bargain we can strike. When your light has gone out, the darkness will no longer be threatened."

Scarlett raised her eyebrows and scanned Myles' features. She could tell he, *himself,* didn't believe it.

"Will fighting the darkness help make people's lives better?"

"If we win? Indeed it will. We can only try."

Scarlett knew that this was no choice at all. *How can I turn my back on my friends and allow people to suffer without at least trying?*

"I'm in. I wanna fight."

"Indeed you do. But that is merely your outer voice speaking. Your rational brain. One must go through the choosing ceremony to allow their inner truth to guide them. Then we will be certain that your path is truly of your own free will and it is the one that you are destined to walk."

***

Drums beat in the background as the crowd parted, allowing Myles to lead her to the clearing's end. A small wooden table appeared before them with three objects: A blanket, a loaf of bread, and a needle and thread.

"If you choose any of these objects, we will bind your Juma permanently, and you will have no memory of the past year. You and your family will go back to Indiana and resume a safe, normal quiet life."

Scarlett scanned the loaf of bread hungrily. Her stomach growled. She hadn't had any breakfast yet, and the bread was looking pretty appealing to her right now.

A second table appeared displaying three more objects: a dagger, a sword, and a crossbow.

"If you choose any of these, you will join us in our fight against the darkness." Scarlett looked over the items. *I'm going to choose the sword. The Romanaskis can train me.* Scarlett took a step toward the sword, but Myles stopped her.

"Uhh uhh, not yet." With a motion of his hand, the two tables became one large wheel with each object spaced out equally along the edge. The wheel spun around and around. Myles placed a blindfold over her eyes. "You must do this with your intuition, your inner truth, not with your eyes."

"But how am I gonna pick the one I want?" she protested.

"Your intuition will guide you to the one that is right for you."

The drums beat louder in a hypnotic rhythm. Scarlett took a few steps towards the wheel. She could hear the spinning table whirring. As she drew nearer, her mouth watered at the smell of freshly baked bread. Scarlett felt the cool morning breeze on her skin as it picked up and moved through her hair. It brushed past her ears with a soft *whoosh*, as if whispering a great secret that could never be told. The hair on her arms stood up, and she shivered as she rubbed them. *I would love a coat or a blanket too.*

A flash of light glimmered from beyond her blindfold. Scarlett instinctively walked toward it, moving past the whirring sounds of the spinning wheel until her feet touched soft clay. There was no mistaking where she was: on the edge of the riverbank. The light flashed again—this time, much brighter. It was coming from the river. Scarlett leaned forward. Another flash of light was all the convincing she needed as she jumped in headfirst.

The cold water rushed over her face, stinging her skin like a thousand tiny needles and the blindfold came flying off. She saw the light even brighter now, coming from the bottom of the riverbed. Down she swam, fighting against the buoyancy of her own body. Moving beyond the logs and reeds, the light became brighter as she neared its source: a long gnarled wooden object with a stone obelisk encrusted in the center of the wooden handle. The obelisk glowed bright white against the murky riverbed, illuminating the mud at the bottom for several feet. Scarlett looked down at her pendant to see that it too was glowing a radiant white. She swam closer. It looked more like a staff or walking stick than anything else. Its gnarled, twisted shape was bone white, probably from years of being bleached in the sun before it was washed away to its resting place. Behind the object lay the gilded mirror. Scarlett swam to it expecting to see her own reflection but was taken aback to see the winged woman and the woman with fin and tail staring out at her. *The elementals!*

The winged woman spoke. "The power of light reverberates. It holds exponentially more power than darkness. As light creates, darkness can only wither. Always trust your light."

The woman with fin and tail pointed to the staff. "This belongs to you now, sister. Take it and never be afraid."

Scarlett bowed her head to the elements and reached for the stick. Despite the fact that within seconds she would be out of air, with the object in hand, a calm strength swept over her. She kicked off the riverbed floor and began her ascent.

She emerged from the water with the staff in hand. The obelisk on its handle glimmered in the morning sunlight. She gulped down the lump of fear forming in her throat and laughed wryly to herself. *Of all the objects I could have chosen, I choose a stick.* Scarlett was met on the riverbank by Myles and hundreds of her allies.

As Myles reached to help her, he looked down at the unusual object she held in her hand and inhaled sharply. Then he nodded as if in confirmation to himself. He turned his smiling blue eyes upon her. "Now, my dear, you must be brave."

Scarlett let Myles help her out of the water with the aid of her new walking stick. Placing her full weight on the object, she felt the handle twist and come loose. Glints of sunlight reflected off the metal that revealed itself as she lifted up on the handle. With the remainder of the stick in her other hand, she pulled further, revealing three feet of razor sharp metal attached to the handle as she unsheathed a sword. It glittered in the sunlight before Scarlett sheathed it back into its gnarled, petrified wooden base and continued to use it as a walking stick to wade up along the riverbank. She scanned the familiar faces of some of her closest friends. Honeybee, Precious, and Snuke hovered alongside the Romanaskis. Grayson, Louzanne, Michelle, and Luke stood behind Myles, *when did they get here?* They had dark circles beneath their eyes from being up all night and the horror they had witnessed but they gave her warm, reassuring smiles, and she felt a rush of relief and newfound strength in knowing that they were here.

She had no idea the significance of the object she had just chosen. She felt the weight of it in her hand. Looking around at the friends she had made over the past year, many of whom she had grown to love, she knew she would never let her light go dark, that remaining a part of the awakened world was the best decision she could ever make. They were in this together, and they were in for a long fight. Scarlett didn't know what lay ahead, but she knew that whatever the consequences, she was willing to see it through.

ABOUT THE AUTHOR

Charmaine Mullins-Jaime lives in Indiana with her husband, daughter, son, and two beagles. She grew up with a love of books and enjoys telling stories, especially ones where the unlikely becomes possible. She also works to help organizations be safer and more environmentally responsible.

www.ingramcontent.com/pod-product-compliance
Lightning Source LLC
Chambersburg PA
CBHW031231120726
47905CB00002B/551